MISSINGVILLE

MISSINGVILLE

Christine Kiefer

What Follows Press

Published by What Follows Press

ISBN (paperback): 979-8-9949391-0-9
ISBN (ebook) - 979-8-9949391-1-6

Cover design and typesetting by Barış Şehri.
Please visit sehricoverdesign.com for more.
Set in 10,5 / 14,5pt Tiempos Text.

For the nonbelievers...
you and me both.

Chapter 1

"I got it from behind," I tell Alvin, a death-by-exposure guy I met in the buffet line. With a wink, I follow it with, "and it's not as sexy as you think."

This is the tired joke I can't help but tell every time I'm asked how I died. Making light of the fact that a man kneeled behind me and strangled me with a rope is a coping mechanism I find appropriate, considering the situation. Being dead, but not in a permanent after-life, pairs well with a sense of humor.

"Oh, I can't tell the suicides apart from the murdered," he says, clumsily using tongs to pick up fried kale. It's a rookie mistake, really; not telling me apart from the suicides is a clear sign he hasn't been here long. I sympathize with his confusion. It's a lot to unpack, being dead and stuck here until our bodies are found.

His lips are so chapped there's blood trickling down his chin. There's a spot on the back of his bald head that's blistered and blackened like a scab that is well past its time to fall off. I can see his collar bones through his LL Bean shirt, and his cheek bones stick out in a way I find attractive, but I've always been into that runway model gaunt look. I guess I had a bit of a death kink, I realize, as I squirt chocolate sauce over my ice cream.

"Can I ask you a question?" Alvin asks, already asking me a question. I nod.

"Have you figured out a way to lead a search party to your body?" He leans down and whispers it, which allows me to see the dried blood in his ear and the worm crawling out of it.

Here in Missingville, this isn't as off-putting as one might think. These idiosyncrasies are par for the course when living in the afterlife with souls whose bodies are strewn about and undiscovered on Earth. I've had full-on conversations with people whose heads aren't even attached to their bodies, so the worm doesn't faze me.

"Alvin, you know we're not allowed to fuck around with the living," I whisper in a way that I can barely even hear. "You're taking big risks even asking me that, but no, I haven't figured it out."

He's a risk taker, I see, which tracks with the fact that he died trying to rock climb while all alone in The Galápagos Islands. But breaking the eleventh commandment, "Though Shall Not Tell the Living What

Happens After Death," wasn't something I was ready to do. Yet.

We eat lunch together and I explain to him how to tell the suicides by hanging from the strangled. Hanging creates a mark higher up on the neck. It's under the chin and comes to a point at the back of the head or the side, depending on where the rope is tied. For me, like others in the murdered-by-strangulation camp, it's a nice, perfect ring around the middle of my neck, with the tell-tale markings at the front made by my fingernails. The murdered will always have scratches on our own bodies where we fought to loosen the thing asphyxiating us. The hangers tend to let their arms fall at their sides, their submission a vital part of the plan.

"I did meet a death-by-suicide who also had scratch marks from her own fingernails. That was a rough one. It means she changed her mind," I tell Alvin as I lick whipped cream off a cherry. His eyes fill with tears, and he covers his mouth like I just told him there was a plane crash.

I continue, "If you're really paying attention, you can tell the difference between us not only by our throats, but by the look in our eyes. The strangled appear startled. We wear an expression made by our eyebrows that says, 'I cannot believe this shit.' Meanwhile, 'Finally' is legible on the faces of suicides." I exaggerate my brows for him, raising them halfway and shaking my head.

Alvin lived a sheltered life. I can tell this by the way his eyes are wide. He's a man who, while alive, said too often things like, "Why would a person do that?" when talking about drug addiction, suicide, self-harm. Bless his heart.

He's void of the guilt that most of us carry here. He fell off a cliff, but he's confident enough that he doesn't feel responsible for his own death. I might beg to differ, but I'm not in charge here. Murder victims like me carry this remorse. Our bodies stay tense, our shoulders seem higher than then they should be, and there's a knot in our torsos where our stomachs used to be, that says, "How could I be so stupid?"

These thoughts stem from staying with an abusive boyfriend, walking down a dark alley at night, getting a ride from a stranger, or selling sex to the guy that looked more pervy than the average perv. I've not met a single murder victim who isn't carrying around a boulder of regret. But it's a different sort from the self-hatred of the death-by-suicides. Most of those folks have a smaller burden that says, "I'm sorry my mom is so sad, but I still believe there was no other option."

Like most people, I thought I'd live a good seventy-five to eighty years. I was too young to think about my cholesterol, but vain enough to get Botox in my forehead, even though my skin was only twenty-eight years old. I was appalled when I saw women walking around with gray hair. I mean, why would you? Youth was already something I feared was slipping away, but that's because I followed too many anorexic wellness influencers on Instagram and most of my friends were already getting collagen injected into their lips. I thought very rarely of death, and when I did it was certainly in a category of "that will never happen to me." Yes, youth really is wasted on the young.

Be it by strangulation, gunshot wound, or the more than one would expect, "murdered-with-a-machete," we're set apart from the suicides in that we spend a lot of time accepting that we're dead in the first place. Suicides, they know what's coming. The murdered spend a whole lot of time trying to accept that we even died at all before we can reconcile the murder part of things. Last for us to sort out is the fact that we're not in Heaven or Hell but stuck in this in between.

Alvin points at his chest and his finger goes through his smoky body. "So, when my body is found on Earth, this body and soul can transfer to the permanent afterlife. Do I have that right?"

He's slow on the uptake. "Yes. This Missingville bullshit is a stopgap. If your body is found, you'll go on to Deadtown, which they say is permanent. It's a catch-22. I want my body to be found, but I'm growing to like it here and the next place might not be so great, if you know what I mean." I nudge his arm with my elbow, and it goes right through him, losing its effect.

Alvin acted like he died yesterday. "You mean the Dark Side and Light Side? I'm terrified of the Dark Side."

I lie to him. "The Darkside may or may not be like Hell, Alvin."

The Dark Side they talk about around here is really just another way of saying exactly that, Hell. But I feel sorry for Alvin. I also tell him I can't imagine a guy like him landing in the Dark Side.

"I was a Catholic," he says, which means he does actually have a bunch of guilt. "I was in kindergarten when I started believing I was bound for Hell. As an adult, I hit a parked car and drove away. I hired a prostitute once, after I was married. I cheated on my taxes and fired a young man with a new baby at home on Christmas Eve."

I find this pathetic. I put a hand on his shoulder and say, "Hang in there, Ebeneezer Scrooge. That all seems pretty benign."

I get up and walk back to the ice cream bar. I'll be damned if I'm going to waste my death eating kale when the ice cream and cookies won't make me gain a pound. Death does have its perks.

Missingville, where I am now, is full of people relieved to be here because, in our last moments alive, we were put into a trunk, a blade sliced our carotid artery, the undertow brought us under.

There's a pause where absolute terror sets in. It's slow motion, a silent film, when the victim lies on the tile floor, bleeding out as she looks directly at the camera. The viewer knows she's done for. And the victim, she knows it too.

Yes, most of you will die in hospitals, in your own bed, or in the ironic Subaru you bought because it was the safest car on the road. You'll die in an arbitrary moment when nothing noteworthy is happening. Good on you.

But the souls in Missingville didn't expire in the middle of a happy moment, or on a regular Tuesday at the office. I succumbed in hiking boots, cargo shorts, and a white tank top. I was sunburned and freckly, with my dirty blond hair in a snarled braid, and my lips white and chapped. Not my best look, which sucks, because I'm stuck here wearing it every damn day. My crime scene, if it's ever found, is clean. There's no brain matter, no blood, at least not mine. My pee is gone too. That's something I was not prepared for, so be forewarned, when you die, you will wet your pants. Probably shit them too, but I was starving so I was spared that, at least.

It's not fair that, for the murdered and the missing, these last moments are the worst of our lives. We didn't get to drive along a coastal highway, blaring Taylor Swift in our convertible, thinking, "I am so lucky to live in Southern California." And then POW, we're hit head on and we're dead, instantly. Those lucky bastards. They die content. You may be one of these people, and I hope you are. I wouldn't wish my kind of death on anyone. That's not true. I do still think that girl Angie from work deserves this kind of death. The octave of her voice and the way she always says, "by the same token," will get her murdered eventually.

Not everyone was murdered though. Some folks, like Alvin, "died of exposure" after getting lost on a hike when they got a little too big for their Patagonia britches and thought they could walk in places called "Devil's Canyon" with just a small bottle of water. Some of those people died from what park rangers like to call "an animal encounter," which means they were coyote candy, their bones strewn all over national parks. There's a guy here with his kids who followed his GPS right into the ocean. He kept watching the little map as he drove into Panama City saying, "The Hotel should be right...." and then splash. He and his two little boys became fish food. People on earth think he kidnapped them in the middle of a divorce/custody scandal, when really it was an innocent, "you spend summers with your dad" little vacation. They may be found eventually in the Gulf, but until then, they're here and there are wanted posters all over Florida for this "kidnapping father."

The common denominator among us is that we died but have not yet been found.

The guy whose body was chewed in half by a shark isn't here. His surfing friends saw it happen. They collected his body, albeit in pieces, but they gathered it right away. A hospice cancer patient gets a direct ride to Deadtown, no stopping in Missingville.

A murder victim found within twenty-three hours doesn't come here, but sure as shit, at the twenty-fourth hour that girl is floating around here wondering when the hell someone will find her body in the "shallow grave" by the meth trailer. My gosh, humans, can we stop with shallow graves? Those bodies always get found eventually, so if you kill someone, just leave them uncovered so they can at least be found quickly.

Chapter 2

I want to say it's okay. Don't be afraid. Death isn't so bad. I wouldn't recommend it to everyone, especially up and coming actors, babies, or whistleblowers. But, if you're just a basic person, know that the end feels like a relief, not at first, but it will. Stopping feels like that nap you took in a sixty-five-degree air-conditioned room with white bleached sheets after a day at the beach. It will remind you of the year you tried to stay up until midnight when you were five. The house still smelled like Christmas, and you surrendered yourself to your dad's shoulder as he carried you to bed.

You'll resist it at first, but once you lean into it, you'll be glad you're done worrying about your future. You'll be relieved that you'll never again fear that your face is going to wrinkle, and your boobs are going to sag. You will never wonder again if you'll have kids someday. You'll get to be done imagining sitting next to your mother's deathbed.

You're probably reading this at the end of a day where you obsessed about the promotion you still hope you'll get even though Sheila, in the cubicle next to yours, has a four-year degree and you just have thirty-one credits from a community college because you smoked too much weed and chased the bad boys. Tonight, you'll watch YouTube videos on interview tips. You'll try on all your professional clothes, iron your most flattering pencil skirt, and tell your dog "I'm gonna crush it. Yes, I am. Yes, I am, Bobo. Momma is gonna crush it."

These mental gymnastics, which most of you have mastered, will seem ludicrous.

Being alive at all, as you are, is going to seem petty. It will be embarrassing. Being you is going to feel like ninety-five percent bullshit and five percent worth a damn. You're going to arrive at the next place with more regret than you can imagine. I'm not going to blow smoke up your ass. I loathe help for self and fuzzies that are warm. I'm not going to say, "stop and smell the flowers." You already know that. If you're old, you've got a bunch of memes on your Facebook page about living life to the fullest. If you're young, you've not stopped taking selfies long enough to think about being unalive. What I will say is yes, your butt looks big in those jeans. And when you die, you'll be stunned that someone invented blue jeans, or all that other stuff that tortured you.

If you believe in God, congratulations. You were right. The atheists were wrong. I was wrong. But let me tell you, and understand that I'm in an ambiguous and baffling death location right now, god doesn't deserve a capital "G." They're a wanna-be comedian, an absolute narcissist, and ironically, a sadist. Keep track of your rights and wrongs. Do more rights. Help people. Be kind. Etcetera, etcetera. But for the love of all that is holy, which isn't god, don't worship them. And don't bother praying. They aren't the marionette masters of anything.

I know this. God has a terrible sense of humor, and a sick propensity for games played for his entertainment. I don't think you should have to go along with the charade any longer. But even this is sugar coating it. God isn't a good person, let me put it that way. But you'll figure that out if you keep reading.

If you've never thought about death, you are a psychopath. For the rest of you, I feel confident that you've wanted someone to come back and talk to you. Don't you wish your grandma would be more than that butterfly that always lands on your pink sweater? By the way, it's the pink sweater; the butterfly has never heard of your Nanna. Doesn't it bother you that ghosts come back just to open cabinets, or drop the temperature in dark hallways? Aren't you angry at the dead?

Why don't we ask for more? Why do we settle for the chair rocking on its own? Why do we set the bar so low that all we want is the movement of inanimate objects? Why aren't we asking for the dead to just walk into the room already and talk to us?

You deserve more. It's high time the dead did some chatting with the living. Real talking, not with slamming doors or swinging chandeliers. I think you have a right to know what to expect. As soon as I got here, I felt compelled to talk to the alive. No one talks about that because no one is alive to tell it. The dead have a lot on our minds once we transfer over, and you can't blame us. But I still find it irresponsible not to let you in on the answer to the biggest question that's tortured you since your goldfish died, or since your parents brought you to Papa's funeral and you had to look at his body in a casket.

When my grandma died, my dad said she was in a better place, but she was still with me. I remember thinking that's weird but maybe we'll still hang out sometimes. I thought she'd come over again with freshly baked bread and cookies made of green-dyed corn flakes and Redhots. I thought we'd chitchat again about the difference between a finch and a robin.

That woman never said another thing to me. I'd ask her to give me a sign. I'd go outside and say, "Nanna, make a finch poop on my head if you can hear me." Never in my life has a bird shit on my head.

Don't you think it's outrageous that we just go on driving cars, working in call centers, dusting furniture and mowing lawns knowing that a moment is coming that will interrupt everything? Haven't you been through enough, with your too small paycheck and your too high blood pressure to have to also go around knowing eventually you'll be unalive, put into a box, and lowered into the ground with no clue what happens next?

Since I've been dead, lots of questions have been answered, and I'll let you in on the things you've wondered about. But what I won't do is placate you. I think you deserve to know what you're up against when you go from alive to dead. Sure, your death likely won't bring you here, but it will take you somewhere similar, and you'll experience the same terror when your lungs inhale and don't do that next expected thing.

Let's normalize asking more from the dead.

I know now that we dead folks are capable of telling you everything, and if I'm the first person to do it, so be it. I'll tell you how I got here. I'll tell you what here is. I'll tell you how being murdered is an absolute shit show.

On Earth, I was nothing special. I didn't cure a disease or win a Pulitzer. I never saved anyone. Hell, I never even donated money to a charity. I never took a sharpie to poster board and stood at a rally. When my eulogy is written, it might be about my smile or my quick humor, but no one is going to go hungry or lose a war after I'm properly buried.

In fact, I was just a basic millennial, naive and shallow, born into privilege to parents that did mostly all the right things. My days included avocado toast and Pilates. I had brunch with my girlfriends on Sundays and went to my job at a downtown Nashville boutique where I sold overpriced fast fashion in sizes 00-6. I fit into those clothes and judged women who didn't. I went to the country club where I'd play tennis and attend bridal showers. I was on a bachelorette party circuit the spring before I died, drinking hard seltzers and gushing over my friends' three carrot engagement rings. I've done nothing with my life that mattered.

But maybe dead me is a better me.

Chapter 3

I realize you may be thinking, "I don't get it, where is this person? Where is her body? Is she a ghost?" Everyone knows that you and most humans believe in things called Heaven and Hell. I'm pretty sure you've spent your life hoping that when you die, you'll go up instead of down. Some weirdos believe that a set number of people are going up, and if you marry someone who doesn't ascribe to that too, neither of you will be in that bunch. There are some of you that pray for a spot at god's right hand. You think about what you'll say to some guy when you get to the pearly gates; I think it's Peter or Paul that guards those gates, or is it Saul? A few of you even believe you've been to this place when you accidentally overdosed on Valium, or had a colonoscopy go bad. Your blood pressure dropped while a tube was up your ass and you saw the white light, even a hand beckoning you to go further. You floated above your body, laying on its stomach with a pillowy wedge under your pelvis, your ass raised up high while your "soul" was tempted to follow the light.

My parents never fell for this folklore. I wasn't raised with the fear of god. I wasn't afraid of a gatekeeping red goblin with a long tail and pointy ears. I never thought, "This is it. This one is gonna send me straight to Hell," after I lied to a friend, denying that I slept with her boyfriend. I am happy to say that I never went into some dark confessional closet to tell a child molester how many times I disobeyed my parents. No one ever told me to trade Hail Mary's for forgiveness. I think I can recite the "Our Father," but that's only because I went to Alcoholics Anonymous for a year to get out of a DWI.

It bothers me that people do virtuous things, or try not to be jerks, out of fear of punishment. Those dreading Hell are like toddlers, looking at the time-out chair and skipping to their cubbies every afternoon relieved they didn't have to sit there. Some of you, like you unfortunate Catholics, think if you eat fish sticks on a few Fridays a year, you'll avoid eternity in flames. You'll skip red meat on Fridays, but sure won't offer your home to an HIV-infected ex-con.

Then there are the those of you that think if a guy dips you back into a pool of water you'll be "saved." I know there was a guy named John the Baptist who dipped people in the Sea of Gally, or Sea of Galileo? Something like that. He also dipped Jesus himself once.

Now this throws me for a loop. The "son of God" had to be baptized? If Jesus himself had to be dunked in an ocean to be saved from damnation, then my friends, there isn't body of water on the planet big enough to save you.

And what are these sheep being saved from? "Jesus Saves" billboards line highways in the Midwest. First, who is paying for these Jesus ads? Second, how many people drove by and thought, "Oh, okay, wow. I think tomorrow I'll go be saved." It feels gross to see advertisements for Jesus, like he's a truck stop with a fake green lawn for your dog to piss on. I have often felt I needed saving, from my addiction to skin products, from my attraction to drug dealers, from the probationary status my sorority was placed on after one of my sisters sent Snapshot pictures of a pledge so drunk, she was lying in her own pee with "no need to consent" as the caption. Sidenote, no, I was not at that party, thank you very much. I just don't think Jesus wants me to be dunked in a pool to be a better person. That seems a little too uncomplicated.

People can't understand climate change, but they're all on board about a human, the son of god, being born to a virgin, making lots of friends, then being murdered for "our sins," only to be brought back to life. Ask a Pentecostal Christian about forest fires or melting ice caps and they can't wrap their brains around it. Ask them how they feel about gay marriage and they'll make a case like you're talking about flatulence. But mention your confusion on praising the virgin Mary while shunning teen pregnancies, and they Christ-splain to you like you just crawled out from behind a rock tomb yourself.

Society accepts the idea of separation of bodies and souls, just like reasonable people, a dying breed, believe in separating state and religion. Loved ones are burned to ash in ovens because we're so sure the soul is separate. Your dad rests peacefully in a mother of pearl urn on your mantle. His entire body was reduced to powder, so fine you can't even gather it in your fingers to throw it off his fishing boat. We've been putting people in boxes underground to feed the maggots because we're so sure their souls go on eternally. What's so weird about that?

Everything is weird about that.

In my former life, I was undecided on Heaven and Hell, and ambivalent about there being a god at all. But most of you have clung to this magic your whole lives. So don't come at me with "How are you in Missingville and your body is somewhere here on Earth?" Turns out, you were right. Our souls come here and live on in these wispy bodies, more smoke than skin and bones. Our souls go to the Dark or Light Side, but oops, if you're like me and so many women before me, you come here because our bodies are in shallow fucking graves.

Lots of people in Missingville, especially American women under the age of twenty-five, are in shallow graves. A few are in sex dungeons or boxcars, but not as many as you might think. One guy here, his body is in seventeen pieces under an in-ground pool. I heard there's a woman here whose torso is in Mexico, and her head is in Belgium. I need to make a note to get her story. We can't even bring hairspray on airplanes.

Regardless of where these bodies are, the rest of them are here. If you can't wrap your brain around this, just refer to your grandpa's funeral where you looked at him in the casket with his glasses still on his face. Your aunt said, "He's in a better place now."

If that's not something you can tap into, how about consider that friend of whose brother died but every year on the anniversary of his death, her alarm goes off at the exact time he died. Maybe it's easier for you to think of us as ghosts; even us Atheists can dip our toes into ghost stories. I may be unable to say the Hail Mary, but I swear neither of us made that thing move when my friend Amy and I played with the Ouija board in seventh grade. That thing rocketed all over the board, saying, "Caleb is into you."

It must suck for my parents, not believing in an afterlife. They can't be placated by the "better place" mantra. My dad was raised in something, Baptist, maybe Lutheran. I just know it wasn't Catholic because he has no trauma from it. Whatever it was, he never told me about it. He wasn't a "practicing" anything. I imagine now he wants to be a believer. I bet he's walked by a church, talked to my grandma who said she's praying for me, got Facebook comments full of thoughts and prayers, and yearned for the beliefs of his childhood.

Instead, I know my dad is picturing me in all sorts of dead poses. He's had me in crawlspaces, under piles of rocks, hanging from a beam in a basement. A part of him knows that a bit of faith would save him right now. He knows that "Jesus Saves" means you can stop thinking the world is cruel, kids die and rot wherever they are, and not one part of them, body or soul goes anywhere. He wishes he could be saved from his perpetual images of me bloody, beaten, drowned, beheaded. Could a billboard nudge him into a chapel somewhere? Could a dose of Jesus stop his constant visions of tourniquets and zip ties, semen and blood, broken teeth, legs spread out with panties around ankles? Is the guy paying for the billboard searching social media for missing peoples' families, ready to go to them and relieve them from the nightmares of white vans, white men, white lifeless faces?

Unless the billboard is doing something like this, the billboard financier needs to fuck right off.

Chapter 4

The end of my time on Earth happened with something around my neck and a person kneeling behind me, pulling on it, twisting it, breathing heavily into my ear as they used all their vigor to take away my last breath. Suffocating, my friends, is no fun at all. Ever have one of those tickles in your throat, like when it feels like spit went down the wrong pipe? You stand up, cough, put your hands on your knees, take heavy breaths in? You swallow a few times, and the feeling goes. I always thought, "Jesus Christ, I almost died" when this happened to me. I had no clue how right I was.

With the rope around my neck, I fought. I clawed and clawed behind my head, scratching a face, a gum line, an eyeball, the hands that were taking my life. I'm sure there's plenty of DNA under my nails. My thoughts in the 4.5 minutes it took for me to be murdered went something like this:

1. Where is she?
2. I'm going to die with a box of dildos on my bedside table. My parents will find them.
3. What if I go to Hell?

And then I was here.

Well, wait. And then I was above it all.

It turns out that some tropes are accurate, like hovering above your body. I guess my dad was right that behind every stereotype is some truth. Turns out, the weirdos who claimed they died and came back to life, people I never believed when I was alive, were spot-on.

My last breath came out and another inhale didn't. That last exhale felt like my lungs weren't just giving up, they were expunging every bong I ever hit, every lie I ever told, every 'Goddamn' I ever exclaimed. There was this satisfaction that I didn't have to inhale ever again, that I had taken in the last ounce of earthliness I could handle, like my body was emptying, free. There was a pause, a nothingness, and then I was hovering above my body.

Like the way camera angles change in movies, there's the perspective of the actor, the buildings outside the window, then the image of the person looking out of said window. The only difference is that when you get the view from above, it's with eyes that don't blink, a body that doesn't breathe, and a weightlessness like floating in the deep end. From this angle,

I could see the top of my killer's head, the way his hair's cowlick pushed yellow hair into a swirl, like a baby's. I could see his bare back, red and blistered, his gritted teeth, and the blood on his hands from the rope's splinters.

I watched my legs move frantically in the dirt. My fingers grasping at a rope that was never going to loosen. I could see the campfire at my feet, and the distance from my body to the trail.

I watched myself die, which is what all of you will do eventually. I left my body but thumped my ghost head on a tree branch. I stopped there and looked down. I hovered as my killer relaxed, fell backward, hyperventilating, exhausted by the intense work it takes to kill someone. My body was on its back, my head turned to the side, my eyes open, my tongue sticking out of my mouth. My legs were wide apart and my arms too. I looked like I was making a snow angel.

After this hovering, I dropped, like a cartoon animal whose balloon has burst. All of us in Missingville fell into this place, quickly like we'd jumped out of a plane, but in the last few feet, a slowing. Our feet were gingerly placed on the ground of Missingville.

So here I am, in an afterlife that isn't a final destination because my murderer is bad at life but good at hiding women's bodies.

God prefers things to be nice and tidy, clean, final. They don't want us to go to the next point while our bodies are still missing, while cops and mothers are searching for us, before we have a "proper burial." Yes, I think it's ridiculous too. Yes, it would make more sense for god to pull some all-powerful strings and just lead someone to our bodies. Or, even better, god could see all souls the same. Dead? Great, go on to Deadtown, no matter the state of your body.

But as I've said, and as you will learn, god is not benevolent. They're a trickster, a bully, the kid in class who raises their hand too much. They're the woman writing a check at the grocery store even though it's 2024. God is the boy sitting in an old timey schoolhouse, dipping the braids of the girl in front of him into an ink well. They're that nephew you caught smiling too much when the dead kitten was found in the road. They're caught up in being the assistant to the regional manager, hell-bent on making arbitrary rules that make it impossible to actually get the job done.

God introduces themself in a building of your choice, like the Taj Mahal, Sistine Chapel, Coliseum, Great Pyramid, Golden Temple of India. I've seen less extravagant options like a T-Pee, the Red Rocks Amphitheater, a hot air balloon, an Elvis Presley concert, The Grand Ol' Opry, the crosswalk on Abbey Road, a mega church with electric guitars and gigantic tv screens. These are all the places where people say they've felt god. I heard one guy got here and went to the set of Jurassic Park, chatting with Laura Dern before he read the "Shout Out." That weirdo was a pedophile who finally got pushed off a cliff by his last victim's father.

Wherever you end up, you'll get The Missingville Welcome, and a nice little note from god entitled: "Shout Out to All Souls Not Yet One With A Body."

You will have a body, kind of.

It's hard to explain to all of you living people what it feels like to be somewhere without your body, but with your body. It's like a hologram. My body became smoke. I felt weightless and suspended. Like the way it felt when I took an edible and walked around in my fuzzy slippers, like walking on twelve inches of cotton. When I wrapped my arms around myself, they went through me, like I was reaching inside a cotton candy machine.

There's no breathing. For something we are so oblivious to when we're alive, it's super noticeable when you're walking around without using your lungs. Hold your breath right now for as long as you can. Feel how still you are? Do you feel a little more dead? I think it's funny how yoga teachers want you to "focus on the breath." What could really get some people to chill out would be to hold their breath, feel perfectly still, feel dead-like. But these are things living people could never understand. I'm not mad at you for the hours you sit in yoga or meditation and obsess about your lungs. Someday you'll realize those things are just distractions.

After I landed, the first thing I noticed was blue grass and a gold sky. I'm using the terms "grass" and "sky" loosely. It's not like Earth. My feet settled on what I can only compare to marshmallows. It's a bubbly, soft surface that we bounce on, like those indoor kids' play-houses. When we want to go a long distance, we bounce hard and then float for a bit until we jump again. Turns out, your wish to be able to fly won't come true here, but it's close so I don't think you'll be disappointed.

The sky is textured, sometimes looking like corduroy, other times moss or ivy. I have seen clouds, but those are just in the Basic Bario of General Population, a place for those with no imagination. I often think those poor souls are more doomed for the Dark Side than the ones in Punishment Prairie, but we'll get to that later.

No, in Missingville the streets are not paved with gold. But again, in Basic I have seen a few yellow walkways. I swear, a lack of creativity really is a sin.

I started walking in large swooping steps, looking at my hands, trying to inhale. I fell onto my knees and put my forehead on the ground. I stayed like that, paralyzed.

I heard a voice say, "Ah, there you are. Welcome."

I looked up and saw a woman walking towards me. She had crows' feet, but smooth, chunky cheeks like a child. Her hair was gray, in an Alice in Wonderland cut, complete with a pink bow at the top of her head.

She wore thick, sparkly pink glasses, too small for her round face. On her feet were saddle shoes and socks with a lace cuff. She was wearing mauve and beige flowy linen layers, like she had on three skirts under two dresses, under five scarves, under beads and turquoise.

"Are you god? Are you god?" I asked.

"No, dear. I'm Rita. I volunteer to greet the newcomers. You're in Missingville. You're going to be fine. You're safe." I jumped to my feet as she approached me.

"Missing what? Where? Newcomer?" I was going to assault this woman.

She started to "shush" me. I started to walk in wide circles, hugging myself and trying to take a breath, moving my shoulders up and down.

"I'm dying. I'm suffocating. But I'm dead. Am I dead?" I called her a hippie bitch and took a swing at her. It was quite a surprise when Granola Grandma tackled me, sat on top of me, and slapped me like we were in a soap opera when someone is told to "snap out of it.'

"If you just relax, I can explain. I'm here to help you, god damnit." I was alarmed that she took the lord's name in vain since we were in Heaven.

"Or is this Hell," I thought, as I continued to struggle and punch her. She was holding my arms, trying to pin me down, and she was winning.

I gave in. I pounded my fists into the blue puffy ground and started crying. I rolled onto my stomach and sobbed into my crossed arms like a toddler. I punched the ground and kicked my feet. A real tantrum.

Rita plopped down next to me, crossed her legs, and said, "Go on, dear. Get it out of your system. I'll wait."

She sat silently next to me before saying, "There's no breathing here. It takes a minute to get used to it. You'll enjoy not having the body of the living. It's much easier here."

"Please tell me I got to Heaven." I pleaded with her.

"Oh sweetheart, unfortunately no, but you're not in the Dark Side either, so it's a banner day. Come on, stand up now. Come here, it's okay." We stood up and she hugged me. Her hands went right through me, but I still felt something like a hug, like the warmth of one, but not the pressure.

"Now, let's get to business," she said, stepping back and putting her hands on my shoulders. "It's time to sit down and hear from god. You're going to see structures, or places you recognize. I want you to decide which building draws you inside. And when you're ready, we'll walk in together." She had a voice like a therapist, and jewelry like a gypsy.

I turned around and saw a café overlooking Capri, Italy. In an instant I could hear the ocean. I smelled coffee and cinnamon rolls. I visited this place in high school and thought "this is Heaven." It was the place I'd think about if some dumb therapist ever told me to "go a safe place." I had photos of the coastline blown up and framed in my bedroom.

Rita took my hand, and I didn't resist. I squeezed her hand the best way a body of smoke can squeeze, and we started to walk. We went up a few stairs to a pavilion overlooking the angry ocean, with loud, monstrous waves pummeling the rock. The breeze was that perfect blend of humid but cool. We were greeted by a hostess wearing a ski parka and one ski on her left foot. The other leg was gone, and she had snow frozen to her hair and eyelashes. I looked around and saw patrons drinking wine and eating flatbreads of tomato and basil. Some had bruises on their faces, or red, pussy sores on the insides of their elbows. Far too many had bloody holes in their temples.

I sat across from Rita at a table covered in a red and white checkered cloth. A man wearing a bike helmet with blood running down his face brought a cup of cappuccino and said, "Welcome. We're so glad you're here." He handed me a menu, except it wasn't a menu because god starts their shenanigans right from jump.

It read:

> *Welcome to Missingville. Let me assure you, dear one, that you are exactly where you belong, because I said so. Whatever your religion (a word I don't like to use, but I must for the newcomers), know that I did not kill you. I do not cause death, but I do think it's endearing that so many of you believe that thing you call "The Old Testament."*

Seriously, asking you to kill your first born? I would never!

I made a few mistakes in my making of humankind. I also think it's a shame that for so long you called it "mankind." Geez, people, I had higher expectations of you. Anyhoo, I forgot to make a rule that bad things do not happen. That's a lie, I didn't forget. I chose not to. I decided to let you all screw the pooch. I had some kind of holier-than-thou moment where I wanted to separate you all from me, from my angels, from the nonhuman. I thought suffering was the best option. Boy, was I mistaken.

When people say the biggest riddle is "Can God make a boulder so big he can't move it?" the answer is, "Yes, except the proper pronoun is 'they'."

But since I made this error, here we are. Humans suffer, their bodies get ruined in all kinds of ways I could have never imagined, and sometimes, their bodies get lost. This is certainly not something I thought of when I was cutting the molds. Bodies lost and dismembered by dingoes? Who woulda thunk?

I realized when one of the first humans died that I needed a stop gap. She was chased and attacked by a monster, or as I have learned, what humans call 'dinosaurs.' Her tribe couldn't find her body. When she passed over, she came before me, and I realized that she needed a body in Deadtown. I like things tidy, final, calculated... think tides, moon phases, DNA, the way pi is an infinite but necessary number. Gosh, I love pi! I was so thrilled when I heard that humans celebrate it on what you call March fourteenth. Very clever! Greeting the mauled woman while her body was in a creek, while her family looked for her, I could not let her in. I do not deal in unfinished business.

I created Missingville, where you will stay until your body is found. When I feel better about the order of things, that is, your body and your soul united, I will send you over to Deadtown. We will have a chat then. Do keep in mind, your actions here count and will be added to my Excel spreadsheet of rights and wrongs. I love Excel, don't you?

Think Heaven and Hell, but without pearly gates or fire. You silly humans and your metaphors!

Choose your actions wisely.

I do hope you find the amenities to your satisfaction. Until you are whole, I remain your loyal but slightly obsessive-compulsive God. Cheers!

P.S. The ten commandments are a nice roadmap, though I didn't make that Moses guy, and I never put rules on stone tablets. But to make it easier for you, I've incorporated those into my spreadsheet decisions. This is very important. The eleventh Commandment is "Thou shalt not tell the living what happens when they die." My favorite genre is suspense!

I looked up at Rita, "What the actual fuck?"

I stared out into the ocean, down the cliff, turned my head, turned my whole body around, looked behind me, looked at Rita, looked at my coffee. I was just suffocating in bum fuck Tennessee. Now I'm in a café reading god's feeble attempt at humor?

"Is this really a laughing matter, Rita? Is this the appropriate time and place to joke about Moses and pi?"

Rita sat silently, sipping her coffee and reaching out her hand across the table. "I promise it's going to be okay. I pinky promise you." She held her pinky up with a grin.

I didn't give her my pinky. I am not a pinky promiser. I gave her a deep, bellowing laugh and spit, "Oh no, fuck this, this is so fucked. What the fuck? Fuck all of this." Rita just nodded, licking her lips and waiting for this expected reaction to pass.

"Finish your coffee and I'll show you to your room," Rita said, like a concierge at the Plaza Hotel. I asked if I could get drunk in this hellscape, and suddenly the bike helmet guy was beside me with a Manhattan.

Rita warned, "It's like Colorado here, the way the altitude affects things. You'll get quite tipsy on that one drink."

"Oh really, Rita, really? I'll tell you what's gonna happen here. I will sit and drink six Manhattans, rip up this ridiculous menu, and figure out how to get the fuck out of here." I could hear my voice trembling, but I went on. "You know what's really fucked up, Rita, if that's your real name, is that I'm supposed to be going home today. I'm supposed to be done with that stupid Appalachian Trail. I should be sitting in my bathtub, sleeping in satin sheets, scheduling a massage and manicure. Instead, I'm sitting here with someone who looks like my high school pottery teacher, reading a menu like I'm at a fucking Applebee's." I couldn't stop.

Rita just kept nodding. "You have every reason to be angry, but anger is a secondary emotion. At the heart of this anger is fear, Renata. I've not met anyone yet who isn't afraid when they get here. It's normal. And you'll get past it because Missingville is really a wonderful place." Her voice sounded slow and syrupy.

I just stared at her. I stopped talking and started to cry. Actual tears came, and I was glad I still had this bodily function. I put my forehead on the table and said, "I can't believe my friend left me on that fucking trail. I can't believe that guy killed me." I sat up and started pinching my arms. "This must be a dream,"

I said, pinching myself and realizing I couldn't feel the pain.

I leaned back, made a sort of "Ugh" sound and said, "Okay, Rita, I'm sorry I assaulted you. What happens next?"

"Oh, honey, I've experienced much worse since I've been on the welcoming committee. Just last week, a newcomer called me a basic-ass, carpet-munching, bull-dyke. I found that interesting since I've never identified as a lesbian. Do I look gay to you? Never mind. Let's just take a moment to acclimate to the real beauty Missingville has to offer." She closed her eyes, smiled, and even let out a little moan.

Rita was right about the booze. I was wasted, slumped back in my chair, my feet on the table, a broken martini glass on the stone beneath me. I closed my eyes too and threw my head back.

"And to think, I was contemplating going gay just before I came here," I said with a wink.

"It's time to go, Renata," Rita said as she stood up. She guided me out of the café and onto a paved turquoise path, lined with purple pine trees and golden grape vines. I put my head on her shoulder. Rita said she made a special request for the path to be paved, so as not to trigger me with a rocky, dirt trail. How thoughtful.

"I want to go home, Rita," I said, thinking of my parents.

"I know, I know, I know," she repeated, as we took a fork that led to palm trees and the smell of the ocean. "You're going to be in the tropical neighborhood of General Population. We knew that was your favorite type of foliage."

The walkway brought us to a beach with white sand and blue water. It looks like god got the colors right here. We walked right up to the water, and I let it come up over my ankles. I tilted my head back and let the sun warm my face. For a moment, it felt like living.

But of course, Rita couldn't let a girl have a normal, life-like moment. She came up behind me and said it was time to go to my bunk.

"My bunk? My bunk? Am I in afterlife prison?"

Rita shook her head. She sighed like she was growing tired of me and wishing her welcome committee shift were over already. "Just come with me, okay?"

We walked down the beach and came upon what looked like a commercial for an all-inclusive. There were rows of huts, the kind right on the water. We walked along the deck and approached a hut that stood out with its yellow walls and pink roof. I'm not sure why I was put in the Barbie Dream House equivalent of a Tahitian hut, but there I was.

"We've decided that having a roommate would be best for you," Rita said as a woman appeared at the entrance.

"Well, well, well, look who finally showed up. I'm Shay and I have the bottom bunk. This isn't up for negotiation." Shay was tall and curvy, black-skinned with long fingers and nails extending three inches off her hands. She wore a yellow bikini and a bright pink sarong around her waist. She was dressed in Barbie colors to match her house, which wasn't a fashion choice I would have made, but who knows who controls these things here. She had scabbed indentations around her wrists. Her lips were purple.

I said nothing as I walked inside. On the top bunk was a blanket, the one I clutched as a child, printed with faded blue bunnies and baskets of flowers. I called it my "Hanky Danky Blankie." On the bed was a bottle of gin and a stack of clothes. All of them matched exactly what I was wearing, duplicate pairs of shorts and tank tops. I thought of cartoons and how the Powerpuff Girls wore the same thing in every episode. There was also one hot pink swimsuit, a yellow sarong, and a pair of white flip flops. Barbie, again.

In the kitchen area there were my favorites- avocados, mangos, kiwis, and a bag of skittles. The fridge was stocked with oat milk, vegan butter, tofu, and spinach.

Shay pointed to the bathroom. "Yes, there's a sink and a shower. That's all you'll need."

Rita hugged me, saying, "Well, I'm gonna skedaddle. I'm here if you need anything. I stay in the desert area of the General Population. You can find me in the airstream, painted with sunflowers. Shay is an old-timer. You're in good hands."

I was suddenly exhausted. I felt like my legs were going to give out on me. My eyes would not stay open. I was going to pass out. The last thing I saw before I went out was Shay, stepping towards me as her sarong fell off and her huge boobs bounced towards me.

That's how the first day went in Missingville.

I hope you never have to come here. I hope you die and someone you love, or at least a nice nurse, paramedic, or friendly motorist is there with you. I hope it's graceful and unsurprising like the tides. I hope you ride the wave to Deadtown, your body buried in the plot next to your wife. I hope you don't need this stopgap, but if you do, know it's going to start this way, on a patio on Italy, or in the middle of the Sahara Desert, or perhaps in your living room where the fire is burning, and your cat is sleeping on your lap. And someone like Rita will guide you to a hut where you'll wear the same clothes every day. My best advice is to think hard before you wear those stained sweatpants and go braless to the grocery store. You don't want your tits bouncing all around for the days, or even years you'll be floating among the missing.

Chapter 5

During my first three days here, I slept. On the fourth day, I woke up on the sofa in the hut, the bunny blanket draped over the bottom half of me. I could hear seagulls and the lapping of waves. I sat up and immediately laid back down. I hear it takes time for the soul to know how to stay awake without circadian rhythm. I woke up again not knowing what day it was. Did they have days here, a calendar? This time I got up and felt like my legs could hold me.

Shay was on the deck, sunning and reading a fashion magazine. She was ruggedly beautiful, with velvety skin of a woman half her age of forty-eight. I envied her perfectly arched, not too thin, not too thick eyebrows. And just like when I was alive, I wanted her double D's. Her arms and legs bore the marks of trauma, with dark spots and keloid scars. Her feet looked as though they never had the honor of wearing shoes.

But those hands, with their slender fingers and classic French tips, I know she was glad she got those nails done just before she died.

I walked outside. "How long have I been asleep?"

"Oh, honey, time is all jacked up here, you'll see. But I'd say in human time it was probably three days. It happens to everyone, the initial Missingville coma," Shay said without looking up from her make-up tutorial article.

"So, what am I supposed to do now?" I sounded childish.

"Whatever you want, girl. This is paradise."

I really wanted this girl to look at me.

I realized that I had been asleep for three days and I didn't eat or pee. And now I was up, and I didn't have to pee. But I did have a change of clothes, food, and booze. "What's the deal with having a body, but not having a body? Do you shower, or take a shit here?"

Shay laughed, looked up at me, and asked me to sit down.

"Ok, Renata, here's the deal. God did us a solid on this one, let me tell you. We don't shit or piss, we don't have to shower, we don't sweat, we don't bleed. It's impossible to get hurt here, so there are no cuts or bruises." I looked at her legs when she said this.

"I know, I know. My body is a god damned mess, but these are all from living. You'll keep those marks on your neck, and you'll wear that same white girl outfit every day, unless you're here, then you can wear your swimsuit. You won't get your period. You won't get hungry. You won't gain a pound, which is almost the best part of it all. You'll eat and drink for the pleasure of it. I can see you were one of those basic bitches who loved her some kale smoothies, so you can have those. Oh, and everything good about a body still happens here, and girl, that means sex!" She hollered "sex" like Oprah saying, "You get a car, and you get a car!"

I told her the whole thing was ridiculous.

"Don't knock it, newbie. You can get a massage, exercise, get a facial, a haircut or even Botox if you'd like. It's heaven, except it's not, but you know that part. You're just here until they find you and then it's on to Heaven or Hell, except it's called the Light Side and the Dark Side. It's important not to sin here, just like on Earth."

She got up and jumped into the water, telling me to get on my swimsuit and get in.

I joined her and there was everything about the ocean you love without the things you hate. The water didn't sting my eyes; it didn't taste salty. I could see to the bottom, and it was full of fish and coral, without any seaweed, jellyfish, or fish you might mistake for a shark. Just a few feet from me, a whale jumped out of the water, blowing out purple water.

You've never seen water like this. God was extra. The water was all the colors, a rainbow, but also teal, salmon, periwinkle, the Crayon colors. But not in stripes like a rainbow. It was more like a Van Gogh, with swirls of colors like Starry Night. I looked down at my body, which, as you know, is just like smoke, and my torso was a swish of color.

Shay and I floated in silence for a bit. I was on my back, my hands out at my side, my legs spread, like the position I died in. I forgot I was dead for a while. In this moment, I was happy to be dead, to be here, to be in a Tahitian resort with my new friend. Admittedly, what I kept ruminating on was this whole "you won't get fat" thing. I mean, thank you, god. As I floated, I put my hands on my smokey thighs, my evaporated stomach, even my transparent ass and thought this was close enough to Heaven.

Someone murdered me.

I am dead.

I'm in an afterlife that I don't understand.

And I was still here thinking about the true gift it was to stay thin.

Stop it, ladies. Stop it right now.

Chapter 6

Later that day, Shay recommended that I explore a bit. "You might get lost, but you're already lost, of course, so what does it matter? Check this place out. There are mountains and farms, crowded cities, and abandoned ghost towns. I once found a prison where a few people chose to go because it was the only place that ever felt like home. Crazy shit out there, I'm telling you."

I changed into my same outfit, but this one didn't have the pee stain. I was grateful for that. But the marks around my neck remained. I thought god could have let us be healed and without reminders of how we died, but who am I?

I was sure I was roofied in the water. I came back outside with a light spring in my step. This wasn't normal. Freaking out and clawing Shay's eyes out seemed like the appropriate behavior of someone who was just murdered and dropped into a kind of Purgatory. But I felt a strange acceptance. Maybe there's something in the water, in the coffee, in the gin.

Still, I thought about god and didn't trust them.

I wondered if I could go back to the café and talk to the one-armed waiter. He seemed like someone who could break it down for a commoner like me. The welcome committee felt like The Man to me. "Rita is not your friend," I told myself. The jury is still out on Shay. I wasn't going to drink the Kool-Aid here.

But that acceptance was fleeting. Without a heart, lungs, or sweat glands, I can't say I had a panic attack. There was no pounding in my chest, no heaving in and out, no droplets going down my cleavage. What there was, though, was a need to be on the ground. My body needed grounding. I dropped to my hands and knees and crawled out onto the deck. Once outside, I laid my cheek down on the hot deck, my butt up in the air like a yoga pose.

"I just need to be down here. I just need to be close to the ground." I whispered.

I looked up and instead of seeing my roommate with a comforting expression on her face, the woman was sitting in an Adirondack chair with a fucking welder's helmet on her head. That's right. She was sitting in her swimsuit, her long legs out in front of her, with this helmet on her head like she's repairing a bridge.

I sat up, the anxiety quickly replaced by bewilderment. I watched her shaking her head, making hand motions, raising her fist, yelling, "You bastards, you dumb bastards." She looked ridiculous in a bathing suit, sitting next to an ocean paradise with a welder's helmet on her head. I went inside and got the gin.

When I came back, she lifted the helmet and wiped her eyes. She shook her head and made a frustrating growling sound. Turning to me, she said, "Well, I guess I need to explain this to you now, don't I?" I stood in front of her and shrugged.

Shay said I could put the helmet on and see what's happening on Earth.

"I'm sorry, what?" I thought I misheard her.

Shay repeated herself.

Stunned, I said, "This is the best god could come up with, a welder's helmet? Couldn't they have made a hologram or something? Anything? They can't at least give us an iPad, a laptop, hell, even a movie projector?" I was gob smacked.

"It's bullshit, I swear, it's absolute bullshit," Shay said.

"Yeah, it's bullshit," I said. "I cannot believe I am in the afterlife and technology is this far behind. Can't god move mountains? Aren't they able to, oh, I don't know, make people come here? For his sake, the water here is a fucking rainbow Picasso painting. And god can't give us something better than a metal helmet to wear to see Earth? I mean..." I was a child, yes, but I stand by my astonishment.

Shay interrupted. "I think you're missing the point here, Renata."

I shook my head, paced, bit my fingernails. I wanted to miss the point here. I absolutely wanted to avoid any points.

"Renata, get over the helmet part, okay. It's dumb, it's old-school, but it's actually sorta modern, considering there are people here who lived thousands of years ago. Either way, get over it. The point is, you can put it on and see what's happening on Earth. You can see your family. You can see your body. You can see whoever put you here." She sounded like my first boyfriend explaining with frustration how to play Fortnite.

All I could do was shake my head.

She continued. "Listen, I've been here two years, one month, and four days. It's cool and all. Shit, the hut, the water, the sunsets, the guy I see sometimes over in the Valley. But I want my body to be found so my daddy can bury me, and I want the mother fucker who killed me to be caught. So, I check in. And you will too. Get over the damn helmet! You're in an in-between here, Renata. You'll want to check on the world."

I squatted down so I was at eye level with Shay. "Okay, okay, this is a lot. This is a lot. Okay, okay, can you tell me about what you were just watching?" I wanted to trauma bond, murder bond, death bond, whatever.

She let her guard down and I was grateful. Shay was born into a normal family. The electricity was sometimes shut off, and she ate lots of bologna, but she had bedtime stories and a dad who'd take her fishing. She walked to school as a kid, passing by boarded up buildings and hypodermics on the sidewalk. Her older brother didn't touch drugs or alcohol. "He not only wasn't out on the streets, he was a damn cello prodigy, if you can believe that shit," she said, shaking her head and letting out a chuckle.

In her wildest dreams, her mother never envisioned that one of her girls would be an addict. Sure, her friends' kids were going down wrong paths with the wrong friends, but not her Shay and Shannon. Her mom was wrong on both accounts.

"It's boring, really, Renata, the whole 'life started to spiral out of control' story. What gets me is how I wore DARE shirts in junior high and told my sister I would never smoke marijuana. I was straight up ashamed of her. Six months later, she and I were snorting mashed up pills in our bedroom as our mom called us down for dinner. My poor mom didn't have a clue."

Eventually, she sold everything she could for drugs, from her body to the X-box belonging to the uncle who molested her when he was nine. She ended up in some shit hole town in Michigan where the cops paid attention when she walked the streets looking for Johns, but sure didn't perk up when she disappeared.

"I'm the classic missing person junkie. Ignored by the cops, my case went cold before it ever heated up."

Shay was animated, her hands talking more than her mouth.

I chimed in, "Isn't it strange that we don't say 'missing people,' but instead 'missing persons? Isn't it bad grammar to say it that way? I don't get it. Have you ever thought about that?" I think this was another example of me missing the point, based on the look on Shay's face.

She told me that on a wind-chilled Tuesday night in 2022, she walked barefoot out of a motel room into a silent, dusting snow, leaving behind an unconscious man and everything she owned, including a forgotten pair of snow boots she lifted from Goodwill. She walked to the edge of the parking lot and into the car of the predator that would put her in Missingville.

There were no clues. The cameras at the crummy, hourly rate motel weren't functional, of course.

"I promise you, every camera is working around America's Pottery Barns and Ikea stores, but an hourly motel outside Detroit hasn't fixed their cameras since it was mostly occupied by white folks in the seventies." I felt uneasy, with my whiteness and all.

Yes, it took four days for anyone to call the police. Some annoyed beat cop finally entered a formal missing person report, and an overzealous new detective told her family they were "tracking down every lead." But the truth is, there never was a lead.

She did not make the news. "I didn't have a home, per se, okay? So, it's kinda hard to say where I was missing from. Does that make sense?"

It made sense and I was ashamed. If missing is not being where you are expected to be, and you're a rich kid with an apartment in the gentrified part of town, a regular salon for eyebrow threading, a favorite bubble tea spot, a preferred hot yoga instructor, there are clear expectations. Women like me leave clues in Pilates studios, Instagram posts, the last order we placed on Postmates.

Cops looked for Shay in trap houses and the camps under overpasses. Shay watched investigators ask a few questions here and there, but not enough and not to the right people.

"Hello!" Shay said. "Women who sell their bodies give a fuck ton of blow jobs to rich guys from the 'burbs. Right now, there's a man with a dad bod and a dead girl buried at his favorite duck hunting spot, but oh no, let's keep looking in the burnt-out buildings near the motel. Fucking cops. Fucking cops." She's shaking her head, making tisk, tisk noises.

"I'm so sorry, Shay." I felt a hopelessness in her that scared me.

"It's not your fault, of course, and I got nothing against you, but poor, brown, black drug-using, sex-selling missing women like me don't get the same kind of detective work you're probably getting right now. No offense, Renata. But my family has just been placated by lazy cops. Watch a documentary about

Samuel Little and you'll see how a man can go around slaughtering brown prostitutes for decades without being caught." As she was talking, I thought how this was another thing that poser of a god could help with, but no.

Shay is surprised at how things have changed since she's been here. There is this trend of woke people, people who want Instagram followers, the Kardashians, or the next pop artist of the day who want to help make people like her unmissing. It's all the rage. Rich people buy pick-up trucks for missing teenagers who get found alive in pedophile's basements. They donate money for rewards. The white saviors flock to stories like Shay's. But none of this leads to the trailer, behind which is Shay's body.

Shay knows all of this because she puts on the helmet once a week. She used to put it on several times a day, something she looked forward to the way she craved heroin. Lately, though, there's nothing to see in terms of finding her killer. She only looks now to see how her nieces have grown or to hear what the doctor said at her best friend's appointment with the oncologist. She watches her brother in the symphony. She knows where her body is and what her murderer is doing now. She no longer looks for him. It's just a matter of watching her family go on without her.

I felt ashamed, thinking of my picture being on the evening news, people saying I "lit up a room when I walked in." My high school friends, my sorority sisters, my spinning class teacher, I imagine they're all making t-shirts, walking in the woods wearing orange vests, making pleas on television for me to come home. They're all clamoring to talk to the cops and have a little moment in the limelight.

Shay's friends don't talk to cops. She explained, "Of course, my friend Maria saw the car. We made eye contact as we drove off, but that girl's not talking. I don't blame her."

Shay tells me she loves being missing, except when she puts on the helmet. These are the best days of her life. She's not getting high, planning the next time she can get high, lying about getting high, paranoid about getting caught getting high, or trading her body to get high.

"Are you ready to see for yourself? Put it on?" Shay asked as she picked up the helmet.

I wasn't, but I did.

Chapter 7

I sat on the deck, my feet dangling in the water, little fish eating at my toes like they do in those cafes in Japan. I put on that stupid, heavy helmet for a morning session of what I like to call, "It's hard enough to accept that I'm dead. Let's take a peek at Earth and see what kind of suffering I left behind."

The helmet is heavy. It's hard to keep my head up, making the whole thing all the more ridiculous. I want to talk to Rita about getting with the times and at least creating a hologram situation.

There's a crowd of reporters and curious Appalachians gathered outside a trailer, which is some kind of excuse for a police station. This, friends, is not reassuring. My parents stand in front of a mess of microphones. Looking ten years older than the last time I saw him, my dad wears a baseball cap and a Tennessee Titans sweatshirt. His trendy tortoise shell glasses fog up as he stands with his arm around my mom. He wipes his nose with a blue handkerchief. I don't remember him having lines on his forehead the way he does now. I don't remember him ever having a runny nose. He worries his legs might give out underneath him. He tries not to lock his legs, thinking about how he heard once that a person will faint if they stand straight legged too long. In his pocket is a crystal he found on my nightstand. He holds it. He hasn't found the box of dildos, and for that, I'm grateful.

My mom's voice is high and cracking as she says, "Renata, please come home." She tries to look normal, approachable, middle-class, someone worthy of having something lost returned to her. She wears a grey sweater that hangs off one shoulder. Underneath is a hot pink tank top. Around her neck is the pendant my dad gave her on her first Mother's Day. It's my birthstone, an emerald, inside the shape of a lotus flower. She wears a bit of foundation but no eye make-up. She's not crying, but her lips tremble like she's cold; at the same time, I can see sweat running down her armpits to her waistline. I can hear her heart pounding, and I see the serotonin monitor in her brain blinking in neon red, "Dangerously Low." She's got the pulse of someone who hasn't slept in days. Her hair is in a ponytail and she's wearing her thick glasses instead of contacts. I wonder if she hired a PR person to help her "look more poor."

Rich people don't get sympathy. Her pleading for me to come home has the potential of being akin to "let them eat cake." She knows better. The shock hasn't worn off, as is evidenced by my dad's blood pressure and my mom's shaking hands.

My mom is still thinking about the phone call. She was on her way to a mani-pedi when Kathleen called her.

"Nora, it's Kathleen. I'm sure this is going to all be resolved quickly, but I wanted to tell you that I can't find Renata. I'm in Lefton and the police are here with me. She hasn't called you, has she?"

My mom pulled over. "Police? You're with the police? No, I haven't talked to her since you two left." I hated that my mom's first thought was something along the lines of "I knew this was a bad idea." A momentary "I told you so" registered in her voice when she said, "Where are you and how do I get there?"

Kathleen talked me into hiking the Appalachian Trail. I wasn't a hiker, and I wasn't a fan of anywhere or anyone that was characterized as "Appalachian," but I was also a huge fan of Kathleen, and I never told her no. I thought I'd get a scratch or two, some mosquito bites and sunburn. I was excited for the opportunity to walk hours a day and lose lots of weight in a week's time. Honestly, the losing weight part is probably why I said yes.

What I did not expect is to die out there. What I did not expect is to suffer death by strangulation. What I did not expect is to be dead and watching press conferences about my murder.

A uniformed woman wearing several tones of browns and beiges says, "We believe Renata Foster was somewhere around the 193-mile marker when she lost track of her hiking partner. We're asking the public's help to be on the look-out for a woman, aged twenty-eight, five foot, five inches tall, weighing approximately 110 pounds. She has long blond hair and hazel eyes, wearing a white tank top and khaki cargo shorts."

I cringed at the explanation of my outfit, the ugliest thing I've ever worn, and here I am, dead and wearing the same clothes day after day. I'd like to take a minute and suggest that you always leave the house looking your best. Don't give in to that temptation to run to Wal-Mart in your Crocs and pajama pants. If you die in such a get-up, you'll wear it here too, and looking good is still important in the afterlife, especially for women, which is disappointing like so many other things here. Misogyny is alive and well among the dead and unwell.

The cop holds up my picture, which I'm pleased to say is one of my favorites. It's from a trip to Maine in the fall. I'm wearing the quintessential white cable knit sweater and my hands are wrapped around a bright yellow coffee mug. I've got a gorgeous orange and green floral Yeves St. Laurent scarf tied around my neck and my hair is curled just right around my face. The freckles on my nose make me look younger, but I was due for Botox, so my forehead says I've reached my late twenties.

"Do you suspect foul play?" The reporters have boners over the first thing to happen in this town since someone was lynched in a year too disgusting to think about.

"We are not ruling anything out," says the cop who is growing tired of repeating these same six words.

"What about the woman she was hiking with? Is she a suspect?"

"We are not ruling anything out."

"Have the search dogs signaled on her scent?"

"That I can confirm, yes." She's pleased she can answer something but keeps to herself that the scent was picked up miles from where she's standing.

I pan out and see people walking around in glow-in-the dark vests, carrying poles to poke the ground with each step. The search parties consist of volunteers who watch true crime documentaries and suffer from low self-esteem. I can hear them thinking, as they walk through the woods, "I hope I find her, I want to be the one on the news. Maybe I could even testify at her murderer's trial." I appreciate these people; deep down, we're all narcissists.

I see the place where I was killed. The circle of stones remains and there's ash in the center. The tent, the rope, the knife, murder things, they're gone. There's no blood; there never was. My piss is long washed away.

The place where I stopped breathing, it's just dirt in the woods. I look closely to see if I can see the place where my boots moved frantically on the ground as I was being suffocated, but there's nothing there. Rain must have washed away any clue of something sinister happening here. My death space is nothing special, nothing identifiable.

I look around the campfire ring. Is one of my earrings there? My watch? The signet ring I wore on my left pinky? A clump of hair? I don't see any part of myself. Not one thing.

I pan out. There are no volunteers near this spot.

Overzealous retirees with matching shirts, saying "Tennessee Missing Persons Alliance," walk around an industrial park fifteen miles from where I died. They're following the lead of an old man who said he saw me walking along a roadway. They don't know that the late stages of dementia are creeping in, that this guy also thought yesterday that he saw Smokey the Bear in his vegetable garden.

Then it occurs to me, I don't see my body either. I'm frantically looking along the trail, around his campsite, towards the road, in a cave. I don't see anything. There are no humps in the landscape shaped like me. I'm looking for a "shallow grave" and realize I don't even know what that means. You've heard it a million times too, haven't you? "Shallow grave." But what is it exactly? A body partially under dirt and leaves?

Should I be looking for branches or rocks? What the hell is a shallow grave?

I hear the thoughts of onlookers, people sitting in their recliners watching the news, the drunk guy at the dive bar watching the TV hanging over the bartender. I hear past classmates, a guy I met on a Tinder date and blew in the front seat of his car, the lady that gave me piano lessons in grade school, a high school teacher who caught me cheating on a history test. They're thinking things like, "I bet the dad killed her. I bet her boyfriend killed her. I bet she ran off just to get attention. I heard she was hiking with her new lesbian lover. I bet she and that brand new Mercedes flew off a cliff."

When I was alive and people asked what superpower I would choose, I'd say I wanted to be able to read people's minds. If you've ever wanted the same, I'm here to tell you it's not all it's cracked up to be. You don't want to know that your friend, chatting with you at a seaside café, is wondering how you missed all those hairs on your chin, or that your work bestie is always thinking how annoying your voice is. When you die, you'll get to hear the thoughts of the alive, and that's all the mind reading a soul needs for one life or death.

Chapter 8

Six days after I died, I had a swim with a dolphin named Tim.

"Renata, since you're new here, can you tell me, does everyone on Earth still believe that dolphins like to hump humans?" He spoke in the voice of a toddler just learning to talk, his "R's" sounding British and his tone high-pitched and piercing.

Floating on a flamingo-shaped raft, a gin and tonic in my hand, I said, "I think it's time you stop worrying about what's happening on Earth."

It wasn't lost on me that I needed this advice as much as Tim. I've been thinking about how I was that girl, a cliché. A murdered girl, like the rest of them, mostly, but being in this crowd didn't make me feel less alone when the breath was squeezed out of my lungs. I was distracted by the mess of it all; being here, everyone else being there, how cruel the divide is, and maybe by design.

Soon after I got here, I met a woman. She was in General Population, living in the Arctic area where the snow was pink, and the sky was apricot. I came upon her because I had a sudden urge to take a stab at dog sledding. When you're dead, you'll be compelled to do things your alive self never imagined. I woke up with a wanting to be cold, to be gliding on snow with animals pulling me like cargo. I bounced on over to Arctic Avenue and found a woman sauntering around pens of huskies, pouring food into bowels, and petting heads.

"It's time for a ride, Indigo. I know you're ready to go, Shasta. Give momma a minute, Roxanne." She had salt and pepper hair in waves around her face, and blue eyes that made her appear more like a Huskie herself than the human she once was. Though she was sporting a fur hat, she wore nothing more than a blood-soaked terry cloth robe. She had on one yellow fluffy slipper and there was a gash from her right eye to the left side of her chin.

"Hi. I'm not sure why I'm here, except I woke up wanting to do that thing you do. I want to go sledding, or be dog sledded, or, I don't know, I wanted to be here." I sounded exactly like who I was, a dead poser.

"Well, hello. I'm Charlene and you've come to the right place. You'd be surprised how many people wake up wanting to come here. I think god knows the healing power of a good run." Her skin was young, white, and smooth, contrasting her hair.

The actual dog sledding isn't the point of this story, so I'll skip to how she motivated me to tell you everything about dying. Out of a modest cabin came a young man. His hair was in cornrows, and he had the whitest teeth I've ever seen. His smile had those perfect wrinkles around each corner of his mouth. He wore a baggy gray sweatshirt that matched his sweatpants. On his feet were muddy socks, pulled up to his knees. I gathered that he drowned because on his head and down the back of his neck was seaweed, housing a small crab that circled the crown of his head.

"Charlene, I've got a pot of chili on the stove if you're hungry," he said as he wiped his hands on a towel.

I said hello and introduced myself. Michael said the same thing about strangers showing up to go dog sledding and that he had never even heard of such a sport until he died.

"I decided I had to be where Charlene was, though, so here I am. A Cuban dude from Tallahassee feeding Huskies and hangin' in the freezing cold." He looked at Charlene like a son, no, like a nephew. I knew they weren't lovers, but I couldn't figure out what they were.

"Do you mind me asking how you all know each other?" I asked.

Charlene told me she was murdered, stabbed to death, and thrown over a fishing boat into the Gulf of Mexico. Michael was the unlucky guy to have knocked on her door the day before, offering to sell her a pest control package. His face recorded clearly on her Ring Doorbell, he was arrested soon after her boss reported her missing.

"I was born with bad luck. My dad had it too. He went up for a burglary he didn't commit, and there I was, headed toward a conviction for her murder. They released me after questioning me the second time, but I knew they were coming for me." Michael was smiling, looking at Charlene like their story was more of an inside joke than a tale of prison and bloody knives.

Charlene explained, "When I got here, I spent the first twelve days with an aching in my sliced open heart as I watched Earth and saw the police focusing on Michael. Of course, I could see my real killer the whole time too. It was my neighbor, a guy with money and letters after his name. I watched that bastard laugh at the evening news while the police asked for help finding Michael, their person if interest."

Michael just kept on smiling. "Yeah, it's some crazy shit. I knew I was going down for it. I kissed my sleeping momma and took her car. I also took her savings from the Folger's can and headed north." He was wiping his bowl with a piece of buttered bread, licked his fingers and chuckled.

"But obviously I'm here. I took a turn too fast on this windy road outside Atlanta and damnit if I didn't end up drowning in creek. Let me tell you, if your car ever goes into a body of water, go to the back window and kick it out. Since I been here, me and the other car-drowning guys talk about how this should be taught in schools, ya know?"

Charlene touched his shoulder and explained that when Michael got here, Rita led him right up to her door and said, "I think you should meet the man accused of killing you."

Michael whispered, "Isn't that just crazy?" His eyes got wide.

Charlene whispered, "It's fucking bat shit crazy." Her eyes got wide.

They lived together in a relationship I couldn't put my finger on because it's this kind: a murder victim and the man accused of killing her. You don't have relationships like that on Earth. These two are bonded in the untruths of the living world. Charlene and Michael check out Earth and see their story on Unsolved Mysteries. Michael comes in at number eighteen on America's Most Wanted. A podcast called, "Find the Monster?" consists of twelve episodes of armchair detectives talking about the murderer on the run, and where is Charlene's body. Charlene's family wears shirts with Michael's picture on them, "Help Find This Man" printed across the chest. Michael's mother pleaded with him on CNN to turn himself in. Even she believed he murdered a woman he spoke to for fifty-seven seconds about how ants infiltrate a home in the spring.

Listening to this story, all I could think about was how easy it would be to clear things up if Charlene just went to Earth and said, "Hey, the perv on the corner killed me. Michael is innocent." If you believe that ghosts can turn your vacuum on or move the toaster, aren't you pissed that they don't clear up some things?

Here's a matter I left out at first. I want to go to the Light Side of Deadtown, yes, like Heaven, after this. I'm in an in between place where my actions are still being judged, and god advised us not to tell you anything. Taboo is an understatement. Turns out, the Eleventh Commandment is "Thou shalt not die and tell the living about being dead." That's right, I'm risking my death for you here. I'm doing the thing.

Michael and Charlene compelled me to break the eleventh rule. I am resolute in telling you my story. The Michaels and Charlenes of the world are up here watching families muddle through messy misconceptions of their undoing, all the while just eating chili and riding sleds.

The way I see it, I'm contributing so much to humanity, it might outweigh god's silly after-death rule. Maybe I'll change god's mind about the whole thing. When Charlene's family gets closure, when the real perp goes to prison for her murder, when Michael's mother can see that he's innocent, won't this cancel out me breaking number eleven? You've watched crime documentaries until the stories bleed together. You know there are executed men, mostly in that god forsaken place called Texas, who were innocent. Michael told me one such precious soul went to the Light Side of Deadtown and met the woman everyone thought he killed. They're best pals like Charlene and Michael. And they trauma bond on a level off the charts. And they watch humans getting it all wrong, and they don't heal the daily pain of their families.

I told Tim I've decided to educate the Earthlings, and yes, there are dolphins-raping-humans jokes out there, but there was a breakdancer in the Olympics who took up all of the comedy space as I was leaving Earth, so no one cared about water mammals and their sexual proclivities.

Tim said he heard about that poor woman, and he'd hoped she'd come to Missingville because he low-key always wanted to learn how to breakdance.

Chapter 9

It may surprise you that we don't spend all our time watching the living. All I can say is, it's a lot. I tripped on mushrooms a few times, and it's like that. After tripping for a few hours, you just want to be yourself already. It's agonizing, really, watching the living not find me. It's exhausting, watching Killer walk around Earth uninhibited. It's a gut punch, watching this person I'm kind of in love with, if I'm honest with you, feel all that guilt over my death.

So, I went with Shay on a tour of Missingville. We walked, but in a way that felt more like floating, through deserts, snowcapped mountains, waterfalls, an amusement park, even a bowling alley. There were people on skis, in scuba diving equipment, walking with parachutes dragging behind them. I saw an old man and woman holding hands, sitting by a lake in airplane seats.

A few women nodded to me as they passed by, with rope burns around their necks like mine. There were more women than men it seemed, but of course that shouldn't surprise you, what with us getting murdered all the time and all. That excludes the millions of men at Valient Valley, a place for those lost in all the wars since war became a thing. It's the largest section here and it's said that when god makes their once every one-hundred-year appearance, this is where they go. Don't get me wrong, the Veterans deserve it, but it's just another detail about god that annoys me. Do they have so much going on that they can't hang out more often? They can't be bothered with Suicide Center, Milk Carton Mountain, or even General Population?

As Shay and I hopped around, Sodom and Gomora came to mind. I'm no biblical scholar, but I do know that these two cities were hotbeds of gluttony. Lots of sex and hollandaise sauce, too many orgasms, and too much Absinth. I was astonished to see so much hedonism in a place most comparable to Purgatory.

Mostly, though, souls here aren't debaucherous as much as they are content. Old timey men with bad coughs and soot-covered faces, who died in coal mines, were grinning, whistling, playing hopscotch, the behaviors of jovial folks. I suppose if your demise came because you were collateral damage of the Industrial Revolution, you'd be skipping along here too. There is also an area called Slave Cenote, which is the most beautiful area here, with its bright blue water and constant sun rays. I thank god for that.

There's a group of women wearing nothing but leaves and vines over their crotches huddled together laughing and jumping, more animal than human. Shay said they were the first ones here and everyone wishes god would give them the ability to speak a language someone here might understand, but true to form, god ignores that request.

It seems that the shittier one's life was, the less burdened a person is by their Earth life. People hunted by bison aren't wearing the damn helmet. Shay said an acquiescence happens eventually to people whose bodies are impossible to find. Especially in cases of dismemberment, it's just not gonna happen.

"Ain't no one looking in the landfill anymore," she says as she takes my arm, and we jump onto a yacht, complete with a captain who's still wildly handsome despite having half his face eaten off by a shark. We sailed for a while, drank wine spritzers, and ate what I had to inform Shay was escargot. She spit it out and said it reminded her of dicks in the August heat. I told her now that I thought about it, she was right.

In the desert area, people who liked a good old-fashioned trip were eating mushrooms, flapping their arms, and saying things like, "I always wanted to fly, and just look at me now." They looked like chickens to me, a flightless bird last time I checked. A guy was hugging a cactus, saying, "I always wanted to embrace something dangerous. I lived a safe life but look at me now." Lame.

In the mountains, we found a middle-aged guy with a classic dad bod, poking a campfire with a stick. He was wearing a bloodied Coors Light t-shirt and had only one leg. Still, he stood steady and strong next to the fire, saying, "I wanted to burn everything when I was alive and look at me now, the head fire starter." I wondered if he also wet the bed and hurt animals.

Around the fire, naked forms, sexing each other in a restrained, hushed rhythm. I have to admit, I gawked. With bodies like smoke, I wondered if sex was just merging into another person. I got closer, but Shay said I was a freak and pulled me away.

I'm uneasy about the orgies. What would god think of the strippers and cocaine? Shay said sins are only sins if you hurt someone, so don't worry about it, and I decide that's good enough for me.

The bowling alley was everything you'd expect. It smelled like feet and pretzels. The pitchers of beer in those cheap plastic pitchers came out of a moldy gun. At the bar sat a chain-smoking woman aged forty-five but looking a solid sixty-seven. Her hair was short in the front, longer in the back, permed into a 1984 mullet. She squirted yellow goop onto a basket of tortilla chips saying, "I always loved waiting tables at the diner, but making plastic food for dead bowlers fills a hole in me I didn't know I had. Look at me now, dead but more alive than ever." Her left cheek was bruised a dull yellow that matched her Fleetwood Mac t-shirt. I envied her Jordache jeans. Those would go for a good $200 on Etsy. The bowlers included a mob man who broke lots of knees, but it finally caught up with him. He's out there with his legs pointed outward, his knees touching each other. He's winning in a game against a bearded man in fish net stockings and a red boa, with white powder around his nose and mouth that says, "Look at me now," with no further explanation.

In a rocky, cavernous part of town, a man with one arm and no legs sat in front of a cave and says, with an Irish accent, "I always wanted to sit by Jesus' tomb, and look at me now." Just a side note, I was struck with an overwhelming confidence that this Jesus guy was just a guy. Sorry to break it to you.

Shay knew a lot of people. She introduced me to Amy, who was stabbed by her boyfriend when she told him she had the clap. There was Sydney, a careless woman who went paddle boarding in the Mediterranean and capsized when an unexpected storm came in. Michael, who was Australian, was attacked by a mountain lion, which I thought was weird because everyone knows it was dingoes wreaking havoc there. His body ended up in pieces, strewn all over the Outback. James was a death-by-suicide English professor. He hung himself from a tree deep in the woods near his boyhood home. Police are still looking for him, and his wife is being accused of his murder. He said, "Maybe I should have thought that out a bit more. I wasn't the kind of guy that watched true crime documentaries, so I was a bit naïve on how these things play out." Poor guy.

Plane Crash Peninsula, now that's a rough one. I don't want you to give up your love of travel, so I won't tell you about it.

People would say to me, "I see you were strangled. Me too. Sucked, didn't it?" One guy said, "I was shot in the leg, I should have lived, but you didn't stand a chance, did you, hon?"

I chatted with a lady who said, "Someone put a plastic bag over my head, which, let me tell you, felt like drowning, but I'm glad I don't have any marks on me. I walk through Missingville and I'm one of the pretty ones." I felt the marks around my neck and hated her a little.

Chapter 10

On day seven, I saw my little brother. As soon as I put on the helmet, there is Liam, sitting on the floor in his room. He's leaning against his bed, Chance the Rapper blaring from his Bose. He's rocking back and forth, with his head down, sobbing. His head full of garbled, twisted cellular misfiring. He's playing on repeat the day he learned to ride a bike, with me standing in the front yard jumping up and down, clapping my hands, shouting, "Don't fall, bubby!"

All the innocent things played on inside him. The walks home from school where he'd be a few steps behind me, trying to keep up, and his chatter. "Hey Renata, did you know Jared got detention today because Ms. Hartnett overheard him say the "f" word? Do you think I should do my project on dinosaurs or comets? I sure hope dad makes pasta tonight. Are we going to the lake house this weekend? Did you know that an atom is smaller than a molecule?" On and on this kid would talk, and each of the memories swirling in Liam's head were distorted in that I had patience with him. He was imagining me as a curious, interested sister, bantering back and forth about how tyrannosaurus rex was his favorite dinosaur, how the Black Hole is too big to even imagine. Me, just loving him.

He thinks of my high school graduation, where he, as a freshman, secretly felt sad that the rest of his time in high school wouldn't include me, how he'd still be known as "Renata's little brother," but without the physical presence of me in the hallways, the assemblies, the cafeteria. He thought about my ignoring him in these spaces anyway, but how he understood it. He was forgiving me with every motion of his body back and forth.

He wrapped his arms around himself as he swayed, thinking of the times way back when we'd nap together, sometimes with our mom, how we'd embrace her, and our hands would rest on each other's shoulders from across my mother's body. There I was hugging him, kissing his cheek when he ran off the soccer field. I was carrying him from the house to the pool, the concrete under our feet so hot, I would tip toe trot, which always made him cackle. He saw me holding him under his belly in the water, his face down and his legs kicking as I taught him to swim.

The last time I saw him was a typical Sunday at my parents' house. He dropped out of college, hadn't found a job yet, and felt like he was free falling. He was in love with a girl who had more ambition than him. She was studying abroad, had already earned one degree, was passionate about international law and women's rights. He didn't even know a thing about national law. He knew women were second class citizens in many countries, maybe even his own, but frankly, he didn't care, not like she cared.

He barely looked up from his phone that night. When I walked in the front door, he was lying on the couch, watching a parkour video. I walked behind him, tousled his hair, and said, "What's up, kid?" He didn't look up and swatted my hand away, saying "Nothing."

My mom called him despondent. His presence made her uncomfortable, like he was someone else's kid she had to babysit until he got his shit together. Her mood adjusted with Liam's mood. And on this Sunday, he wasn't giving a shit about us. The atmosphere was strained, not only because Liam wouldn't look away from his phone, but because my mom's disappointment and desperation were congruent, making her talk in a high-pitched voice, nervously saying things like, "Liam, why don't you come help your dad grill these hamburgers? It's okay if you don't want to. Hey Liam, tell Renata about what Grandma said last week, it's hilarious. Oh, never mind, I'll tell her."

My mom couldn't tolerate disconnection. She wanted her family members to melt into each other, the way she always melted into us. She wanted to hear her boy talk about dinosaurs again. His bearded face still looked like a kindergartner's to her. She told me once that when she talked to him, she'd imagine his baby face covered in chocolate ice cream, or his little body in a diaper, taking his first steps.

While my brother rocked and thought about that day, he felt an ache in his stomach. He saw me sit down beside him and say, "Dude, get off your phone. It's time to eat."

He stood up, looked down at me, and said, "Jesus Christ, Renata, you come over here like you're the fucking queen. Just leave me alone."

He stomped off to his room and slammed the door. My mom put her hands on the counter and bowed her head, making a tiny whimper sound as she tried not to cry. My dad said, "Well, let's just eat."

Dads get to be one digit removed from such family irregularities. He didn't imagine Liam as a baby; he didn't long for the toddler days. Liam was a grown man now, going through some existential crisis, and it would pass. Few things were a big deal to my dad. He'd often say, "It is what it is," and I will forever abhor that expression. My dad looked at us through rosy glasses.

My mother could never see her family through this lens. It isn't just "what it is." It's so much more than what it is. Everything was so much more, especially when it came to Liam. What my brother didn't realize, but was starting to now as he rocked in his bedroom, was that I didn't trigger my mom in this way. She loved me, she was supportive and, in many ways, my best friend. I didn't have the capacity to break her heart the way he did. He understood that every move he made was too powerful in our family, that he set tones he had no right to set, that his selfishness and immaturity sent electrical shocks through my mom and then bounced off the rest of us.

I ate dinner with my parents, talked about my upcoming trip to Gatlinburg with Kathleen, and listened to my dad give all his advice on what highway to take, the best places to stop in the Smoky Mountains, and how Gatlinburg itself was a gluttonous, embarrassing part of Americana.

My mom would chime in, but she kept looking towards the hallway, hoping Liam would come out and eat with us. Liam knew that's what she'd do if he abandoned dinner, yet he sat in his bedroom with Snapchat and told himself all of us were ridiculous and unreasonable.

He never came out of his room that day. I knocked on his door to tell him goodbye and when he said, "Yeah," I opened it and said, "I'm headed home."

He looked didn't look up, but said, "Ok, love ya, bye."

Liam was an "Love ya" kind of brother now. Not the kind to make eye contact and say, "I love you." This hurt my heart a little, but honestly, not a lot. I resented him for being such a little bitch if I'm honest. I left thinking, "He needs to grow the fuck up."

As he sits in his room, me gone for seven days, it's all making sense to him. He damaged our family with his indifference. He bruised my mom as he made sure not to show her one thing she wanted to see. As he admitted to himself that he knew this all along, his shame felt like bricks in his stomach, his head felt pinched in a vice. I could feel his deep desire to be nonexistent, that feeling I surmise every human feels at some point. He didn't want to die; he didn't want to hurt himself, but if an airplane crashed into the house and instantly killed him, he wouldn't be outraged.

Liam, the baby my mom couldn't let grow up, the four-year-old I carried to the pool, the teenager my dad took to football games, he knew who he was to all of us. Being with him now, as his music blared and his heart pumped fast, I felt his self-loathing, his remorse, his embarrassment. He was adored beyond what he deserved, he thought.

The helmet was an agonizing headpiece, make no mistake. It was wretched and raw, sending me into a kind of sorrow I couldn't sit with, but I couldn't escape from. Liam was twenty-four years old. He didn't know who he was, or why he was. He was running in place since he got out of high school, going through motions orchestrated by my parents and the American dream. Being a grown up, he didn't want it. He wished he could see himself the way we saw him, innocent, and worthy. How did he harden so quickly in his short life? He asked himself this as he imagined me standing in his doorway saying goodbye. Over and over, he saw himself on his bed, looking down at that goddamn phone, saying, "Love ya."

While I watched Liam though the helmet, I started pacing on the deck. I was frantic. I was yelling, "It's okay, I understand. You're perfect, I love you, you did nothing wrong."

Again, this being dead and not talking to the living is bullshit. I want to be more than a light flicker. I don't want to be a slammed door or a ball bouncing down the stairs. I want to be me, in Liam's room, sitting next to him, telling him what happened to me and where I am. I want to be so much more for the living. I didn't ask to die, I was too young to die, I had no reason to expect that my last day at home was my last day at home. But god and their shitty sense of humor has me here, silent, and stuck.

I can want all day long, but the truth is I can't figure out a way to talk to him. The archaic helmet is just a Ring Doorbell. The kind you can get for free where you can't talk through it. I've got nothing to offer Liam except a ceiling fan, his stereo, curtains, windows, his wrestling trophy sitting dusty on his desk. Like a cliché,' I stared at the light, saying "turn off, turn off, turn off already." Could I touch him? I reached out into nothingness. I tried to blow hard; could he feel my breath on the back of his neck? I have no breath. Can I send a bird? I looked outside, saw birds in trees, and willed them to unalive themselves into his window. Nothing.

I went to his phone. I stared at it, imagined my thumb on it, put my hands in the position of holding a phone, scrolled through his music. I found it, "Mr. Brightside," by the Killers. When Liam was just a toddle, I'd play it and dance with him. I think the lyrics in this song made up the first full sentence Liam ever spoke. We'd ask our dad to play it on his CD player and Liam and I would sing it into hairbrushes, jumping on the couch, dancing in our pajamas. With every cell in my dead body, I willed Spotify to go to this song. I had to sit down. I was getting lightheaded and queasy. My legs felt like Twizzlers. My arms were wet noodles, and I could hardly keep my eyes open. I lay flat on the deck, curled my hands in to fists and whispered, "Change the fucking song, just change the fucking song, change it, change it, change it." My ears popped, my eyes watered, my stomach cramped and for a second I thought I'd die again, if that were possible.

It was too much. I put my hands on the helmet to take it off, and just before I did, the song came on. I saw only a second of Liam's reaction before I lost consciousness. He stopped rocking back and forth, he looked up, all around, and said, "Oh my god, Renata?"

Chapter 11

Helmet wearing this morning.

1. A search party reconvened on the trail. I'm no surveyor, but the bird's eye view tells me they're about two miles from my body.
2. Dogs from Texas are there, because of course they are. Everyone knows that the best searchers are from Texas and Washington because these states have an ungodly number of weirdos and gun owners. Want to wind up missing? Feel like taking a little trip the M-Ville? Go to Washington and wander around in the woods, if you're a woman, that is. If you identify as a man, still go, but know it will take some time and concerted effort to get yourself murdered.
3. My killer. I don't see him. Zooming in on his campsite, I see there's a pit full of ash, a square of

matted dead grass where his tent sat, and some stumps standing up like stools. I look closer at the ground and see one stake still left, and if I look just below the dirt, a rubber mallet.

4. Looking into the mind of a member of The Texas Find 'Em Coalition, I see she's done this thirty-two times before. She's looking not only for my body, but for evidence of someone else. She's walking in a straight line with a pole thingy, moving leaves and grass with every step. "This terrain is too flat; she didn't just fall. I'm stuck on that eyewitness who saw a man camping near here. He said the man was talking to himself about skinned knees. Maybe it's nothing." But she's looking for the man, for any man. This girl, who I still want to make fun of just a little bit, might be my liberator.
5. Other search party members are thinking the same thing, I realize when I do a quick glance into twenty-five of them. These aren't just voyeurs wanting to locate a skull, or Reddit users preoccupied with crime. They've got the real deal out there.
6. I zoom out, way out, and I can't find Killer anywhere.

Chapter 12

I played a lot of tennis in my Earth life. I found a court here and have been playing almost every day. The ball moves a little slower here. It lands and bounces like it's pushing through syrup, giving me about two seconds to reposition my body and the racket. Two seconds is like a lifetime deathtime in this game. I think it's god's way of giving us the impression that we're good at it. I was already not too shabby at the game, to be honest, but with the deceleration in Missingville, I'm a damn Williams sister.

I've got a doubles team going with this woman named Stella. She's fifty-nine years old, but robust and agile. Her arms look like Michelle Obama's, and her legs like Tina Turner's. She's better than me, by far, but she's tolerant, taking my mistakes in stride. She says things like, "Shake it off, kiddo."

Stella died at the hands of her husband, a fate handed to about thirty-seven percent of the women here.

I expected that statistic to be higher, but you must keep in mind that there are people here from all over the world. In lots of other countries, men don't loathe women. Wait, that's not true; they hate and resent them, but they don't go on killing them.

Stella was a realtor. She had new money and enjoyed six figure commissions from the mansions she sold in and around San Francisco. Stella never thought much about marriage, and having children "sounded like being put in a cage with a starving boar." Calling herself an introvert, she enjoyed a silent house, a tranquil hike, and long solo road trips.

She met Mitchell at a showing. "The first time I saw him, he was standing in front of a bay window. He looked like James Bond." I'm not sure which James Bond, but all of them are pretty hot. They got coffee after the first meeting, and he then pursued her like she was the first pot of gold in California.

Mitchell was wealthy, divorced, and handsome, with a full head of hair, an anomaly for a man at sixty-seven. Sadly, Mitchell was also addicted to porn, the kind that brings the FBI to your door if you're not careful. Stella didn't know this, of course, but only one year into their marriage, the FBI did just that.

The cops tore up their house, but they didn't find anything. His computer, her computer, both phones were clean. Mitchell explained that this must have come from his computer at work, which "anyone could access after-hours." Stella believed him, hired the best attorney in the Bay area, and slept soundly for a night or two, thinking this mess would be quickly cleared up. Bail was paid, he was out, no confession was given, no evidence was found.

Funny how the guilty make such huge mistakes when they should be on their best behavior. Mitchell never sold his old condo. After they got married, he moved into her house and he "rented out his place." Mitchell handled collecting rent, oversaw repairs, and vetted the tenant. But Mitchell never rented it out at all. The cops hadn't figured this out yet. Either way, stupid, perverted Mitchell didn't mop up the mess he made at his other place.

Stella said she knew there was a god right before she died and asked me if that was the most ironic thing I'd ever heard. I said almost. In the middle of one night sleeping next to the husband she knew would be exonerated, she woke up in a panic.

"I swear, god shook me awake. I felt something on my shoulder, and it wasn't the pedophile sleeping next to me. He was snoring away when I got up."

She said she got up and started walking through the house like she was being pulled.

"It was like there was a rope around my waist dragging me to the spare bedroom. I went right to the desk Mitchell brought when he moved in. The son of a bitch had a trick drawer, with a compartment in the back.

Can you believe that? The cops didn't find it, but I did, thanks to the good lord guiding me." She made the sign of the cross and kissed her thumb.

She popped the drawer open and found photos of a girl.

Stella said, "I will not describe this picture to you, but let's just say, this isn't one of those 'but she looked eighteen' situations." The girl was standing in front of a window and out that window Stella could see the light blue walls of the building, the white awning, and the view of a golf course. She recognized it as Mitchell's condo. She'd find out later that he used this property as the location for his twenty-seven counts of producing child pornography.

Stella fell to the floor the way wives do when they find out their husbands are sick fucks. It was swift, as you'd expect. Her back was to the door. Mitchell crept into the bedroom, saw she had the photo, and knocked her over the head with a heavy crystal trophy Stella received for "Realtor of the Year." She fell back and he clobbered her some more.

"I didn't let that kill me though, oh no sir," Stella said as she stretched her legs on the tennis net.

Mitchell had the M.O. of most wife killers. While she was in and out of consciousness, he strangled her. Stella said the thing that bonded us together, "Men just love to squeeze the life out of women, don't they? Why is that do you suppose? I think it's because so much of a relationship, at the beginning when there's that special smile, later when it's a glare of disapproval, after marriage when it's sheer boredom, is expressed with the eyes. Men like to look into those same eyes as a woman become shocked, terrified, and then dead."

I told her I was killed by a stranger, but he, too came around to face me when I took my last breath.

Stella said all the men who murder with two hands around one neck think, "This murder is dedicated to all the bitches I wanted to kill." She thinks they're surprised, then delighted at how long it takes a woman to die this way.

Stella hates that Mitchell's face was the last thing she saw before she died. She wished he had done it from behind so that she could have been looking at the blown glass vase she bought at a gallery with her first commission check.

In case you didn't realize what a bad ass this woman is, let me bring it home. Stella doesn't know why she's here and not in Deadtown. She's got conviction. She has never worn the helmet. Not one time. The woman has never taken a gander at the world she used to occupy. She knows he killed her. She understands that she's here because no one found her body, but she doesn't know where Mitchell disposed of her.

Rita explained it all to her while she sat at Wimbledon watching a match between Billie Jean King and Chris Evert. She sat, turning her head left to right,

right to left, left to right, when Rita handed her the program. Stella opened it and read the "Shout Out To All Souls Not Yet One With A Body." Rita told her it was okay to be upset, but Stella just asked if she could stay there until the match ended.

When she got to the Joshua Tree section of Missingville, she got the tutorial from her roommate, Maxine, who was eaten by a crocodile. Now that's a lady who's never getting out of here. Maxine gave her the helmet and told her how to visit Earth. She also said, "Now I know you're upset, but it might help to get an idea of where your body is. I'll be right here while you take a peek."

Stella looked at the helmet and said, "What's done is done. Can I play tennis here?"

I'm dying to know if Mitchell got caught. Where did he put Stella's body? He must be suspect number one in her murder. Stella, she gives zero fucks. For this reason, I love her.

There's more to my love for Stella.

A year before I died, there was the beginning of this thing I had with someone named Kathleen. My mom met her first at the country club when she was having her racket restrung. They had lunch and then played a match.

My mom told me about her. "This Kathleen, she loosened all my strings in that game." The innuendo was lost on her. She told her she had a daughter who might be a suitable fit for her. And, well, I was.

Kathleen looked confused in a tennis skirt. She was boxy, with broad shoulders wider than her hips, like a wrestler. She was a bit blotchy, a red head who reacted to the sun with patches of pink bumps. Worn in a short pixie cut, her hair was the color of peaches, orange, white, bronze. Her stomach was flat and her chest almost concave. She had a long neck and high cheek bones, and round, green eyes with lashes that separated out nicely with a layer of mascara. Full lips, but not the injected kind, were her best feature, I decided.

Kathleen made me reconsider what was beautiful. I looked at her and decided hourglass figures were overrated. I found myself staring at her hips, her waist, especially when we'd meet up for drinks and she'd be wearing an Earth Day t-shirt tucked into jeans, with a brown belt and a chunky buckle. The way her clothes covered her body, the way her chest and stomach were flush, the way she carried a wallet in her back pocket, it made me imagine her laying naked on a poolside lounge chair.

I daydreamed about laying my hand on parts of her, wondering about her belly button, thinking of the ankle tan line I discovered when she took off her socks. I mulled over a day with her where she'd take off her shirt and mow my lawn, like a suburban dad. I thought of her drinking a Stag beer, the condensation falling onto her nipple, her sliding under my car on one of those wheely things, me handing wrenches to a topless, genderless human. I once asked her if she shaved her pubes, in a way that I hoped sounded like a normal girt chat, but underneath I wanted clarity for my masturbation fantasies.

Kathleen talked with her hands, bigger than mine, with the joint at her thumb and wrist jutting out, just like the one at her big toe. I watched her hands on wine glasses and forks, how she ate like the British, her left hand flipping the fork over to eat her steak. When I went to her house for the first time, I inspected her medicine cabinet and took a stick of tinted Chapstick. We went hiking and I walked behind her staring at her hairline, how the red hair grew wispy on her neck, thin and barely blowing in the breeze, like these were the same baby hairs with which she was born. She would come to my apartment and make dinner, chopping onions like the pros do on the cooking shows, the tips of her left hand holding the onion just right while the right-hand chops in a staccato motion.

She wore a turquoise ring on her left pinky finger. She twirled it when she sat back from the dinner table and commenced with her questions, "So, Renata, I told you the things I'm afraid of, what about you?"

I told her how when I get on highway ramps, for a split second I think I'm going the wrong way. I often picture the bodies in the car I might hit head on.

She started sentences with things like, "Ah, true, touché," an affirmation I didn't know I craved.

She'd reply to me with things like, "Ah, good point, but did you ever think about how the mouse feels when he realizes he's stuck in the trap?"

Or, "Touché, I'll give you that. But I often wonder if the pharmaceutical companies are paying off the marijuana growers so there isn't an alternative on the market."

Or, "True, true, I get that. But there was more to the rise of Hitler than just raging antisemitism."

No one talked to me like this. She listened like I was teaching her, but then ever so gently nudged me to turn my thoughts on their heads. We deliberated how to help unhoused veterans and thought that asshole Elon Musk should build tiny houses all over the country. We agreed that AA shouldn't be the only way to stay sober. She explained how much she respected Steven Spielberg for vowing to never remake E.T., how some things can never be touched, like classic movies or arrowheads she stumbled across on "lesbo float trips in Arkansas." She admitted to shoplifting when she was old enough to know better, and how it gave her a tingling in her crotch every time she lifted something from the "evil empire that is Wal-Mart." I told her I hit a parked car when I was old enough to know better because it was just last year, but I got a thrill out of driving off.

Kathleen talked about the last man she slept with twenty-seven years ago, and how she felt like her vagina was happier for it. She said, "I sometimes wonder if my skin cells down there would look different than yours under a microscope."

She told me how she never really "came out." She just went to her parents' house during a break from college and brought home a "super dykey volleyball player." She sat close to her. She kissed the woman's cheek while she sat on the couch playing Trivial Pursuit with her parents. She had a brother who married a Jesus freak, and he was a hard sell, but they just never talked about it. He did once used the term "faggot" when has weaving in and out of traffic with Kathleen in the car. When he got to a stoplight, she opened the door and got out, saying, "This faggot can walk." He later said he didn't get it because only guys can be faggots. Kathleen gave up on him.

Old enough to be my mom, if she got pregnant that last time she had man parts in her vagina, she had wisdom I couldn't yet, dark humor I thought was mine alone, and a willingness to delve into things most people only write about in journals. She was a therapist; she'd heard it all. She placated neurotic people all day, telling people to "practice self-care, give themselves some grace, remember this and that are not your fault." But her own acts of self-care included polishing off bottles of Malbecs on the weekends, smoking weed during the week and popping left over Percocets when she was particularly haunted by clients who talked about cutting themselves with razor blades, or watching their children die. Those days called for the hard stuff and Kathleen wasn't ashamed.

Other women envied her tennis skills, but not her looks, which made her approachable. The country club housewives weren't intimidated by her, so they related to her in a way that wasn't playing quid pro quo. No one tried to one-up her; they liked her enough not to mind losing to her. She was completely undangerous.

Kathleen wouldn't steal your husband. But she just might steal your daughter.

It started off as tennis. Being set up by my mom because we had the "same speed and feistiness on the tennis court" was later a joke between us. It was a blind tennis date. And my mom was right; she was my perfect match. She served better than me, and aced me at least a few times each game, but otherwise it was like we went to the same Arthur Ashe tennis camp, like we learned the same game at the same time, on the same court. The challenging, but smooth back and forth brought me to what my mom called "flow."

We'd play three to four times a week, always at dusk. Midway through, the lights would come on with the sound of metal clanking. Before the lights, she looked damp and red-faced, quietly lobbing back and forth. Once lit up, she was sparkling, the sweat catching the light on her collar bones and forehead. It was around that time in every game that she'd start to grunt each time the ball hit her racket. It was low-pitched, short, like she just bumped her head into a cabinet. By the last matches she couldn't control it. She grunted like it was twenty-seven years ago and something had entered her that she liked, despite herself.

I objectified her.

As a general rule, I'd say women don't objectify men. We find Chippendale performances to be comedic, not a turn on. Most of us don't put calendars in our offices of shirtless firemen. Women don't cat call. I've not seen a man who made me come in my pants the minute I saw the white of his teeth or the premature wrinkles around his eyes. I didn't analyze men's wrists, armpits, or my god, feet. I never dated a guy because I wanted to touch the back of his knee or watch him tuck in his shirt.

Ah, yes, I know. Am I gay? Who knows? Are you? I don't know what I am. I don't know what I'd be doing if I was still alive. Would my experience lead me to lesbian pickleball leagues and pride parades? Would I meet Kathleen's friends at her queer book club? I don't know, and it won't need to be worked out. I died at a moment in my life when a woman captivated me. My life ended while I was learning how to move into a person without all the basic tools I had always known. During my last moments alive, I was thinking about how I was going to fall into her and succumb. I was picturing us on vacations in exotic places, arm in arm as we walked through fish markets and old ruins. I was wondering what kind of dog we'd get. I imagined myself kneeling in her flower garden, planting tulip bulbs as she flipped portabella mushrooms on the grill.

All of this kept my mind off the aching in my feet, the burning in my thighs, the cracks on my lips. I hiked, too far behind her. I strayed off the trail. As I was dying, I saw Kathleen and I laying in a hammock, putting our palms together, noticing her fingers were the exact length as mine.

Chapter 13

They do something super rad here, if you like to sob as if your dog just died, or if you're into stabs of pity slicing through your chest; you know, things god likes. When someone is found, we get to go eavesdrop on their eulogy. Each morning there's a list on the kitchen counter entitled, "Those whose bodies have been found – Hooray!" Then a list of names and next to it the time their eulogy will be shown in the Virtual Reality Rotunda. That silly god thinks it's essential for us to know who our friends were on Earth. They also revel in reminding us how barbaric it is that people are yanked from the world to this thing called death.

Again, god is a sadist. They just can't leave well enough alone. They whisk our friends away when their bodies are found, then invite us to witness the suffering happening on Earth since they've been gone. It's a self-masochistic venture I have availed myself to a few times. And, truth be told, I like it. I've always been a voyeur, looking into people's houses as I walk by, listening in on conversations at the coffee shop, glancing over the shoulder of the guy sitting next to me on a plane to see what he's reading. Some folks here share their whole stories, chatting on and on about their lives. I don't attend their eulogies. But the folks that stay tight-lipped, those are the people I creep on. Their eulogies pack a punch. Who knew the sex kink guy, who crawled around here on his hands and knees wearing a dog collar, was the Director of the Society for Old Fashioned Family Values?

It takes all kinds.

Chapter 14

The eulogy of Thad.

Thank you all for coming to pay your respects to Thad's family. While we have closure now, the loss of this kind man is palpable in our community.

Thad was a giver, a sharer of his wealth, his time, his talents. From his gifts to the local university to his position on the Board of Directors of the Mystic Society of Taos, he bettered this world. Thad believed he was a sparrow in his last life, and as we all have come to understand our last role in this temporary world, we celebrate the sparrow in him that lived on.

Thad flew, sang, and hovered through this realm. He was confident enough to spread his wings, leaving Orlando and its plastic, fabricated Mickey Mouse mystique. He hovered above Boulder, Salt Lake City, Albuquerque, before landing on the branches of Taos. And we thank the stars, Mercury, and the planet formerly known as Pluto, for his arrival here.

Thad's home became a nest for those who were also birds in their former lives. They came to sing, play in drum circles, cling the chimes, and speak to Mother Earth about what this life means without wings, but with human capabilities and frailties. The Bird Drum Circle is here today, and we were quite touched by their performance. Thank you, cardinals, and blue jays, for your gift to us today. Especially the blue jays, for we all know your temperament.

In this life, Thad traded his wings for arms and hands, which he used for massage, acupuncture, and an occasional colonic cleanse. And Taos is better for it. Everyone in this room has been freed of plantar fasciitis, irritable bowel syndrome, and the curses that afflict us when our bodies are not aligned with our chakras. Thad did all these things for me and also led the meditation that brought me to realize I was a flea in my past life, a discovery that has changed my life and my love for dogs in a whole new way. I only wish I had one last chance to thank my sparrow friend.

We have come full circle, neighbors. After a late-night session with the humans closest to our sparrow friend, we came to know that Thad was happily bathing in Garnet Lake when the mountain lion approached. We saw Thad welcome the animal, knowing that, in fact, the lion was first on this earth as a lamb. Thad spoke to the lamb, invited him to bathe with him, told him that as a bird he once took a ride on his back.

We felt Thad's disappointment when he realized he was wrong. As the lion approached, Thad became keenly aware that the lion was in his first life and was indeed a real-life mountain lion. We forgive the lion, because of course we do. We honor Thad, because like a sparrow, he flew toward dangerous things knowing he could always rest on a high tree branch. Today, we are thanking the universe and the mountain lion for leaving Thad's tibia behind. We came to understand that the mountain lion, naive in his first life on Mother Earth, was guided by the Planet formerly known as Pluto to leave something behind. We thank the lion for this gift of identification. We must not forget that the response to animal violence is always forgiveness.

Last night, as we charged our crystals under the quarter moon, we could hear Thad's wings flying right next to our ears, but as we listened closer, we heard him say, "I am coming back as an Instagram influencer. You will be able to find

> *me on YouTube where I will offer classes and mediation for a small fee, where I will deny science, where I will spread misinformation, and where an eventual scandal will send me into a Netflix documentary like none you've seen yet. And yes, there will be a cult."*
>
> *Fly high, Thad, as a sparrow. I hope your new presence as an influencer will let me meditate with you for a fraction of the cost.*

I never took Thad for a sparrow, but he's going to rock it on Instagram.

Chapter 15

A guy left today. He transferred to Deadtown after staying here only five days. Eric had shaggy black hair that he flipped out of his eyes in an exaggerated shake like a golden retriever. I half expected his tongue to stick out and flap around. Tall and slender, he was fragile like the breast of a baby bird. Poor guy was only nineteen years old. He wore a Dave Matthews T-shirt that his mom got at a concert in 2001. As he walked toward Deadtown he said, "I hope my mom buries me in this shirt." I was sad knowing his mom would likely put him in a suit and tie.

He was in a hiking accident, or a "climbing accident" as he corrected me. What the hell is the difference? He fell something like ninety feet, so he walked with a limp and had blood trickling down the side of his face. He wiped it with the back of his hand, the way a toddler wipes his mouth after eating spaghetti for the first time. Sometimes the blood landed on his lip, and he would lick it. This made me want to try this dead sex thing, but he left before I could find out.

When he got here, I happened to be on my way to skydiving club and darn it if the hipster didn't land right in front of me. He was more confused than the average arrival. I guess the head injury is the best explanation for his behavior, though I always thought head injuries were bullshit.

"Are you one of the first responders?"' he asked.

"No, kid, you're in a different place now," I answered. He hadn't yet been greeted by Rita.

He looked at me sideways, which made the blood go all over his shoulder. I resisted the urge to hate him for his shirt.

He asked, "Will you go canoeing with me next weekend? I promise I won't try to get down your pants the way I did at the Phish Concert. Are you the girl who gave me herpes in my mouth? I should have known you were dangerous based on the smell of your pussy."

Now I liked this kid. I went with it.

"Honey, you can go down on me right now if you wipe that blood off your face," I said with a wink.

He started sobbing, his narrow shoulders rising and falling in quick hiccups. He was patting his pants, his shirt, his pockets, like smokers do in that panic when they think they lost their lighter.

No cunnilingus for me.

I hated the obligation of comforting people. I'm the person that gives a distant hug and says "there, there" with a pat on the shoulder, which is what I did. I was proud of myself because I was willing to get blood all over myself in my pseudo-embrace.

He realized that he wasn't in the real world anymore, that he had ascended from the climbing trip and the girl he ate out despite her nasty vag. He got this wide-eyed look the reminded me of my grandpa's face when someone said something a bit racy. Most people cry, often a slow-moving, subtle lip quiver followed by silent tears. It's weird how women here probably sobbed their eyes out when they learned their boyfriend cheated on them, but when they discover they've been offed, they produce only a silent tear.

But Eric, between his sobs, said, "Where's my dog? Where's my dog? Where's my dog?"

Jesus Christ. One thing I had never considered is if there are pets here. I have a pulse for god's sake. Of course, I don't, but I haven't turned to stone. I cannot handle the thought of lost dogs. I hadn't seen any, so my guess is they don't get to transfer. The thought made me want bourbon and a Golden Retriever. Yet another thing that makes you think twice about this god person. Who the hell would ban dogs? I would have to ask Rita about this.

To Eric, I said, "He's here, hon. He's in Pet Plains, on the other side of that hill there." I thought he'd ask me to take him there, so I regretted this. Being compassionate has its downside. It's the follow-through that sucks, and I wanted no part of that.

But Mr. Head Injury didn't ask to go to the dog park. Instead, he said, "Do you have a one-hitter? Have you seen my Zippo? Can I play my ukulele for you? Will you get high with me before the show? Are you in the drum circle?" My god.

Sure, I had been to Coachella, I was a cliché, a caricature. I was a rich Nashville girl. I took horseback riding and tennis lessons. I got Brazilian waxes and even had my asshole bleached once before spring break. I had 4,532 Instagram followers, and I'm sure that number has probably doubled since I died. I was a little bit bulimic, a lot anorexic, and recently had a consultation for a boob job. I get it, I was a cliché.

But this guy.

I told him, in a disingenuous voice, not to be afraid. Then, I channeled Rita, "You're dead, but you're not in Hell so it's a banner day."

Eric proceeded the way you'd expect, taking the posture of someone about to be eaten by a bear, and telling me I was a cunt. The typical fodder. I gave him time, hoping I wouldn't have to tackle him.

"Once you're finished with this little fit, I'll take you to the Welcoming Committee." This was not my best choice of words, but he started to chill out.

Then, Rita came up behind me saying she was sorry

she was late; she was greeting a toddler and that takes more time than the usual Newcomer. I told her he was looking for his dog and, "By the way, can we talk about the animal population here, please?" She waved me away.

"Let me tend to Eric, dear. Come back later," she said as she wrapped him in an afghan. He leaned on her shoulder and bloodied her linen dress, stark on the cream linen. The redundant sound of a jam band started in the distance and Rita said, "What a wonderful place to get the Shout Out, Eric." This explains the t-shirt, though who can tell the difference between Dave Matthews and Phish?

After seventeen days, Eric transferred to Deadtown. But during that time, I learned all the things about Ayahuasca and Nahko and Medicine for the People. He mostly rambled about his efforts to tidy up the dog park, which I found insufferable. Rita later explained that of course dogs are here, and parakeets, but all other pets were out of luck. I asked why dogs and parakeets and not dogs and cats. She told me everyone knows that cats are the most hated of all animals.

"I disagree, Rita. What about opossums and slugs?"

She said I was getting lost in the weeds.

I didn't like dogs. I realize this is akin to me saying I burned crosses in people's yards, but I'm asking you to let it go. I considered getting a puppy to up my Instagram game, but otherwise I found them to be smelly and arrogant with their demands. I wasn't going to leave work to let an animal out of the house and I wasn't keen on picking up an animal's shit, so I walked by the dog park with Rita but never went back.

I did learn that Eric's dog came to Missingville and is still here. Eric was located wedged in between sandstone rocks, but his beloved dog remains missing. So, Jerry Garcia, the black lab, still runs around here in his Bob Marley poncho. Eric doesn't have him where he is now, and that was enough to make me cry in shaking hiccups.

Chapter 16

Kathleen and I planned an adventure in the weeks leading up to my death. After reading about Grandma Gatewood, who hiked the entire Appalachian Trail like it was a cakewalk, Kathleen wanted to take on a slice of it and pretend to be a real hiker. She was a real hiker, actually; I was going to fake it. I disagreed with few of Kathleen's suggestions. I don't want to say that I was codependent or manipulated; I just thought her smarter and better than me.

In our tennis matches, I'd tire before her. At dinner, she always ordered the right thing while I often said, "Well, I guess I should have stuck to what I know and ordered the fish." She volunteered for things, like something called the Rotary Club which honestly, I still don't understand, but I went to a church basement trivia night for this woman. At work, she fixed people. At my job, I moved tiny sweaters around a showroom, and swayed shoppers toward high-priced crop tops.

While I was keen on pop culture, often referencing actors, musicians, or reality TV shows Kathleen had never heard of, she spouted off literary themes in Tolstoy. While I forced her into a Billie Eilish concert, she talked me into the symphony, and once, the fucking opera, where I fell asleep. With velvety chairs and dim lighting meant for sex or naps, how could a person stay awake?

She didn't have any bad ideas. I never heard her say, "Well, I screwed the pooch on that one" or "I should have known better." It's not that she was egotistical, it was just that she knew herself in ways I suppose I might have if I lived to be forty. She understood people in a way only a therapist can. Watching a bit too much MSNBC for my liking, she had her finger on all possible pulses. She didn't walk into things blindly, unlike me, who was in a constant state of pinning the tail on the donkey.

So, when Kathleen said, "Let's hike seventy-one miles of the Appalachian Trail," I said, "Sure."

She announced, like it was an ordinary statement, that "we'd do it in seven days." I'm no math whiz, but I calculated that to be ten miles a day, with one to spare. I pictured myself crawling towards marathon tape with scraped knees and sun-poisoned shoulders. Who knew how right I was about the knees.

I took to Google.

Average difficulty of a hike in the Smokey's - 5-8.

Average number of deaths per year on the A.T. - 2-3.

Number one cause of death on the A.T. - heart attack.

Other deaths on the A.T. -tree falls on man, a thirty-six-year-old folksinger.

Murders on the A.T. - a young woman killed by a man with a hatchet; young woman held captive for three days, then killed with the handle of a car jack; holy shit, lesbian partners' throats slit in a tent.

Some tree huggers thought it an eyesore to have chain linked fences around the camps. Meant to keep bears out, they've all been removed, leaving hikers a billion times more likely to be mauled by a bear.

I had as much desire to hike as I did to get doxed on the internet. If a hotel didn't have a fuzzy white robe waiting for me, I was roughing it. I once went camping with hippie friends I envied and wanted to emulate. On the second day, I was scratching mosquito bites until blood caked under my fingernails. I had a hangover like milk rotting in my stomach. I stayed in the tent all day, sweating like an Evangelical at a drag show.

So, when Kathleen recommended not only hiking, but with tents strapped to our backs, of course I said, "Count me in!"

There are few things this woman couldn't talk me into, especially when she wasn't trying. She had a quiet way of coercion. I didn't blame her. She was the hand on many a yo-yo in her life, without ever trying to be a puppet master. Some people just have their shit together so well, the rest of us feel like we're swimming in mud to catch up.

Kathleen was giddy when she showed me the map; yes, an actual paper map that I couldn't decipher, but I faked it. I don't think she realized I was young enough that this was the first map I'd ever had the pleasure of reading. She had all the lean-tos mapped out. That's right, we'd sleep in something called a lean-to. The word feels good in my mouth. I thought it romantic to sleep between three walls, off centered and crooked, with a woman who could talk me into eating beetles and drinking water previously shat in by mountain lions. I remain baffled though; if you're going to build three walls, why not go ahead and put up the fourth one, Paul Bunyan? They also had things called privies, which is a polite word for holes into which I was expected to piss. I told myself I wouldn't shit the entire time, no way.

We entered the hellscape in Pigeon Forge, with crisp cargo shorts, stiff boots, and shaved armpits. We walked, then we walked some more, then we drank hot water, after boiling it on a fire Kathleen made with a spark thing I couldn't operate. But this little thing she repeatedly scratched on made me think about rubbing mine against hers, even if we stunk like labia sweat and overzealousness.

Next, we walked. Then we'd stop for a few minutes. Then we'd walk. After that, we'd walk. We'd find a lean-to at dusk, keel over with fatigue, then wake up and walk.

"After this, I'm using a Segway to get from the couch to the kitchen!" I'd yell to her, always ahead of me, sometimes so far ahead, she was out of sight.

"What doesn't kill you makes you stronger!" She'd shout back at me.

"I swear to god, the sixth hour of walking on the A.T. is not the time for cliches, Kathleen," I'd say to myself.

"Where's the next lean-to?" I asked when I caught up and held her hand. I'd be sweet and gentle with her while my thoughts were, "If I don't sit down in the next four minutes, I'm going to break your skull with this ridiculous walking stick you got me for my birthday." Absolutely the worst present I ever got, by the way.

"We've only got four more miles for the day. Hang in there, kid." The sixth hour of walking on the A.T. is also not the time to call me "kid."

I continued to envision the walking stick hitting her head or impaling her chest.

On day five, I was worthless. My feet felt like boulders, and my legs had no interest in lifting them. My thighs felt like someone was using that damn fire starter on them, twitching like a trigger point under a needle. With the eighteen-pound pack on my back, I was hunched, with a knot in my low back and a rope tied between my shoulder blades, stretching, and pulling them out of their sockets.

I guess none of this happened to the A.T. queen, Kathleen. She said the night before, "I'm sorry I got so far ahead of you today. It's like I'm in a trance when I'm on that trail. I can't explain it, but I have no awareness of anything but my feet." The A.T. gave her flow.

Same, Kathleen, same. But when I say feet, I mean blistered, burning things carrying me further into Hell.

On day seven, we hiked the first two miles close to each other. We weren't speaking. When we stopped to eat tuna, soggy crackers, and squishy over-ripe grapes, we smiled at each other. I brushed hair out of her eyes. She rubbed my neck and shoulders. I took off her boots and got fresh socks from her bag. Something about this made me want to fly away with her, to water, or sky, somewhere where feet wiggled freely. She gave me the last of the Gatorade, and I let her eat the last of the chocolate protein bars. We didn't talk; we just passed things back and forth, keeping each other alive, which in retrospect is quite ironic.

I loved her then. I loved her when I died, just one hour and twenty-six minutes later.

It's because of her that I'm here now. But when I put on the helmet, and I go to her, I can see the guilt; it's a snake coiled around her intestines and stomach. It travels, sometimes to her heart, where the weighted twinge makes her pace. There's no relief, no release after she sat in a Ranger's office and told him "Yes, I got too far ahead of her. Yes, I had most of the water. No, if she screamed I might not have heard her."

My disappearance is a malignancy growing insider her at a much faster rate than that of my forgiveness. I'm not angry with her. Wait, sometimes I am. I'm mad at her when the helmet goes on and she's smiling. But when she's in the fetal position, sobbing into a pillow, I'm forgiving. When I wore the helmet and saw her playing tennis with another human, I was irate. She was back in Nashville, on our court. On the other side of the net was an old man, far too skilled for his age. I wanted him to trip and break a hip.

I want some anguish for her, but just a little. I don't want her to drown in her guilt. I just want her to wade it in a bit, wetting her legs and splashing regret water on herself.

Chapter 17

I put on that godforsaken helmet.

I've seen plenty of true crime stories where friends and family set up "command posts" at the local Knights of Columbus, or the Veteran's Hall. There are folding tables and metal chairs and just watching it, I can smell burnt chili and Bengay.

My family set theirs up at the country club. I don't love this. I want my family to be mindful and act like the middle class. I want the news outlets to portray them as people deserving of a miracle.

The room is too elaborate; it's lit with crystal chandeliers. The chairs have too soft, green velvet cushions. The tables are covered with white tablecloths. My god, waiters in black vests and ties are serving people cappuccino with hearts made out of foamed milk. The buffet line boasts shrimp scampi and caramelized Brussel sprouts. Women in their seventies are buzzing about.

Their hair is colored in shades only natural in toddlers. Their diamond rings cast shapes on the walls as they arrange flyers in stacks and hand them to retired men lined up at the tables. They're in golf shoes, polo shirts, and shorts in shades of yellow and pink. There are far too many gold and diamond pinky rings on chubby male hands for my liking.

Yes, I am thinking the same thing. What are they doing with flyers in Nashville when I went missing from bum fuck Tennessee? I see a table of cops, scarfing down crème Broulee and smiling too much like it's just another upper-class beat at a Sunday morning donut shop. One of them isn't playing along, a guy who can't be older than me, with thick hands and a jolly belly. He's not eating, and he asks the server for basic coffee, black. He has never eaten food that requires a blow torch. He's never drank a beverage containing steamed milk. He's typing away on a laptop, googling mile markers on the Appalachian Trail. Looking up at the gang of idiots, he says, "What are we even doing here? This girl isn't in Nashville."

A middle-aged guy with a crew cut and posture that says Marine replies, "Nathan, we got the tip about the Starbucks. We have to focus our attention here." I get the feeling he wants to be right more than he wants to find me.

A girl from my high school class comes into the room. I haven't seen her since a graduation party where a coffee table collapsed under her dancing body, leaving her paralyzed from the waist down. I left the house before this tragedy took place, and I'm glad for it, because I heard she lay there being laughed at by drunk kids who thought she was faking. I think now that if I had been in that group mocking her, I'd likely be headed to the Dark Side of Deadtown.

She wheels up to a table and says, "How can I help?"

A man I don't know with a gray ponytail says, "Thank you so much for coming. I've got a stack of flyers we'd like to put in the library, which is right next door."

She takes the flyers and starts to turn around but stops and goes back to him. "I knew Renata, and I keep having dreams about her. I know this sounds crazy, but I keep seeing a walking stick with her initials on it. Has anyone found that?"

"Oh, honey, I don't know. The police don't tell us much, except someone saw her at Starbucks on Maple, so we're putting all our efforts around there." He sounds like Mr. Rogers but looks like a Hell's Angel.

She starts to leave, but turns around again and makes a bee line for Nathan and Marine Cop.

"Ahem, I'm sorry to interrupt," she says as she approaches the cop table. Nathan turns around and asks what he can do for her.

"I know this will sound crazy, but I don't think Renata is in Nashville. I know she was hiking on the trail, and I keep having this same dream. There's a man carving her initials into a walking stick. He's blond and sunburned, covered with oozing blisters on his back. I can only see the back of him, but I can see what he's doing with the stick." She stops and blinks fast.

Marine Cop overhears and says, "Thanks, dear, but I see you've got some flyers there. Handing those out in Nashville is the best way to help locate her."

Why everyone is calling her pet names, I don't know, except men find this to be a simple way to tell a woman that her thoughts are ridiculous.

Nathan leans towards her. "Tell me what else you see in the dream."

"Well, the man is sitting either at a stoplight begging for change, or he's in the woods, sitting on a tree stump with a pocketknife and a long piece of light wood, white like Ash. And I heard about the witness at the Starbucks. Don't you know that guy was our P.E. teacher? He was fired for streaking at a track practice. He was carrying on about how he saw Michael Jackson at the laundromat and maybe he's the return of Christ. He said he saw this guy Matt Davis who was the school's soccer star, killed in a car accident the year before. It's very Sixth Sense. But of course, you fine gentleman know that already, I'm sure." She speaks in the voice of someone who is called "honey" way too often by people who tower over her.

"Of course, we know that," says Marine Cop as he stands up and nervously wrings his hands in a white, silk napkin. I expect him to say, "now run along now," but Nathan stops him.

Nathan asks her name and when the teacher thing happened. When she says six months ago, he stands up and says, "Thank you, Madison. Would you mind coming back to the station with me?"

Nathan and Madison file out and Marine Cop follows, shaking his head like a douchebag who, if he ever admitted he was wrong, would get laid a lot more often than he does.

Chapter 18

Rita has been missing for thirty-seven years. I heard she got special privileges on the thirty-fifth year when she sent a memo to god asking if she could continue here as the adult she thought she'd be had she lived. So, somehow, she's in an adult body, with a child's haircut and wearing clothes all wrong, but being sensitive and benevolent so it's okay.

She's been missing more years than she was unmissing. When she was nine, she went on a field trip with the Brownies and "fell off a cliff," as the humans have said for all this time. If the unmissing used some common sense, they would have found her right away. But instead, the cops, the family, the Girl Scout leaders, the Boy Scouts and their pervy leaders, all searched at the bottom of the "cliff" she was "hiking" on when she said, "I have to pee, I'll be right back." The unmissing are idiots if you ask me.

First, she was at the top of a steep hill, not a cliff. It was grassy, not rocky. It was on a clear path, not rough terrain. Even if she tripped, she likely would have rolled down the hill, maybe sprained an ankle, maybe skinned her elbow. But the girl wouldn't have died. Still, so much time was wasted on the fall theory.

Did anyone think she went to the actual bathroom that was about fifty yards away? Did anyone think about the parking lot she had to walk through where the old WHITE VAN had been parked for the entire day? Seriously, a white van? With no windows! No one noticed a white van when they unloaded all these children off the bus? Had no one ever watched Unsolved Mysteries in the whole fucking Brownie troupe?

Did anyone think she had to drop a number two? How about, maybe she went to the actual bathroom because no nine-year-old girl, or any other person, shits in the woods when a toilet is nearby. Yes, she said "I have to pee," but that's because we all say pee regardless of what business we're doing, especially if we're a girl.

No one mentioned the man parked by the bathroom, the man that asked her if she knew where a certain trail head was, the man who got her to come closer to the van, threw her in, and drove seventy-five miles into Idaho. He took her to a trailer, took some pictures, and had his way with her, shot her, and buried her on the 200-acre property he inherited from his dad who went to prison for killing his mom. The guy is not a choir boy; the guy is known all over his small town as a creeper. HE DRIVES A WHITE VAN FOR THE LOVE OF ALL THAT IS GOOD! But no, they were hooked on the "fell off a cliff idea." They concluded that coyotes or bears ate her body before she was found.

Rita was dead before the first real search started in the park. She was dead before the dogs got to the parking lot. She was dead before those stupid dogs went right to the trail, giving no signals in the parking lot from where she was snatched. Search parties spent twenty-one days searching the woods. By that time, she had maggots in her eye sockets and worms crawling in and out of her nose and ears and who knows where else.

Rita never going home.

Rita is never going to transfer to Deadtown.

Rita knows these things.

Had she continued with the living she'd have been a midwife or a nurse practitioner. She understands science, decomposition, the flimsy search that ended years ago but was a waste of time from the beginning. She's done her recognizance on the living. She knows the habits of the man who took her.

The fact that this bastard is still alive and free should nullify any cute little notion you may have had about god or Jesus or whoever. The pedophile's pleasant, leisurely life better rid you this second of any of your "everything happens for a reason" bullshit. Take a minute and compute the reason a child gets murdered.

Rita is a leader here, a politician who wears a Green Party pin on her smock. I find that odd since it's not like we need to worry about the environment here. She likes to use podiums when she speaks; she paints yard signs and plans elections.

Rita means well. It's not her fault she went missing at nine, and is now forty-six, having gotten old in Missingville. She hates when we talk about gender identity, George Floyd, and "that internet thing." She wants it to be 1987, and who can blame her? I will say she has great taste in music. She plays "I'm Still Standing" by Elton John and though I had never heard the song before, I appreciate its simplicity. She also plays "Mr. Roboto" and it makes my stomach hurt to watch this middle-aged woman try to dance like a robot. I sympathize with her. She desperately wants to be found. Her dad died, her brother lives in a commune in Brazil, and her mom prays the rosary every night from the dementia ward at the Catholic nursing home. I heard that every six months or so Rita goes to visit her mom, dips her hand in holy water, and sprinkles it on her while she sleeps. Once she woke up and said, "Is the roof leaking?" before going right back to sleep. I'd like to tell Rita that she should try something else, but I'm basically afraid of her. Anyone here for that long becomes less human and more ghostly, and I don't believe in ghosts.

Still.

Chapter 19

Today is Kurt Cobain's birthday. Every year, the old-timers get together to commemorate the four days he was here in 1994. They perform Nirvana's MTV Unplugged verbatim. A plane crash guy named Sam plays the drums with those wiry things instead of sticks, and a guy named Rodney dresses up in a green cardigan and sings ironically about Jesus and sunbeams. Rachel, a fellow strangulation victim, plays the guitar and Kurt/Rodney calls her a "certified honorary punk rocker."

Rodney has penetrating blue eyes and chin length, greasy blond hair. I hear he arrived with a buzz cut, wearing an orange jumpsuit. My guess is he used to wash his hair and present himself like the preppy guy he was on Earth. But on his seventy-fifth day here he met Kurt Cobain. Rumor has it they were fast friends during Kurt's short stay.

Rodney was twenty-two in 1994. He was about to graduate from Utah State University. Like every basic guy in 1994, he was getting his bachelor's degree in business administration. He was a Mormon, which in itself made the guy pretty fucked up, but he survived his religion and carried it gently, like an egg he had to carry around and keep from cracking.

Raised with a heap of dos and don'ts, he kept his virginity all through high school and college. This wasn't the impressive, unique feat it appears to be. Afterall, he was in Utah. While lots of righteous Mormons were secretly getting it in the ass with veiny dildos, Rodney wasn't a hypocrite. He was like most of his friends; he believed in John Smith and the trouble he went through to have the rules engraved on gold plates. He didn't even drink caffeine, which was difficult because Red Bull had quite a rise in popularity in the early 1990's.

These guys do lots of missionary shit. Over Christmas break he went to Appalachia with a "Spread the Word" group. While I thought all these guys went to Africa to convince people to of the golden plate story, I gotta hand it to them. They took their self-righteousness and their weird gold plate fantasies and helped people. My feelings about the Mormon Church went from mocking scorn to puzzled acceptance when Rodney told us about these acts of service.

Choosing Appalachia was a great idea too, since every house in Kentucky had slanted porches, crumbling foundations, and broken refrigerators in the carport, their doors half hanging off to protect kids from dying in them. Those same kids were knee deep in abuse, hunger, illiteracy but "I'll be damned if I'm going to let my kid suffocate in a freezer."

This was before people looked at these houses and called them "methy." The public didn't yet know that things were in disrepair because everyone was smoking drain cleaner out of a glass pipe. If a house burned to the ground, drivers-by assumed it was because a mom let the oil get too hot when she was frying frozen burritos. It was a good time to be poor because everyone just thought "You live in rural Kentucky. All of the coal mines are closed. We expect nothing more from you."

Rodney replaced rotten boards, hammered nails into roofs and trailer siding, and learned to change flat tires. He jacked up a Ford truck while a four-hundred-pound woman watched from her kitchen window, eating pork rinds, and drinking out of a two-liter bottle of Mr. Pibb. They went from house to house in their little Jesus bus and though they left those ridiculous pamphlets with paintings of Jesus holding a lamp, and words like, "I am the bread of life," and though they invited everyone to their evening services, they really didn't deep throat the Jesus message to the Appalachians.

At night they would sleep in the local Mormon Church basement, on cots spread out with boys on one side and girls on the other, sheets hanging between the groups. They would sing:

Father, all my heart I give thee;
All my service shall be thine.
Guide me as I search in weakness;
Let thy loving light be mine.

Rodney sang this, but not in his Kurt Cobain voice. One day towards the end of the trip, the mission leader asked Rodney to go on a separate side job. The principal of the local high school heard the Mormons were in town, and he asked the leader to send someone over to paint the bathroom. Someone in the ladies' room wrote in thick magic marker, "Kayla is a slut" all over one of the stalls and they wanted this rectified immediately.

Rodney was dropped off alone as the church bus went on to repair more clothes lines and remove water heaters from people's yards. The principal gave him a bucket of green paint and a brush and led him to the bathroom. It didn't cross his mind at first that he was in a women's bathroom, but then he saw the bloody maxi pad poking out of the little box and sticking to the wall. He says now, "I will never be able to explain this, but looking at it made me lustful."

Not long into his painting job, a student came in. He was in the second stall so when she walked into the first one, she didn't see him. Rodney held his breath and stood perfectly still wondering why on earth the principal didn't put a sign outside the door. He decided he had to make his presence known so he coughed and said, "I don't want to alarm you, but I'm in the next stall painting. I'm sorry, I should have put a sign out."

The girl just laughed. When she stepped outside of the stall, Rodney did the same. They stared at each other for a second like kids in the bra section at what they used to call department stores. He apologized again and said he was on a mission trip to do repairs around town; the principal asked him to paint the stall. She was the tiniest thing. Barely five feet tall, she couldn't have weighed more than ninety pounds and had the most delicious southern twang.

The two chatted a bit. She asked him where he was from, and he asked her how she liked school. He discovered she was sixteen years old and on the basketball team, which he found amusing if not impossible. Then, before she walked out, she said, "Maybe I'll see you after school. You could walk me home. My house could sure need some help. By the way, my name's Kayla."

Rodney describes this exchange as the most sexually charged moment of his life. He prayed while he continued to paint her name off the stall. He kept looking at the bloody pad and, though he was alone, was blushing with embarrassment as he tried to push down his hard-on. He leaned down and smelled the pad. With his enormous boner, he walked into the hallway and found a supply closet. He wrote a little sign saying, "Under repair, use other restroom" and taped it on the door. He then went into Kayla's stall and jacked off for exactly thirteen seconds before he was relieved of the anti-Christ erection.

Killing time until the end of the school day, Rodney used the smallest brush of the bunch. The job could have been completed in twenty minutes, but he made it last an hour so he could be there when the bell rang. He went outside, crossed the street, and leaned up against a tree, like all grown men do when they're waiting to groom an underage girl. He had on khaki pleated pants and a t-shirt that said, "Visit Utah, Where God Loves You."

Kayla came out and looked around; he was so relieved she was looking for him. He waved and she crossed the street. "Hey, Mission Man, I'm glad you stuck around."

Nervous and red-faced, Rodney said, "Uh, yeah, which way to your house?"

She pointed and they walked. He tried to make small talk about her day at school, what was her favorite subject, did she have a lot of homework.

I interrupted Rodney to say he sounded like a creeper, and I didn't like where this was going.

When they got to the house, Rodney tried to hide his shock. Hers was the worst of all the houses he'd seen so far. The home itself may have been in okay shape, but the yard was a hoarded mess. Full of wheelchairs, bedpans, rusty bikes, and dog houses, it had fake flowers meant for gravesides stuck in the ground. Rodney said he knew the inside had seen cigarette smoke yellow curtains, fried bologna, and beatings with a belt buckle. Kayla said, "Well, I guess we really don't need repairs as much as we need a dumpster. Think your Jesus squad could help with that?"

Rodney nodded. He felt he couldn't speak as he eyed the mattresses, a washing machine, two console TVs, a portable toilet and a shower chair, boxes of Christmas lights, a kitchen sink sitting in a wheelbarrow.

"We also could just put all this stuff in the shed if you can't get a dumpster. Let me show you," Kayla said.

She walked him through the overgrown yard to the back of the house. There was a shed, tilted to the right with spray paint across the front reading, "Don't Tread On Me." Kayla told him she hadn't been inside it in some time, but she thought it was mostly empty.

Rodney looked at Kayla's ass, walking behind her and wondering if she was bleeding, or wearing a maxi pad. He felt the pre-boner tingling going down his stomach into his groin.

Inside the shed, they found it was empty, except for an old truck. Rodney said he thought they could help, and he'd talk to his mission leader that night. He'll get back to her tomorrow. He had to get back to the school since the bus would be there to pick him up.

Kayla said, "Do you think less of me because my name was on that wall?"

Rodney stuttered, "Oh, of, of course, I mean, of course not. People, kids, um, high school kids make up stuff all the time."

Kayla moved closer and pushed Rodney against the truck, saying, "I had a Mexican boyfriend for a few weeks, and it turned into those lies on the stall. I'm the only one around here who's not a racist piece of white trash, you know?"

Rodney's knee was in between Kayla's legs. She put her crotch on his thigh and pressed down. He told her he didn't think she was white trash at all. He said, hoping some Jesus talk would stop his hard-on, "Jesus teaches us to love our neighbor. Discrimination is not Christ-like."

Kayla kissed him, wrapped her arms around his neck, got up on her tip toes, and bent her neck back so she could reach his lips. He put his hands on her waist and pulled away.

But she quickly had her hand on the bulge in his pants and simply whispered in his ear, "Yes you can."

Rodney said, "I had free will, but I decided to give up Heaven to lay with this girl. Jesus would no longer want me for a sunbeam."

Nineteen years of pious commitment to Christ, gone. He said it left him in a muffled moan into Kayla's neck. How could he be so good for so long and then renounce it all in an act that lasted forty-seven seconds? Maybe it was because no one ever tempted him in this way. Maybe it was because he abided by his church's rule that young men are never left alone with young women.

It was all worth it, he thought. But then, a man walked into the garage, toothless and holding a shot gun. Rodney was standing next to the truck wearing just his Jesus t-shirt and socks. Kayla was giggling in the back of the truck.

Yes, the man was Kayla's father, who drank more than he worked, and yelled more than he talked. Rodney said he looked like a man who got in frequent bar fights and often told Kayla her tits looked good in her blouses. He was a dumpster diver, a car thief, a seller of pills, and more than happy to make this missionary the bad guy.

The dad called the cops and kept the gun pointed at Rodney until they came. He was put in a cell by himself, "which was certainly a blessing," he said, as he thanked Jesus for this act of mercy. Unlike the movies, Rodney didn't get a phone call, he wasn't offered a lawyer, he didn't get to talk to his mission leader. He took a ride in a van three days later to appear before a judge. His hands and feet were shackled. He was attached by a chain to three other men, and he went before the judge for seventeen seconds.

"Mr. Ross, you have been charged with Rape of a Child, Sodomy of a Child, Kidnapping, False Imprisonment, and Indecent Exposure. How do you plead?"

A man next to him, who he assumed was his lawyer, though they had never met, nudged him, and whispered, “Not guilty,” so Rodney repeated it.

“Your bond is set at $500,000,” said the judge, and Rodney was led back into the small room in the corridors of the courthouse.

The next day, the lawyer came to see him and told him his parents hired him, they needed to talk about the charges. Rodney told the story just as I’m telling you now. Kayla said he forced her into the garage, held her there against her will, and assaulted her. He told Rodney, “You’re looking at shit ton of time behind bars, kid, but I’ll do my best.”

I told Rodney none of that mattered. She was a child. He said he has come to understand that.

The worst of it, said Rodney, was when his parents came to visit. His dad sobbed while his mom was stoic. They begged him to tell them he didn’t do it. But Rodney wasn’t interested in any shortcuts. He told them the charges were mostly accurate. His mom said she prayed about it, and she couldn’t justify paying for the lawyer when he committed such a sin. Rodney’s dad said they were seeing the pastor the following week to decide on how much they would help him. A public defender was appointed ten days later.

When it was his turn to go before the judge again, he was again taken out of his cell, cuffed, and put in a van. This time it was just a driver and one other prisoner with him, but they weren't shackled together. On the drive to the courthouse, Rodney moved his feet and realized that they weren't shackled together. He was able to spread his feet far apart. Each one was cuffed, but they weren't attached. He wondered if it was hard to run with hands clasped together.

When they got to the sallyport of the courthouse, Rodney got off first. The other prisoner was old and wobbly. He fell when he stepped out of the van and the driver was struggling to help him up.

Rodney ran.

This was not a big town. He was in Shit City, Kentucky and the courthouse was in a little town square with Chinese take-out, a tavern, a secondhand clothing store, and closed anonymous storefronts. The square was at the end of a rural road; it was surrounded by woods and farms. Rodney found it mostly easy to run with his hands in front of him.

After several hours he came to a river, with rushing white water and boulders jutting out. Rodney sat on a log and cried. He prayed two words over and over as he rocked back and forth, "Forgive me."

He climbed to the top of a cliff, picked up the heaviest rock he could lift, and jumped.

Kentucky news outlets ran the story daily for weeks, "Be on the lookout; this man could be armed and is extremely dangerous." There were interviews with the other missionaries, and the missionary leader guy.

Everyone raved about what a great, god-fearing young man he was. His parents stayed out of the spotlight, and Rodney used the helmet to see his family was relieved it ended this way. They assumed he was dead. They wouldn't have to go through a trial or ever look their sinning son in the face again.

People speculate he's living somewhere under a new identity, continuing to assault girls. He did see that a documentarian who focused on crimes committed by Mormons, and there were a lot, included him in the film. After drawing lines with string from push pin to push pin on a corkboard, he concluded Rodney committed suicide. Good on him. But regardless, his body has never been found, so he's here with us, impersonating Kurt Cobain and doing a mighty find job at it.

When Rodney got here, he knew there was a band called Nirvana and saw a glimpse of the MTV unplugged show where Kurt wore the cardigan. But he wasn't necessarily a fan. He listened mostly to Christian Rock which none of us can believe when we see Rodney play "Heart Shaped Box."

Regardless, when Kurt got here, and spent those short four days with Rodney until his body was found, Missingville was transformed. I hear Kurt was nervous, jittery, and drifted around here like he was a neon sign, buzzing and flashing as he went from anger to relief to regret. Missing folks "drowned Kurt in love and acceptance," as they said during the birthday ceremony today. "We let Kurt know that he was loved, by us and by the unmissing, and that he would be forgiven for taking his own life. We told him we would transfer easily to Deadtown and despite any worldly beliefs otherwise, he would get to the Light Side."

Rodney perked up at this when he saw everyone comforting Kurt, who received lots of hugs from people who affectionately wiped blood off his head and said, "You changed my life." Rodney was in awe of Kurt, but he was sure that Hell was Kurt's next stop. The two of them spent a lot of time alone, or in suicide support groups. Those here due to suicide have some serious shit to work out before they transfer over. The main affliction is shame and "I left Francis Bean" guilt.

It was through Kurt, his songs, his sweater, his dirty blue tennis shoes, the way he talked about Courtney and the success of his band, that Rodney was able to forgive himself. Spend hours telling Kurt Cobain that he is forgiven, worthy of love, and a person deserving of the Light Side, and you'll start forgiving yourself for your menstrual fantasies and sex with someone who cannot consent.

Kurt saved Rodney. Rodney saved Kurt. Rodney tried to be Kurt.

The birthday bash wasn't so bad. Rodney, who's been here over twenty years, has mastered the guitar. Wait, I should say, he's mastered Nirvana songs. He plays nothing else. He does the full set of MTV Unplugged and moves his hair out of his face the exact way Kurt did. He sticks out his tongue between songs the way Kurt did. Rodney says that Kurt wanted the set of the Unplugged session to look like a funeral, so he recreates it with the same flowers and the chandelier; it's chilling. Rodney even says, just like Kurt, "Fuck you all, this is the last song of the evening," as he smokes a cigarette.

Chapter 20

I took a shift over at Milk Carton Mountain today. I didn't understand the reference at first, but Rita told me about how back in the day, the faces of missing kids were printed on milk cartons. She said people would pour their milk, see the picture, then read the back of cereal boxes while they ate. I found the lack of internet to be more haunting than pictures of dead kids on milk.

I say, "dead kids," which I understand are two words, that when together, sound crass and insensitive. But I want to get across to you that they won't come home safely, and no, they didn't run away. If you have a kid and he's missing, I'm sorry, but he's dead and he's here. But don't get too freaked out; Missingville takes great care of their minors.

On my way to The Mountain, memories of childhood songs and games came over me.

Miss Lucy had a steamboat. The steamboat had a bell. Miss Lucy went to Heaven. The steamboat went to Hell.
Wait.
Now I lay me down to sleep. I pray the Lord my soul to keep. If I should die before I wake....
Wait.
Criss cross applesauce

How can it be that there exists a god and also a million dead children? They wrote me a tongue in cheek letter, joked about dinosaurs and Pi, gave me a sweet deal with my ocean hut, but at the same time, the happenings on Earth require a place in Missingville for dead, missing kids. It seems god would have put a referendum on letting kids die after cholera was such a debacle, but who am I?

To those of you praying for your missing child to come home, I understand. I'm not mad at you for grasping at straws. But the same god you want to bring your son home allowed him to disappear. If god can cure childhood cancer, why can't they keep cancer away from your son or daughter in the first place? I'm just saying, if you lost a little one, you have every right to suspend all beliefs.

As I approached the Mountain, I smelled funnel cakes and popcorn. The sky was purple with green polka dots. A unicorn circled above, throwing glitter and lollipops and singing "If you're happy and you know it." I tasted strawberry ice cream on my lips as the wind picked up, carrying pink dust up from the sidewalk-chalked path I started skipping on as I approached. I walked over stick figures and suns, and haphazard chalked words like "Mommy, I love you, Jane, Elmo." My skips turned into jump roping, a yellow rope suddenly in my hands. I started singing, "Mary Mack, Mack, Mack, all dressed in black, black, black."

I wanted my mom. I felt a sting on my finger and a desire for a Blue's Clues Band-Aid. I whispered, "Mommy, I have a boo-boo." I sat down on the chalked path and saw my mother, or a cloudy version of her, kiss my tiny thumb. I felt her smokey arms around my smokey body. I sniffed her hair and smelled lilac. I rested my head on her shoulder and put my arms around her neck. I twirled her hair between my fingers.

She sat me down and disappeared. I was left wanting a blanket and something to suck on.

Once at the top, I saw a roller coaster, water slides, trampolines, swing sets, ice rinks. Thomas the Tank engine chugged along a track. Elsa from Frozen stood three stories tall, with kids hanging off her arms.

My job was to help prepare for the evening's event, a bonfire and camp out with s'mores, sing-alongs, star gazing, and intense denial that we're all dead. I followed the signs, written in crayon, which said

"Volunteers This Way." Along the way there were kids playing Duck, Duck, Goose, Red Rover, and hopscotch. There were some old timey kids throwing marbles and running with sticks and tires. I caught a glimpse of a one-eyed, one-legged, one-armed girl playing tick tack toe with a no-eyed boy.

When I got to the wooded area, a lady welcomed me.

"Hi, I'm Esther. I'm in charge of the camp out. You must be Renata." Her collar bones protruded out of her potato sack "dress." Under her eyes were half-moons of black, hollowed out like the rest of her. Standing at her feet, holding on to her knee was a child, in a white, but stained yellow night gown. I'd never seen a child with blackened circles under his eyes, but here he was. I could see each disk of his spine and his elbows were like bent matches.

Esther's son wasn't the only little one clinging to a mother's legs or nestling in a father's neck. I started to imagine ways that starving kids could be left for dead with a parent, never found, and forced to hang out here. I pushed those thoughts out of my head, and I'd rather not speculate.

I followed Esther's instructions, breaking Hershey bars into small squares and setting up telescopes. The tents were all set, the fire had a nice steady burn, and hot dogs, buns, chips, and Cokes were nicely displayed, along with the fixings for the s'mores. Jessica, a very soccer mom type, with extensions in her matted, bloody, blond hair and a bloody Louis Viton purse on her shoulder said, "Let's start this party like it's 1999. Bring in the kiddos!" She laughed and looked to me for some supportive laughter, but I didn't give it.

A man told me to watch out for her. "She was the type who called her kid's teacher to complain about Aiden's bad grade on a second-grade spelling test." There's not a lot of subjectivity in spelling, so that explains a lot about Jessica.

Esther went to the carnival area where the kids were lined up. She shouted, "Come on in, little ones!"

I wasn't experienced with kids. My little brother was four years younger than me, and while I taught him some things, I never actually had to take care of him. I didn't have any younger cousins. I never babysat for a neighbor, and none of my friends have kids yet. So, everything I said to children felt like it was coming out of someone else's mouth. Hearing myself talk was like hearing your voice when someone records you and it sounds like a stranger. My voice went up two octaves when I said things like, "Oops, the mustard squirted all over your shirt. Good job on the swing! Yes, I love your purple barrettes! Wow you're quite the artist!" All these things were perfectly appropriate statements, but each one sounded more ridiculous.

What I wanted to say was, "What monster did this to you? Is your murderer in Punishment Prairie? Why did you get in the car with that man? How long have your parents been keeping your room set up just like you left it?"

Other volunteers seemed so natural, even though they talked in the same kind of syrupy, just-breathed-in-helium voices. I kept comparing my voice to theirs, sure mine sounded fabricated while they were professionals at entertaining the souls of dead children. I was either overly observant or a narcissist. I've been unsure about this fine line most of my life.

Things went smoothly, with dead kids singing "100 bottles of beer on the wall," talking on and on and on about how crispy a marshmallow should be, throwing horseshoes, collecting sparkly rocks, just your typical group of murdered kids having a nice, innocent campout. There were moments when I forgot they were dead. I spent a good eight minutes evaluating with a nine-year-old the proper way to layer chocolate, marshmallow, graham cracker. I spent a good twelve minutes helping a kid take off her sticky gloves. There were eighteen minutes where a girl with pigtails and red dots on her face beat me repeatedly at hang man. I acted naturally, purposely losing over and over to a preteen girl, taken by a disease god didn't think to prevent.

Getting these kids to go to bed reminded me of why I wasn't pining away for motherhood when I was alive. I don't have the patience for manipulations that start with "I need a glass of water, I have to pee, read me another story." Fuck you and go to sleep. But these kids were murdered, so I was accommodating. I brought twenty-one kids a glass of water, read Goodnight Moon and portions of the Hunger Games, and walked twenty-eight of them to the outhouse before finally sitting down by the fire and cracking open a beer with the other grown-ups.

They were all chatting about how cute it was when one of us did this or that with a kid, how sweet it was to watch me play with Zoe, how funny it was to watch my friend Blake giving horseback rides, how one kid, Garrett, asked if he could leave the Mountain and stay with Blake on his fishing boat. Blake had no such boat, so they laughed at how sometimes kids here get confused about their lives at home and their lives here.

The adults were mostly volunteers, except for the ones who died with their children. Some were murder-suicides, others likely killed by their husbands who went on Earth acting like both their child and wife were kidnapped together. One mom said, "Bless his heart, Garrett really wants to go back on that boat, even though that's where he died. He's such a hoot." Umm...a hoot?

A dad asked me about my prior life. I told him my full name and where I was from. His name was Ricky, and he had a bullet wound on his chest. His son had the same, but to his temple. He freaked out.

"You're Renata Foster? Holy Shit. I just got here. I'm from Nashville. You were on the news nonstop.

How the hell are ya?" He said as he stood to shake my hand.

"Oh, ya know, I'm pretty good for being dead. What did you see on the news?" I shouldn't have asked.

He was way too excited. "They said you were last seen at a Starbucks. But there was a person of interest they wanted to talk to, a chick. I heard you were killed by some old dyke. Is that part true? Were you on some lezzy romantic getaway?"

I stood up and yelled, "A lesbo what? What did you just say?"

Ricky said, "Relax. What do I know? Maybe it was some guy and not your homo lover. You know you should never go to a second location, right? When the guy tried to put you in his car, you were toast. You do know that, right? Were you carrying mace? Every girl your age, if they look like you, needs to carry mace."

I stood up, taking a defensive sort of posture I don't recall ever taking in life. The other adults looked down at their beers. "What the fuck do you know, you fucking loudmouth prick?"

Ricky laughed, "Calm down, honey. I'm just saying, watching the news, I knew you were murdered. Shame you gotta stay here with that mark on your neck. That had to hurt."

I lunged at him. Pushing him by his shoulders, he fell backwards like a kid. I yelled, "I hope you're in the Dark Side by sunrise!"

Ricky chuckled, stood up, brushed off his clothes.

Esther asked him to go to bed.

Ricky walked off saying, "fucking bitch" under his breath.

It was all going so swimmingly until then. I left the Mountain. But not before asking Esther, "What happened to that asshole anyway?"

She said, "His story is that his wife shot him and little Albert, then burned the house down with them inside. But then you'd expect their bodies to be found right away, right? I suspect there's more to it, but I'm not here to judge. He's nice enough."

Someone's definition of "nice enough" was certainly skewed. I thanked everyone for having me, said how much I enjoyed everyone's little ones, and said I'd love to when they asked if I'd come back for the field trip to the firehouse. I was lying, of course.

That fucking Ricky. Who did he think he was anyway? More importantly, an abduction into a car?

Too distracted with disdain for Ricky, god, the Appalachian Trail, and Kathleen, I ended up good and lost. The terrain went from rocky trail to tall grass, as high as my thighs. Walking through it felt like the time I went skiing in Vale and had to push through the snow to find my brand-new Chanel sunglasses. I took big, leaping steps, bringing each leg up like I was some nerd in marching band. Burrs stuck to my socks and shorts.

The sky was earth-like, blue-black with sparkling stars and a full moon. I smelled kettle corn and fire. I thought I could hear chanting. I slowed down, spun around, thought about walking back, but I didn't know what back was. I came over a hill and saw a billboard lit up with plastic angels holding spotlights.

It read, in Old English font, "Welcome to Punishment Prairie."

Chapter 21

I stopped. Said a few "Well, fuck's" out loud, thought about turning around. But Ricky soured Milk Carton Mountain and I remembered I was already dead. Why be afraid of sinful ghosts running around? I've been to Vegas. I can handle a city of heathens.

I walked on and came to a clearing. It looked like an Andrew Wyeth painting, golden wheat grass as far as I could see, with the occasionally perfectly shaped oak tree. God has really done something with the place; I'll give them that.

Like that longing to be a child when I approached Milk Carton Mountain, going towards the Prairie made my stomach drop, like when I was in junior high and cheated on a math test. I felt that 'getting caught' sensation. But then, absolution.

I saw myself at thirteen, when I pushed my mom during a nonsensical, pubescent argument.

Right afterwards, she hugged me as I cried and apologized. She rubbed my hair and whispered, "It's okay, I still love you." This was getting something I didn't deserve. Punishment Prairie was the old man whose car I hit at a traffic light when I was sixteen. He got out and asked if I was okay, saying, "No biggie, accidents happen." It was undeserving compassion.

I started walking again and saw cabins lined up like spokes in a wheel. They were A-frames, the size of trendy tiny houses, built with rugged logs jutting out the sides. They looked like a child built them with irregular shapes and leaning roofs. Clothes were hanging on lines, dogs sat on porches, and hammocks stretched between trees. Each house had a different color door in bright yellow and robin's egg blue. Chimneys with perfect lines of smoke rose to the sky. I was struck by the smell that I had to assume came from the chicken coops and pigsties.

Like the churches along the High Road to Taos, there was an orange adobe altar in the center of rows of cabins. It was long and narrow, as tall as my chest. Draped over it were rosaries made of pink crystal, onyx, pearl, even some that looked like diamonds. There were locks, like the ones on that lover's wall in Paris, attached to hanging vines, lilies of the valley, and ribbons of purple and white. Sprigs of sage sat on top, with clay statues of Buddha, wooden crucifixes, golden menorahs, stone carvings of totem poles, pentagrams, and burning incense.

Written on the altar, with sharpie and paint were phrases like, “Forgive me. Lord help me. Brahma save me. In Him we find redemption.” Candles burned at the base. They were those tall, narrow candles I’ve seen in churches and bodegas, with images on them of Jesus, Elvis, and Dolly Parton.

I stood in front of it, touching the velvet ribbons and silk Tibetan flags.

“Touching it can be too intense for some people,” said a voice behind me.

I spun around and there was a man. He wore a plaid flannel shirt, held an axe over his shoulder, and had blood stains on his jeans. He was broad, his chest wide and thick. With a beard covering most of his neck, wide brown eyes, and tanned, leathery skin, he looked dirty in that sexy way men are dirty after repairing your car. Though he had a full head of hair, he had crow’s feet around his eyes that reminded me of my dad.

“I think I’m lost, I um, I’m sorry, which way to General Population?” I wasn’t afraid, but the feeling of being held and rocked by my mother disappeared.

“Oh, I have no idea. I’ve walked for miles it seems and all I’ve ever seen is this prairie. The last guy that came through here walked straight north trying to get to General. I assume he knew where he was going.”

On Earth, I hated when people used north, south, east, west to give me directions, so here I was clueless. I had to ask, “Which way is north?”

He looked to his right, squinted his eyes, and pointed, like the brainless Scarecrow.

I looked to the supposed north and saw nothing but endless prairie grass. It was also starting to get dark. Not like night comes to Earth or in Milk Carton Mountain. Rather, the milky sky started to turn dark blue and sparkly, like being under a dome of sapphire.

The guy said, "Is the sky like this in general population? I'm guessing not based on the look on your face."

Now I was scared. He looked normal enough, but Rita warned me about there being serial killers, rapists, and child abusers in Missingville. They're dead and missing, but humans, thinking they're alive, search for them to bring "justice to the families" of their victims. Being a bit of a jerk in life didn't land you here. If that were the case, I would be this guy's roommate. Instead, it was reserved for the doers of super shitty stuff.

I introduced myself anyway. "It is beautiful, but I'm not sure I can get home in this light. I'm Renata by the way."

He stepped forward and shook my hand. "Ben. It's nice to meet you," he said. He was smart. He set the axe down first.

"We have some tents and sleeping bags if you'd like to camp out for the night. I can build you a fire. It's not a bad night, sleeping under this sky." He looked up as he said this and his mouth opened a bit, revealing a space between his two front teeth. He looked innocent like a child. He looked back down at me, silent.

I accepted the invitation. He walked off towards a shed. I started collecting sticks and stopped wondering why he was here.

Ben popped a tent, gave me a sleeping bag and a pillow, and started a fire with a stick and a string. This, I have learned from Milk Carton Mountain, is much easier here than it is on Earth. It took him about three seconds until the flames were glowing, lighting up his face in a way that made him now look like a madman.

We sat on logs in front of the fire. Ben walked over to one of the A-frames and came back with a hot chocolate and a bottle of whiskey, saying, "Pick your poison. I'm a whiskey guy myself."

I took both the hot and cold tin cups. "Tonight, I think I need both if that's okay."

He sat quietly for a bit, and then said, "I started a forest fire once as a kid." Ah, is this bad enough to put him in Punishment Prairie? "It was a fire about the size of a queen mattress, but still, for a second, I was sure I'd burn the whole park down. After we put it out, I started sobbing. I told my dad I was afraid I'd killed all the squirrels in the forest."

We stayed silent a while, and I started to feel exposed. I didn't mind it.

Ben went on, "I never chopped wood in my real life though. Here, it's like therapy. Every man should chop wood. It settles the testosterone, minimizes the frontal lobe's compulsion to be angry, if that makes sense."

Somehow, he did make sense. I said, "I've never chopped wood before either, but even without testosterone, I can be pretty angry. I was just thinking about this time I pushed my mom while we were in an argument. I felt like I was forgiven for it. What is it about this place?"

Ben wasn't ready to divulge. Changing the subject, he said, "How'd you end up here tonight? Where were you coming from?"

I told him I volunteered on Milk Carton Mountain. "I made s'mores and wiped the sticky faces of lost toddlers."

Ben just looked down into his cup of whiskey, his elbows on his knees, tapping his feet. He nodded his head a bit. Holy shit, did he kill a toddler? My Earthly instincts kicked in, my fear of being abducted, beaten, raped, the way we all (women) go through life afraid of the man who's coming to kill us. Am I hanging out with a murderer? Am I going to survive the night? When will they come looking for me? Maybe I should just leave right now.

"Maybe I should get back. I don't want to worry my roommate," I said as I stood up and looked behind me.

Ben laughed, just a couple little sounds tumbling out of his mouth as he smiled and looked up at me like a child. "Renata, you can't get hurt here. You can't get lost here. Sit down, enjoy the sky. I'm in the Prairie where I light candles and ask for redemption every day. Do you think I would ruin that? You've never been safer than you are right now, kid."

I sat back down and said, "I want to go home. And I mean home, home, not General Population home." I felt that sting in my eyes, that ball in my throat as I held back the tears of a lonely woman in the middle of a forgiveness fire.

"What would you be doing if you were at home?"

I told him that I would be watching Netflix and taking selfies, eating peanut butter and celery, warm and cozy in my fluffy pajamas and wool socks. I'd go to work, have happy hour cocktails on Thursdays, and go to the winery on Sundays. I'd go to my parents' house every few weeks for dinner and I'd go shopping with my mom. I'd be making my bed and watering my plants. I'd be taking trips to Lake Tahoe or Vegas, planning my bestie's bachelorette party, and envying my friend who just had the most beautiful gay wedding in Kansas of all places.

"Ah, I do miss Vegas," Ben said. "I lived there for a while. It's suffocating to be in a place that feeds on loss and gluttony. But it's so electric and constant that it's like breathing cocaine and caffeine. I always felt like I was missing something. I had no right to just relax and watch Netflix in my fluffy socks. No one takes naps in Vegas."

I told him I felt that way in Hawaii or San Diego. "It's so beautiful every single day that there's such guilt if you're not swimming or laying on the beach. I prefer seasons, where there's permission in the winter to be a fat sloth."

Ben laughed. "Yes, I was a sucker for a nice snowstorm and a pantry full of mac and cheese. I lived in Chicago for a while too. That wind is no joke. It's not just a cliché, but the snow allows you to hibernate, like a reset."

I said I was from Nashville, and yes, I was all the things that come along with it.

I felt like we were about to sit on a freshly painted bench. There was a hesitation, a halting, rearranging. Ben felt it too, the need to hold his cards closer to his chest. He stood up and said, "Well, I better hit the hay. I put extra blankets in the tent, so you should be warm enough like when you wore the Netflix pajamas. Good night."

When I'm uncomfortable, I laugh. After Ben got in his cabin, I sat staring into the fire and chuckled. What the fuck just happened? After I was done laughing, I cried, looking up at the sky and licking the tears off my lips.

Chapter 22

I had the best sleep of my life, or my death, in Punishment Prairie. I woke up with the roosters, and the sound of hummingbirds whipping around my tent. When I went outside, the sun was rising but not like it does where you are. It was moving upwards, a huge ball, changing colors from orange to blue to purple. I guess that clever god thought it would be nice to give the sinners a bit of extra beauty since they're likely going to the Dark Side once their bodies are found. Nice move.

I got out of my tent and sat by the fire. Yes, I was worried about my bed head, combined with my skull fracture, in case I saw Ben again. Rubbing my eyes and combing my hair with my fingers, I heard commotion behind me. When I turned, I saw a group gathered around the altar. Bald old men with white beards and blood running down their backs and middle-aged women with round bellies and scars in the crook of their elbows, were skipping like children. A dark-skinned woman with feathers in her hair and a seeping slash across his face chanted, "Forgive me, redeem me, save me from myself." A teenage girl in a poodle skirt and saddle shoes, a rope around her neck, dancing wildly, shouted, "I am more than the sum of my parts."

They held hands, formed a circle around the altar, and then went to their knees. They all bowed down, foreheads touching the grass. A pre-teen with slashes across his wrists stood up and started playing a drum attached to his waist. He beat the drum and hummed like a Buddhist, his eyes closed, his head tilted toward the blue sun. I heard him say, "Forgive us our trespasses and lead us not into temptation." The crowd responded, "Deliver us from evil. For thine is the kingdom, the power, and the glory."

A woman with no hair or eyebrows took the adolescent's place. She had a hula hoop spinning around her neck and said, "Forgive me for killing myself instead of letting the cancer get me." The crowd responded, "When you know better, you do better."

A man with a gun strapped to his back and a hole through his forehead said, "Even I am worthy of forgiveness." I thought otherwise when I noticed the swastika on his shoulder.

There was what looked like an entire family wearing matching white robes, blood-stained from what trickled out of the corners of their mouths, saying, "We poisoned ourselves for the Lord, which must count for something."

In a black and white striped jumpsuit and chains around his ankle, a man with algae in his hair said, "Forgive me for the crime, but I stand by my escape."

I saw Ben, shirtless. I noticed the black hair on his chest and the definition in his stomach. He was clasping hands with a topless bald woman on his left and a man with an Amish beard and hat on his right. Down on one knee, he kept his forehead to the grass as the hairless woman exclaimed, "We are all deserving. We will be delivered to the Light Side of Deadtown." Ben looked up with an "Amen."

This is the kind of behavior that my living self would have mocked. I would have called it some "New Age, mamby, pamby bullshit." I found those that shouted in front of altars, or my god, danced to a drum circle, to be grifters. But my belittling laughter didn't come. Disgust at Ben didn't come.

Instead, I got up and walked toward the altar. No one noticed me at first. I stood just behind the circle. Ben stood up and started dancing, moving his hands in the air in front of his face, stomping his bare feet in step with the drum. From his mouth came sounds. With rolling "R's," Ben was doing what I can only describe as speaking in tongues. Group members responded like they understood. Still, I didn't have an urge to make fun of them.

Damnit if I didn't close my eyes and start swaying. I bowed my head and shifted my weight from left to right, my hands dangling at my sides with palms up. The dialogue around me registered in my brain as "I'm so sorry. I'm ready to move on."

Then, they sang. "This little light of mine, I'm gonna let it shine."

Ben looked at me the way only a dead man making penance might do. I smiled and sang, "Let it shine. Let it shine all the time."

Chapter 23

To get my mind off things, I went to Angelique's eulogy.

She was a forty-year-old beauty, with long, curly, black hair and green eyes. She had tiny hands and rings on eight fingers. Her body was small, her nose was small, and the number of stabs it took to kill her was small. It took one knife through one piece of skin, through one heart to knock her dead and bleeding out within forty-three seconds. She walked around here in a blood-stained, tulip print top that didn't match the striped pattern of her skirt. Risky, yes. But she pulled it off.

She was one of those people who said sorry too often. Sorry she accidentally was in your path when you walked to the buffet for more potatoes. Sorry you misunderstood her when she very clearly said, "Of course I will." Sorry she continued to date the married doctor who lavished her with gifts. Sorry she allowed him to put her up in her own apartment and then control her life, and death. Most sorry she died without having a show at a gallery. Sorry her art barely sold. She went to all the festivals, Earth Day, Pumpkin Festival, Indigenous Pride Day. She set up her table, her canopy, her brightly printed tapestries, and all those vases, bowls, and soap dishes. She'd say sorry to shoppers who said her art was out of their price range.

And in her eulogy, her brother knew how sorry she was too.

> *Angelique was the bravest person I've ever known. When she was little, she'd skateboard in my dad's cowboy boots. In the heat of summer, she'd be coasting around wearing a Cookie Monster stocking cap, pink corduroy pants, and a green Kermit the Frog t-shirt. My mom would tell her to put on tennis shoes, but she'd just run off and pick flowers, putting them in her hair, holding bouquets of dandelions as she danced in the garden.*
>
> *Later, she'd up and move from Oklahoma City to Brooklyn. She was the first of a long line of Proctors to ever leave Oklahoma. We were safe people, with pride in our hometown and fear of the unknown. But not Angelique. She found it her responsibility to see the world. It never*

dawned on her that a person or place could be dangerous. She saw the world as a child would, full of wonder and awe.

She worked as little as possible to pay the bills and while some may find this un-American, I loved it about her. She was a creative, not a cog in a wheel. Her pottery was loud, bright, and shaped wrong, twisted and tangled, confused but going somewhere. She once gifted me an ashtray with a spiral six inches high on one side, painted with the words, "Maybe it won't kill you after all."

You'd want her on your team if you played pop music trivia, but not geography. She once asked me if she could take a train to Puerto Rico. You'd want her to teach you the subway system, but not to give you a ride. There was too much outside those windows to see. She'd ask, "How can a person watch the road when the leaves are changing and letting go?"

She didn't like romance, or so she said, but she'd let people fall in love with her, because what choice did they have, anyway? Things went sideways for her in love. Her forgiveness came too easily, and her apologies came unwarranted. It is not lost on me, our collective fear of her being taken advantage of. It is not lost on me that we are all here wishing we'd done more, or less, or something else. It is not lost on me that this tender heart was fish bait for the wrong shark. But I am also keenly aware that she died having never hurt a living thing in her life. She died having not once let me down. My sister died with the same innocence she had on the blacktop, in cowboy boots and a stocking cap. She left us all a little more innocent, a little more likely to skate when it's dangerous and to love even though it'll kill you.

I know she is skipping with a rope and a flower in her hair, a pink polka dot shirt with an orange striped skirt looking at all of us today, saying, "Love yourselves the way I did."

Chapter 24

I went for a swim with Tim today. He said he's feeling a little blue because he heard the Earth's oceans are the new trash dumps for humans. I told him it's not so new. We've been assholes for a long time now. He said a little bird told him that, what with pollution, climate change, and whack jobs running countries with nuclear weapons, god is preparing for the inevitable moment when every inhabitant of the planet comes to Missingville.

"If everyone is dead, no one can find them," Tim said.

I told Tim I knew god would come up with a fucked-up way to handle it and I'd better be in Deadtown by then. Tim said to watch my mouth.

I floated on a flamingo-shaped raft and put on the helmet.

Nathan the cop is outside Bum Fuck Tennessee, in front of a supply store on the trail. There's a tent set up and it's raining sideways, so he and another officer are wearing thin, soaked ponchos that make them look incapable of finding a thought, let alone a person. Nathan is looking at a map and asking an elderly man where, within twenty miles, is a stoplight.

The man, toothless and with tobacco in his cheek, says, "Fredericktown's got a light. Though I don't suppose I ever saw it do anything besides blink yellow."

He tells Nathan it's seven miles north. The cops look like they're in a 1970s action film. They look up at each other with a that's-the-tip-we've-been-waiting-for look and run to the cruiser. The old man spits and walks slowly out from under the tent, rain be damned.

I decided not to follow the car. My body is nowhere near a stoplight.

I floated as Tim jumped over me. I clapped for him and thought about the fat fingers of old white men pushing big red buttons, mushroom clouds, plastic tampon applicators in the ocean, the homes of celebrities sliding into the Pacific. I asked Tim why god doesn't do something to stop it, and he told me the Agnostics got it right. Make the world in seven days, etcetera, sit back and watch it go up in flames. For the first time, sweet little Tim sounded cynical.

Chapter 25

Yes, I have been thinking about Ben. I've met a lot of people here. We're a bunch of traumatized, edgy, guarded souls. We've been through some serious shit. This isn't a peaceful place, no matter how much Rita wants it to be, no matter what god says. Sure, the amenities are beautiful, the "foliage" as they call it, is serene. The weather is always a perfect seventy-six degrees in Gen Pop. There's no humidity so my hair never frizzes and there's no winter to make me cracked and ashy. Pineapples taste like orgasms, the bedding feels like silk, and the air smells like orchids. There's no acne, no vomiting or diarrhea, no need for yearly mammograms or vaginal exams. No one is going to put my feet in stirrups and ask me to "scootch down some more."

But the people, my god. We're annoyed and bitter. It's like everyone here is in a constant state of PMS. No one gets their period, but many times I've thought,

"I wish I'd just bleed already so this can pass."

It doesn't.

That prickly, scratchy feeling in our bellies stays. It's like we're all weary from the longest road trips of our lives. Like when my dad woke us up at 3:00 am so we could get to the beach before noon. A middle of the night wakeup call that leads to a cramped car where your brother ate all the Oreos and your mom says every two hours, "I'm sorry, Julian, but I have to pee again."

Your dad sighs in frustration, saying "I'm going to skip this exit and wait for the next one." Except another exit doesn't come for thirty-seven minutes and mom is squirming in her seat trying not to piss her pants.

Everyone here has to pee. Their dad won't let them. They're stuck in traffic, and the radio is staticky.

But I'm putting Ben in a category I often referenced in life called, "Not Like the Rest." I was usually wrong about it as every man I classified this way ended up being transferred to "You Should Have Known Better." So, sue me, I'm not fucking self-actualized.

Ben wasn't on the road trip; he'd already arrived. Ben was already in the mountains or at the beach, sleeping in a jeep or the bed of a truck. He was well-rested, not woken up at 3:00 am like the rest of us. He wasn't in the throes of PMS.

What's surprising about the other side is that in Missingville there are still players, fuck bois, phonies. Just yesterday I was standing in line to get to the most crowded eulogy yet. Brian, a father of six foster kids who ran a food pantry, was stabbed by an unhoused man he picked up on the highway. These good Samaritan types, they pack the funeral homes.

A guy standing behind me said, “Hey, I couldn’t help but notice we died the same way,” as he pointed to his neck.

I barely glanced at him, but I knew enough to say, “Nice try. We all know men with rope marks are death by suicide, not murder.” They try to get down your pants any way they can, ladies. And when you die, they’ll keep on trying.

I’m confident Ben would never use such a tactic. Maybe I’ve had the misfortune of never meeting a genuine man. If you’re thinking that this genuine man might be a serial killer, this is not lost on me. I’ve entertained way too many daydreams dedicated to the possibilities that landed him here.

As I mentioned before, I’ve done some abysmal things, and I’m not in the Prairie. Shay said, “Oh, girl, it takes something like hurting animals to end up there. He’s the bottom of the barrel. Don’t go back there for some lumberjack fuck.”

I just knew Ben hadn’t hurt an animal. Yes, he probably hurt a person, but let’s be honest. Don’t we all get a lot more worked up over animals?

But I don’t want to go back for a lumberjack fuck. There are plenty of other lumberjack types in General

Population. One legit lumberjack is here. He died while poaching some super rare trees in New Zealand. A tree fell on him, and before he could be found, some sort of animal encounter left his body in thirty-nine pieces. He's sexy and edible, like I want to take a bite out of him, but he's an anti-vaxxer and dabbles in flat Earth inquiries, so I got the ick.

Ben looked like he was a brick layer on Earth, or a welder, a union type. I imagine him driving a truck with a ladder in the back, a red bandana tied to the end. He had lots of these bandanas, sometimes he wore them around his forehead, sometimes just in his back pocket to wipe off July sweat. He had his own little square house with white siding and an outdated kitchen, but a deck he power-washed every spring. He had a Golden Retriever, an unsightly, enormous flat screen tv, and a leather couch with white cracks coming through. He drank Miller High Life and smoked an occasional bowl, but he made burgers with ground turkey and had bouts of too many protein shakes and bench presses.

I gave Ben a story. I imagined he went fishing with his dad on weekends. His mom still sent him home with leftovers, packaged in recycled Country Crock containers. His parents loved each other, his brother gave them grandchildren, and his niece was his favorite person on the planet. He had a few serious girlfriends, but nothing stuck. He was losing friends to wives and children, which aggravated him and made him should all over himself.

Maybe he dabbled in a little embezzlement, sold drugs to a kid, pulled a knife in a bar fight. Maybe he snapped at waiters, tailgated too much, and ignored cross walks. He could have flipped the bird a little too often with unnecessary road rage. It's possible he teased a boy in high school who wore nail polish and lipstick. I bet he showed a nasty temper a time or two and had it in him to make a woman feel small. Maybe he stayed quiet when a friend used the N word. He might have been that guy who always raised his hand when, at the end of a college class or work meeting, the lecturer asked if there were any questions. It's possible he worked at a customer service job where he talked the elderly into reverse mortgages. Perhaps he put one of those card readers into the pump at gas stations and robbed people of their pin numbers and hard-earned paychecks. Maybe he taunted women as they entered abortion clinics or signed a petition against the expansion of Medicaid.

I'm willing to consider scenarios worse than these. Murderer, rapist, new age grifter who sells teas and supplements. Those people that made fortunes fabricating hauntings and exorcisms, maybe he was in that crowd. I don't think he was a politician, but I can only assume that all missing members of congress are in the Prairie. I do see him as having the propensity to join a cult. Maybe he killed someone for his leader, all Charles Manson like. Jeez, I hope it wasn't a cult since that pairs so well with child brides.

Whatever the case, befriending someone in Punishment Prairie must help my numbers when I pass to Deadtown. Not only did I volunteer at Milk Carton Mountain, but I walked right on past those gluttonous orgies. I held my tongue when I wanted to tell people to get fucked. I hugged people that needed comforting, even when I thought they were just being insufferable babies. But to really put a feather in my death cap, to show god I deserved the Light Side, to highlight my empathy, my good nature, my knack for forgiveness, why not buddy up to a wicked soul in the Prairie?

Altruism it is.

Chapter 26

When I approached the Prairie, the same feeling came over me. It was beautiful in the way old time pictures of people without smiles make you long to be in their bleak, drab moment. It felt old and sacred, the way the trees were gnarly and winding, the way the prairie grass waved in the wind. The ground felt old, dry, and crumbly under my feet, while the sun felt new. There was a warmth that I hadn't experienced on Earth, even when I baby oiled myself and sat on a Caribbean beach. It was warm like putting your cold feet right on the rocks around a campfire.

I approached the pasture with a dry mouth and a stir in my stomach. My body felt almost alive. With what smelled like rye rubbing up against my legs, and the breeze blowing in my face, I recalled being a baby, when my mom would hold my hands up as I learned to walk, the wind taking my breath away. My eyelashes rose and fell, slow and careful. I once read that we blink less when we're in moments of happiness.

Ahead of me was a row of something I couldn't make out at first, identical figures standing in the same pose. They were in a line as far as I could see as I looked to the left and right. Horses. It was a row of horses. I started to run towards them. They stood still, like they were waiting for a command. They were black and white, like a grandma's hair when she first becomes a grandma, not later when she's all gray and everyone has forgotten about her. Salt and pepper manes flowing behind them as long as their tails, wagging back and forth in unison. It made me think of a symphony, all those violin reeds back and forth like they're making music out of the push and pull of living.

I stood on a rock and watched them approach me. I raised my arms, the way I stood naked in the hot springs of New Mexico. I lifted my head and closed my eyes. "I'm sorry" coming out of my mouth over and over.

They walked slowly with their heads high and their steps a regal, slow gallop. They all came towards me. In unison, they looked straight ahead and nodded their heads up and down. I approached one and put my head against its side. I rubbed its head and listened for a heartbeat. Of course, there wasn't one, but I swear it felt like my heart was beating again. "I forgive you," said my pulsating chest.

I heard, "Yes, you are forgiven for that, and that, and yes, even that too."

Cheating on a history test in sixth grade, the time I promised Emma Flynn I wouldn't tell anyone she was adopted, then immediately called Maddy Clark with the news. The way I made fun of a classmate's acne-covered face, the time I laughed about a customer who left the store because nothing we sold was plus sized. The day I spent in bed with my best friend's boyfriend. That time I faked like I was sick to get out of the father daughter dance, just to sneak out of the house to blow Ian Banks in his Mustang. My dad was so disappointed. Oh god, my refusal to make eye contact with pan handlers at stoplights. The knack I had for sarcasm used most often towards people not smart enough to understand that I was actually making fun of them. My lack of donations to any charity. My failure to show up on the mornings my sorority volunteered at the Ronald McDonald House. The fact that I never visited my grandpa in the nursing home, even after I heard he was asking for me. The lies I told:

"No, I didn't cheat on you."

"Yes, I locked the safe before I clocked out."

And, trying to get him to stay with me, "I'm pregnant."

The horses nodded. They didn't speak, their mouths didn't move, but I heard, in the voice of a thousand Morgan Freemans, "Every human does these things. Here are grace and mercy."

Then, they turned around, and all in unison, and ran away in a perfect line, like animals trained for a circus. They galloped to a chant of, "You. Were. Human. You. Were. Still. Good."

On Earth we're so daft, stepping into closets and confessing sins to men in white collars. Begging on our hands and knees at our bedside for a chance to get into Heaven, despite ourselves. We hope we're still allowed into the speakeasy, praying we have the right password, even though we coveted our neighbor's wife. Walking to the front of a congregation and saying, "Yes, I accept Jesus as my savior," wearing linen and plunging into a pool.

What are we actually sorry for? Sorry we screwed up our chances of going to the Light Side. Sorry we looked foolish when we got caught. Sorry we have to kiss up to someone to make them not mad at us anymore. Sorry we lost the righteous upper hand. After our apology, we rinse and repeat. We know when we walk out of the confessional that we're going to do it again. Sometimes the guilt feels worth it. Aren't there times when the wrong thing just felt too damn good? Think having an affair with a younger woman. That kind of guilt, we're willing to carry it around in exchange for feeling young again.

But of course, the guilt sometimes feels like a thousand disapproving looks from our mothers. The shame builds up as if we're going to pop from gluttony, chocolaty and sweet. Humans run on a hamster wheel of wrongdoing, apologies, forgiveness if you're lucky, and shame. When I was alive, I wasn't interested in amends. I don't think I looked in the proverbial mirror long enough to see what needed fixing. I mostly took the low road.

But line up a thousand horses and make an inventory of your failings as they accept you, that feels like the last time you'll sin. It's an invitation to just cut the crap already. I stood up, stretched tall and looked to the warmest sun in any universe and said out loud, "I am so glad I died."

I'm sorry, friends, there's just no way to get to this place without coming to this place. You're not going to get out of the pits of Earth alive. I don't know what Hell is, and maybe I'm about to, but where you are right now, ironing your shirt, stepping in gum, paying your taxes, sweeping the kitchen floor, standing in line at a self-check-out, and envying scrolling faces on a screen, it's worse than this.

As I approached the Prairie, I saw a man in a tuxedo churning butter, a drag queen splitting firewood, a teenager with half a face hanging clothes on lines. A woman in a Cinderella ball gown clanging away on a horseshoe. Men in uniform were lined up picking strawberries and a woman who looked 100 years old was carrying a bucket out of an outhouse. With that job, I'm guessing she definitely hurt an animal.

I found Ben, walking towards a truck, carrying a kayak on his head. For a minute, it felt like Earth.

I was approaching a guy I liked, admiring his muscles. But mostly I was curious about every single thing he had inside himself. Trying to fix the matted hair at the crown of my head, running my hands down my hiking shorts, I cleared my throat. Just a young woman about to talk to a young man about kayaking and the weather.

I approached him as he slid the kayak into a red truck. I'm not good with cars, but it looked super old, with rounded fenders and rust spots. The kind people take wedding pictures in, the kind a person might pose in front of for a country album. He jumped when he turned around and there I was.

"Well, well, if it isn't the Nashville girl coming over to the wrong side of the tracks," he said as he ran his hand through his wavy brown hair. I wanted this to be nerves.

"Hey there, Mr. Vegas. I guess there's some water around here?" I nodded to the kayak.

"Heck yeah, you don't know? Oh wait, of course you wouldn't. The Prairie has the clearest, coolest river. Better than any I ever saw on Earth."

Without hesitation I said, "Can I join you?"

Without hesitation he said, "Absolutely."

Hopping into the passenger seat, I heard the staticky radio playing what I think is Thirty-eight Special, or REO Speedwagon, maybe Night Ranger? You get the idea.

"So how does radio work here? Do we have a station? Are there dead people turning vinyl or can you think of a song, and it comes on?"

Ben said, "I have no idea. Every time I get in this truck, it plays three songs on repeat. This, Piano Man, and something in Spanish that sounds like a polka. I don't know any Spanish, but I can sing every word to whatever that is."

"My god, god is weird," I said as I rolled down the window and stuck out my hand. We were on a country road, corn stalks on both sides, a sun in front of us that looked like the kind I'd draw as a kid, just a round hump of yellow with lines coming off in every direction.

Ben talked about kayaking in his Earth life, fishing with his buddies, floating down rivers with his dog, and drinking too much beer. I was right about him.

"I'm a wine girl myself. I always wished I could open a cold beer in the summer to quench my thirst. Instead, I feel like I'm drinking bread."

He laughed, then paused, looked out the window, looked at me, looked at the road. "Beers, and then whiskey, they abused me as much as I abused them when I was alive. I'm the guy stumbling around and getting kicked out of bars. How any of my friends could tolerate me, I don't know." He frowned.

"Well, there's a whole mess of horses here who will forgive that shit in a second."

Ben's eyes opened wide. "You sat for the Horse Brigade Forgiveness Pageant?"

"Well, I never would have called it that, but yeah, I did. I wish that kind of stuff happened on Earth.

After the nodding horses, I felt glad to be dead. Those are some powerful animals."

Ben shook his head. "Those fucking horses. I was here over a year before they performed the Pageant. What the hell?"

I wondered why it took a year for him. "Well, maybe if I lived in Punishment Prairie it would have taken awhile for me too." I walked into words I shouldn't have.

Ben didn't say anything. He fidgeted with his hair, ran his hands over his beard, kept looking to his left, rearrange himself in his seat, all while Billy Joel said we were all in the mood for a melody.

Pulling off onto a gravel road, I started to worry. You're driving down a secluded road with a killer, a rapist, an animal abuser. What the fuck were you thinking? He's going to kill you. I know, I know, he can't kill me. But Missingville doesn't wash away all the fears you've carried around your whole life. Driving down dirt roads with a man you just met is on the list of no-noes. And yet, here we are.

Ben turned into a paved area that led right to water. Not like natural Earth water, more like animated water, water like the time I tripped acid in Hawaii. Clear but blue tinged, or green, or a combination of blue and orange, mixed with a neon pink. All the colors.

I sat in the truck with my mouth open, my bottom jaw unable to join the top. Ben got out and put the kayak on the edge of the water, then walked over to my side of the truck. "I know. It took me a minute the first time too. Another thing to make you glad you're dead."

How many times have I kayaked you might be wondering? The answer is zero. But, unlike on Earth where I would have faked it and told a new crush I was a pro, I just blurted out, "I've never done this before and all the sudden I feel like you're going to regret this because I'll crash the boat into a rock, or I'll tip it over and somehow break the entire thing in half and we'll almost drown and all of Missingville will talk about the girl who was creeping around a Prairie guy and what was she doing there anyway?"

He exhaled and smiled. "Renata, you're not that special. Also, no one calls a kayak a boat."

I wanted to put my tongue down his throat.

Chapter 27

You probably know this, but if you suck at kayaking you sit in the front. It's the back guy who does the steering. I thought he was just being a gentleman when he said, "Ladies first, sit up here," as he handed me an oar.

But my pal Halim clued me in later when I told him about my "date." Unlike Shay, he said, "We're dead. The rules don't apply. Go ahead and creep on that Prairie lumberjack."

We floated along. It smelled like earth, like mud and pine. It smelled alive. The breeze kissed my face the way a person touches your chin right before they kiss you. The sun remained a child's drawing, and the water changed along the way, a wave of color coming towards us and running under us in rainbows. Ben pointed out different birds, telling me that one was still a dinosaur that god thought would be cool to put here. He said he heard god was still obsessed with dinosaurs and thought them his best creation.

Ben said, "I imagine god likes dinosaurs more than humans, to be honest. And who can blame him?"

I corrected him. "Who can blame them?" Ben rolled his eyes.

We pulled up to a sand bar. Not my most graceful dismount, as I slipped and fell onto my knees into the water. Me and these damn knees. Ben rushed over and helped me up, and I laughed. "It's not easy to get off a boat, is it?"

"A kayak cannot be called a boat!" He yelled and laughed.

Ben went to the rear of the kayak and damn if he didn't pull out a picnic basket. A man, with a picnic basket. Not a cooler, not a paper bag, a woven basket with blue and white checkered fabric lining the inside. I looked at him like, "Are you serious?"

He smiled. "I live in the homesteading capital of Missingville, what can I say?"

I asked him if he had a butter churn hidden somewhere in there.

We sat and drank lemonade, the kind full of pulp, likely made by the same woman who wove the basket. We ate fried chicken and strawberries. Ben's jaw popped when he ate, a little muscle by his ear pulsating as he chewed. My dad's did this too and I wondered what he was doing at that very moment.

"I miss my parents," I said, with a mouthful of chicken.

"Yeah? I miss mine too, but mostly in a guilty, how are they handling my disappearance kind of way." He said they were agoraphobic, always keeping to themselves, but becoming paranoid hoarders as they got older. "I haven't been in their house in twelve years."

I said, "My gosh. I bet that's hard to watch them crawl into themselves like that."

Ben was older than me, I could tell. I figured he hadn't relied on them in a long time, but maybe he never did. "My sister is who I really miss. Beth is her name. She's the funniest person I've ever met. Goofy, clever. That girl gives zero fucks, and I love her for it. She tells my parents to stop being such pussies, says their fear of living is melodramatic and tired. She kept me in line. Well, until she didn't."

I thought about how she might have done that. What was Ben doing that needed to be kept in line? If she hadn't stopped, would he be in the Prairie?

"I bet she misses you like crazy," I said. I imagined her at their parents' house, yelling at them to join the search party, begging them to take part in finding him. I imagined his mom sitting on a tiny section of couch, with stacks of magazines on one side of her, a mess of China dolls on the other saying "I'm just being patient. I'm staying right here until he comes through that door."

We ate quietly for a while. I laid back and closed my eyes, happily not wondering what Ben was thinking of me. Happily wondering if his bare back tanned on these trips to the stream, or if he died with this dark, leathery skin. I wanted to touch it, to feel the heat of his skin. So, I did. I placed my palm on the small of his back. He didn't move away.

"Ya know, I've been here for three years. Eleven hundred and twelve days to be exact. And you're the only person to purposefully come to the Prairie. People get lost all the time, like you did at first. But they all run off to wherever normal people go, and they don't come back. I don't blame them. My next-door neighbor killed a toddler, and the blacksmith ran a dog fighting ring. Shit, the woman that made that basket, and this food, she was a Columbian Cartel boss. The number of bullets she ordered to be put into peoples' heads is staggering."

I was confused. "So, is everyone trying to do their penance? Trying to get good with god so they can go to the Light Side of Deadtown?"

Ben explained, "Well, it's a conundrum, isn't it? If they never get found, they'll be here forever. Most hold on to the hope they'll be found, so they act like angels here. But the guy whose head is at the bottom of the Atlantic, and torso is washed ashore on an uninhabited island in the Pacific, he's still scary as hell. He won't be found. He knows it. He has no reason to ask for forgiveness."

I went for it. "And what about you?"

He paused, took a deep breath. "Last time I put on the helmet, I was sure I'd be found. But even if I'm not, I can't help but ask for forgiveness in the Prairie. The energy in that place, the altar, the horses, you must be a psychopath to not ask to be forgiven."

I asked, "And you're not a psychopath, eh? Thought this was a perfect segue for me to just get that settled."

He chuckled. "A psychopath I am not. A selfish, careless idiot, that's me. I took a whole lot more from living than I gave, that's for sure. An absolutely wasted life." I found this hard to believe.

"You're crushing this dead thing though, Mr. Vegas. You had me at picnic basket." I sat up, turned to him, and made my best "kiss me" face. He left me hanging, though I wasn't embarrassed.

"Let's get back, eh?" he said as he stood.

Floating back, he whistled now and then. Serial killers are likely whistlers. My personal opinion is that not every whistler is a serial killer, but every serial killer is a whistler. I sat in front of him wondering if he whistled when he cut up a body in a bathtub. Did it brighten the mood when he shoveled graves? Did he whistle before he struck a girl with an oar? Maybe be brought a proper picnic basket on Tinder date with the girl he killed on a blanket beside a sunflower patch. Perhaps he killed a man on the banks of a river and stole his kayak, whistling as he paddled downstream.

I turned around, rocking the kayak as I tried to situate myself. I sat staring at him while he paddled and whistled. He didn't look away. I smiled. He smiled. He stopped paddling. He put the oar across his lap. He stopped whistling. He smiled, exhaled through his nose, and nodded, the one does when they're giving up, or giving in.

I felt that warmth you get when you exchange a knowing glance with your sister while your uncle is talking about immigration at Thanksgiving dinner. I remembered the inside joke with my brother about how my mom "can't lift a finger" with the rock on her hand my dad gave her to celebrate twenty-five years of tolerating each other. It felt like opening a school lunch with a note from that same mom saying, "You've got this!"

On the drive back, I thought about how Missingville was just Earth, only differentiated by the color and texture of the sky. Just a bunch of broken humans trying to untangle the knots between self-preservation and trust falling. We're out here in the same push and pull of "I'm willing to trust you and also armed for when you inevitably fuck me up." You'd think that death would resolve these dichotomies. It turns out, it doesn't. We're just a mess of categorized people, put in slots of good and bad by a being that made us susceptible to the seven deadly sins in the first place.

I'd like to see god and punch them in the throat.

Chapter 27

After I parted ways with Ben and walked home, I had something like butterflies in the space where my stomach used to be, that "I have a crush on you" physical response. I might have had some tingles in between my legs if I'm honest.

I told Shay about Ben.

After a long pause, she said, "Well, I suppose if you went for bad boys on Earth, this tracks."

I told her that on Earth I went for everyone. Everyone that went for me, that is. From the bad boys to the choir boys, to the woman who made me wonder why I ever wanted a man in the first place. She raised her eyebrows at the woman part. I waited for a word of shock or disapproval, or the worst, "You're not going to try to get with me are you?" But she did none of those things.

Instead, she said, "Girl, I went for anyone that loved me enough to give me drugs, or who loved me enough to hunt me down, chase me, then bend me into whatever knot they wanted to. Falling for a guy in Punishment Prairie is something I'm surprised most women here haven't done."

I shrugged. "I don't know what put him there, but I'm filled with this impulse to inhale him until whatever he did becomes a part of me too, and he forgives himself while I tell him it's okay." I started to cry.

She got up, kissed me on the forehead, and said, "So do it. You've got nothing better to do."

Chapter 28

The eulogy of Ramone.

Good morning. I'm Ramone's brother, Rene. Thank you for being here.

Ramone was a good man. He was a devoted husband and father. He cared for our parents in their final days and was a loyal and supportive brother.

We are saddened by his passing but know he is with the Lord.

We are especially grateful to the Sacramento police department for their hard work in finding Ramone and bringing him to rest.

He....

I'm sorry...

Umm...I...give me a second. He looked down, shook his head, and then looked up, closed his eyes, and continued.

I haven't seen my brother in twelve years. He put my parents in a filthy nursing home and never once went to see them. He cheated on his wife and ran his family with an iron fist. Look around. His children aren't even here. Growing up, he bullied and tormented me. If you look at me, you can see the aftermath of Ramone and that damn BB gun. (Rene had one eye)

I mean, let's be honest. He started crying and shouting, banging his own fist on the podium.

Is anyone surprised that he was finally murdered? Are you? Are you surprised? It's a wonder he lived to be seventy-five. I mean, my god, that lucky bastard got seventy-five years on this Earth. If there is a god, he has a fucked-up sense of humor. My oh my, how right you are, Rene.

If there is a god, I do hope he is forgiving, and I hope I also can find forgiveness. But right now, I don't care if Ramone is here or there. He pointed up. He pointed down.

Ramone taught me what not to be, and for that I am grateful. He made me a better person as I went through my life trying to be everything my brother was not. I am a better person because of him. We say that a lot at funerals, don't we? "He made me a better person." Well, that is also true of Ramone. Without him, I might not have

> *found a moral compass to steer me towards right. Without him, I might not have known what not to be.*
>
> *Thank you, Ramone, for making me a better man.*

Well played, Rene. Well played.

Chapter 29

Today, I found my murderer. The helmet felt heavier than usual as I watched him. At first, I jerked the helmet off, held it on my lap and said out loud, "Are you sure you want to do this?" My hands shook when I took a deep breath and put the helmet back on.

He's living in a tent that looks to be miles from the Appalachian Trail. He's sitting on a tree stump sharpening a knife, a fish laid out on a log in front of him. His teeth are white and perfect. With yellow hair and long, blond eyelashes, his face is surprisingly handsome. The bright sun is hard on his blue eyes, and his eyelids look sunburned. He wishes he had a pair of sunglasses, a thought he has several times a day when he forages in the woods, puts a fishing line in the water, bathes himself naked in the stream.

He shakes his head and laughs. At first a quiet giggle, then a bellowing, loud belly laugh. He tilts his head back and looks up, saying, "That was some crazy shit, wasn't it?" He's completely alone. The closest people I see are a man and a toddler walking on the A.T. at least a mile away.

Images in his head are spinning like a Scrambler at a fair, a roaring tornado. He sees himself in bed with a woman. He's sitting up in her bed, against the headboard, while she straddles him and says, "You are perfect." He looks into her eyes, pushes her hair off her forehead, says, "I don't deserve you." He sees her falling off him, laying back, and stroking his collarbone. He says, "I love you," and gets up. In the bathroom he does a line of coke and comes back to her, spooning her quietly, but with restless, shaking legs.

"What a cunt," he whispers. "What a cunt, what a cunt." Laughter. Oh, but she was my soulmate, he thinks. She was everything. He smacks himself in the head. "No. She was a cunt. She was a cunt."

Next, his mom. He goes to the last time he saw her. She bonds him out of jail, walks to the car ahead of him, never looking back, never looking at him at all. She brings him, not home, but to a homeless camp and says, "Good luck," as he gets out of the car. He watches her drive away and thinks of how he used to bake pies with her. The feel of flour on his hands, under his feet, in his hair. She never minded childhood messes, but the kind he made later, she couldn't tolerate anymore. "I love you, mom. I love you, mom." Laughter.

He adds a log to his fire and thinks of how his sister and dad taught him how to live in the wild. The three of them would drive to a plot of land in his dad's family for generations. They'd set up camp, sleeping in tents instead of the little cabin his grandpa built fifty years ago. He heard his dad say, "If I wanted to sleep with a roof over my head, I'd stay home." His dad showed him how to fly fish and how to shoot a deer. His first bloodletting of a doe, when he was just twelve. Reaching in and pulling out the organs; his dad told him not to puncture the colon. The ritual of biting the heart after a kill. Blood and more blood. He always wanted to crawl inside the deer and sleep in its guts. What if he never killed an animal before, would it have been harder to kill a girl? "Kill a girl. Kill a girl. Kill a girl."

Then, his dad crying, the day he found Killer on the bathroom floor, another overdose, another ambulance. "Dad, Dad, Dad. I shot just a tiny bit too much, my bad. That's hilarious." Chuckles.

He starts a fire. Lydia was the best fire starter, he thought, smiling, twitching. His sister was affectionately called "The Pyro," not just on camping trips, but at home too. She taught him how to collect the best tinder, the way a bow drill works best with wood like Aspen, and how to position a foot on the fireboard. Lydia always used a bare foot, so even if there were shoes nearby, he'd take them off to secure the board. He says, "Spindle, spindle, spindle. Lydia spins the spindle. The spindle, the spindle." He pulls the string, laughing some more.

The sun is going down and he whispers, "Twilight, twilight, twilight" while the embers light up. He blows into them saying, "Fire, fire, fire." More laughter.

Swirling in his head next, the last time he did meth, with a guy he met at the food bank, both lighting spoons behind a day care center, of all places. Then he thinks of his grandma's funeral, where he was so drunk, he fell into a row of flowers and blackened his cousin's eye with his elbow. His uncles threw him out into the snow. He crushed up pills and snorted them in the cemetery.

He stands up, wearing only mud-covered, tattered, denim shorts. His skin is red, not the kind that can tan. His shoulders are blistered and his back is covered with bites and scratches. He circles the fire and starts to dance, a hopping maneuver with his arms raised above his head. "The girl has melted into the Earth. Maybe I should have set her on fire. You're such a pyro, Lydia."

He's clicking his tongue and moving his eyebrows up and down. "You'll never find the girl!" Cackle. "I'm a Goddamned magician!" Chuckle.

Then, he replays it. He sits down, closes his eyes, and with an exaggerated exhale, he touches himself, an erection starting. I don't have to look into his mind. He says out loud, "She was just there, what else could I do? That poor little girl with her skinned knees and an empty water bottle. Bloody knees. I love bloody knees. Bloody knees."

He imagines himself in an interrogation room. He plays the scene in his head, in black and white, a wobbly metal chair, a cigarette burning on the table. "I saw her walking alone, up a steep incline. She fell and busted up her knees. She called out the name, Kathleen. She screamed, 'God damn this fucking trail' while blood ran down both legs. She opened her backpack and, like an idiot, poured water on her knees, wiping them off with a t-shirt. Then realized she had no water to drink. She started crying and calling out for someone named Kathleen."

Out loud, "Who the fuck was Kathleen anyway? Anyway. Anyway."

He plays the scene in color now, fondling himself. I close my eyes; I stop watching him and play out the scene myself. Crying as I wiped my bloody legs, I heard, "Looks like you could use some help. I've got water, and some bandages."

I thanked him as he asked me to follow him. He said he had just set up camp a little ways off the trail.

I thought, "This man is gorgeous." Pretty people get jobs easier, and they also have a leg up on murder. I followed him, without one ounce of trepidation. I followed him. I was hungry, thirsty, exhausted. I couldn't believe Kathleen was so far ahead of me. I was abandoned.

At his camp, I sat down on a log and let him clean me up. He gave me water and offered me some almonds.

I accepted both. He very gently cleaned up my knees, wrapping them like he'd done this a time or two.

I hear him, "She had such pretty knees, pretty ankles, my god." Laughter, stroking himself.

I told him my hiking partner had gotten too far ahead of me. I wasn't a particularly good hiker. I had no business being out there. I needed to find Kathleen.

"Find Kathleen, find Kathleen, find Kathleen." He takes his shorts off, spits on his hand, and I stop watching.

He told me to stay where I was, and he'd walk ahead to look for her. Telling me he knew the trail well, he could walk a quick mile or two up the trail. "Don't worry, I'll find her. You just relax here. Those knees aren't going to get you very far." I agreed.

"Walking up the trail, Kathleen, walking up the trail, Kathleen."

He was gone for ten minutes when I heard something behind me. I ignored it at first, assuming it was a squirrel or a bird. Then, as the noise got closer, I turned, and he was behind me. He put a rope around my throat, pulled back, then twisted. I fell backwards and hit my head on a rock. Keeping his hold on the rope, he had me on my back, tightening the rope from behind, then moving in front of me.

"There's no Kathleen. There's no Kathleen." Laughter.

With one hand on the rope and the other unbuttoning my shorts, I begged. "Please don't, please." But he did.

Next, a sock in my mouth, pushed down, my throat contracting.

The tightening of the rope.

The last breaths.

The hovering above my body.

Back to the helmet. He gets up, picks up a pot of water and a shovel. He walks down into a ravine. "Let's check on her. Check on her. Check on her. Check. Check. Mic check. Mic check," he sings and cackles.

Tree limbs, leaves, and dirt cover my body. Above ground, in a half-ass attempt at a grave. I'm surprised to see how visible I am, even from a distance. He was a good murderer, but a bad hider of bodies. How in the hell had I not been found? I can see one bandaged knee sticking out of the branches. I get an ariel view and see how close to his camp, how close to the trail he had brought my dead body. I've watched enough true crime documentaries to know dogs and humans had to have been looking for me here. How was this man free, and how was I here?

"Bury her, bury her, bury her better. Better. Better burial." He's naked, digging, laughing, still stopping every few minutes to spit on his hand and move his hand downward.

It looks effortless, his digging and singing, masturbating, and laughing. "Six feet under, six feet under."

He takes drinks of water and lets it run down his chest, rubbing it in with his filthy hands, beating his chest, snickering, and repeating, "Bloody knees, bloody knees, bloody knees."

He lays down next to me, reaches under the brush and grabs my hand, mostly just bone now, and finishes himself off, saying, "I love you, little girl. I still love you."

He digs next to my body. All the while, singing, laughing, dancing on my grave. The hole was nowhere near deep enough, but he found it suitable. "This will work just fine. Fine. Fine. Like cherry wine." He laughs.

I look away when he uncovers me. I don't want to see myself covered in maggots. I want to watch the madman, though. I don't want to miss one gesture, word, or laugh.

While I'm being rolled into the grave, I open my eyes again. "Bye, bye lover girl, bye, bye bloody knees," he sings as he covers me back up. There's plenty of dirt over me now, and he piles all the branches on top again. He then walks into the dry creek bed and brings up stones, piling those on top of the branches. Then, more branches, fallen tree limbs, all on top of me.

Before taking off the helmet, I watch him lay on top of my grave. On his stomach, he stretched out his arms and legs, running his fingers and toes into the dirt. "You're the best thing that ever happened to me, bloody kneed baby."

I don't know what to say.

Chapter 30

Shay has been spending a lot of time at her man's place, over in Suicide Center. She says he's a pussy for killing himself, but she can't get enough of his cologne. When she comes home, she smells like a middle-aged man who has lunch martinis at one of those clubs that still don't allow women.

"I can't help it. When I leave his teepee, I spray it on myself. There are worse things to be addicted to."

Coming home today with extra musk clinging to her hair, she sat next to me on the sofa. I put my head on her shoulder. "What's wrong, honey? What have I missed?"

I told her about the grave fucker. Shay is the kind of woman who doesn't respond to words like a normal person. Without surprise in her voice, she kept stroking my hair and said, "Mm-hmm...Then what happened?"

I asked her isn't that enough and she said I should

lower my expectations of a guy that strangles a woman to death.

She went on. "When I was a teenager, there was a guy who worked at the city pool. I saw him once looking at porn in the little snack shack. Turns out, he killed a woman in Utah of all places. I didn't think they had Black people in Utah. Anyway, he ran off to Detroit and was arrested right there at the pool. It came out at his trial that he hauled the dead woman from Utah to Detroit and kept her on ice. He thawed her out when he thought the cops were on to him and was doing nasty things to her body when the cops showed up. My point is, which is worse, the murder or what he did with her body? Does it matter, once the soul is here? Come to think of it, I bet that lady was in Missingville for a while."

She made a good point if you're talking about someone else's body. I wished the woman were still here so we could trauma bond.

In a pouty voice, I said, "I want my body to be found, but I'm terrified of what's next. I've come to like Missingville, in a way."

She shoved me. "You like your sinning lumberjack is what you like." She's not wrong.

I told her she and Tim were my best friends and I'm afraid I won't make friends in Deadtown. Shay said there's probably no such thing as friends on the Dark Side so don't worry about it.

I punched her in the arm.

Chapter 31

To cope with watching someone move my dead body, I opted for denial and distraction. I was craving a latte. No, I was craving the smell of a coffee house, but regardless, I walked over to the New York City side of town and walked into a Diner.

I met someone new. She did like Virginia Woolf and simply walked into a river. She didn't know how to swim, so she didn't have to mess with tying boulders to her feet. I've always wondered about this because if I walked into a river, I would tread water for a while until I got tired and then I would just sink, but maybe the human condition makes us tread and tread and tread and the only way we can really die as if we attach weight to ourselves. Maybe the will to live really is that strong; maybe even those that can't swim learn in that second before they die. Either way, the woman couldn't swim, so the whole thing seemed easy. She told me that she walked into the river until it was above her head and took a deep breath.

I sat at a table with my mocha latte with oat milk blah, blah, blah, and noticed a woman sobbing at the table beside me. She had short spiky purple hair with a weird sideburn that came to a point all the way at the bottom of her jawbone. I thought this look was giving, 'my favorite past time is posting negative Google reviews,' but it somehow worked for her. She had pretty fingers with eggplant purple, oval shaped nails. She was a summer, the type of person that looked good in pinks and yellows and the flowy top she was wearing accented her body well. She looked like a woman whose teen pregnancy had destroyed her belly, but she was determined to stay young with her hip hop Spotify play list.

I don't know where this disposition of mine came from, but I asked if I could sit with her. I sat across from her and looked at my coffee and then up at her and then back down at my coffee, waiting for her to stop crying. She took a deep breath, sniffed loudly, wiped her face with those beautiful fingers.

"Well outside of the fact that you're dead and living in this limbo, what's the matter?" I asked in the voice I've been practicing, called 'empathetic alto.'

"You were strangled, huh? You poor thing." I put my hand to my neck. Why I'm embarrassed about my scars when I'm literally dead, I haven't done quite enough soul searching to determine.

"Yeah, I got the old rope around the neck. Got it from behind, not in a good way." There I go again with the joke.

She chuckled. "Well, I was killed by my husband, of course. I'm just another cliché. He's having an affair, I found out. He'd rather I die than give me half of his shit, you know the story." She stands up so I can see her shirt, blood stained around the midsection.

"He stabbed you in the stomach? Did it take a while to bleed out?" Questions like these are like talking about the weather back home. Harmless.

"Well yes, I'm afraid so. I stayed alive for quite a while before I started floating above myself. The bastard rented a storage unit under a fake name, and no one has smelled my rotting carcass yet. I imagine once the air fresheners and bleach wear off, someone will smell death. I just want to be found." Her sobbing turned into a more reasonable, quiet cry.

"Does this bother you because you want him to be caught, or because you want to transfer to Deadtown?"

She wants him to be caught. "He's that prick that's all over the news, begging for my safe return. He's that caricature of a husband, smug and innocent for the cameras. I want him caught and punished. More than that, I want my kids to know the truth about him. I'm really tired of them comforting their dad, defending him, holding him while he fake cries on their shoulders. I've hardly thought at all about Deadtown."

I get the feeling this is the first time she's felt such a desire for revenge.

"Guys like that, they always get caught. He's an idiot to have killed you, and he's not smart enough to cover his tracks. They'll get him. Maybe stay away from the helmet for a bit."

I invited her to come swim with Tim and Shay and me. As we walked to the tropical section of town, I told her we had fish pedicures, swimming with dolphins, and the best cocktails in the Ville. Her name was Lindsey, and her kids were named Lola and Lionel. Her husband was Lloyd. I know families with names like these. On Earth I made fun of them, but here, I love this little lyric of alliteration. She told me her kids were out of the house, and she wanted to be that independent woman who loves the freedom, but the truth is she misses them. She spent lots of time wondering if she's bothering them, was she asking too many questions, was she smothering them, should she be upset if she hasn't talked to Lionel in seventeen days? Should she worry when Lola talks about going on a jog? Could she ask her to share her location with her, or will that seem over the top?

I told her, "I wish it didn't take me dying to see my mom as a real person. When I was alive, I thought of her as a constant, that thing you can count on like the electric bill. She'd never skip a month, she'd be predictable with the seasons, and even if I ignored her, she'd give me grace periods. I'd never ignore it long enough to get it shut off, but I'd come close."

Lindsey said she hoped when she got to Deadtown she'd be really dead, the kind of dead where you don't look back on Missingville or Earth. She hoped it was the kind of Heaven that was so joyful she didn't miss her kids or her parents. She hoped she'd be so happy to be with her mom again, and her grandparents, her friend Carol, and that poodle she loved so much as a kid, that she wouldn't miss the survivors. I told her I hoped for that too.

At the house, Shay was asleep on the deck. I made martinis and brought them out on a tray that said, "Summer Fun in the Sun!" and told Lindsey, "Let's jump in and splash Shay awake."

I cannon balled into the water, and Lindsay did the same behind me. I came up to the surface to Shay screaming, "You bitch," but with a huge smile on her face.

"This is Lindsay, Shay. Her douchebag husband killed her, and the bastard is doing that whole cry on TV bullshit." I felt like a kid, showing off my new friend.

Shay said, "Oh, girl, I know the type, sure do. Don't worry, those pricks always get caught."

"See, I told you!" I squealed. Tim jumped through my arms and gave me a kiss on the nose. "Tim is my spirit animal," I shouted, throwing in, "And no, he doesn't rape me, that's an urban legend Tim is working through."

Lindsey laughed and dove under the water, her legs above the surface doing kicks and making Ys like a synchronized swimmer. She came up for air and said, "I miss those days of going to the pool with my girlfriends. I thought I was fat, and god, I'd give anything to be as thin as the first time I thought I was fat. What a waste."

I thought about my body, how I hated my hips, wide like my mother's, and my ankles weren't delicate. When I'm Lindsey's age, will I miss this body? Oh wait...I know. Never mind.

I told Lindsey she was beautiful now as I know she was then. I said, "You've got really nice boobs, you know that, right?"

She smiled and grabbed them with both hands. Her mouth opened like she had a rhetorical quip to lobby back at me, but no noise came out. She froze in this open-mouthed, sarcastic lipped gesture. I heard the sound of a train.

"What the fuck?" I yelled, looking over my shoulder at Shay, now lounging half in the water, half on the deck. She put her finger to her mouth in a "shush" gesture.

Looking back at Lindsay, she was the same, frozen. Then, she looked up to the sky and put her arms up in that "I'm being saved" way I see Pentecostal Christians do on TV. The water started to drain around her, until she was standing on sandy ground, a path cleared out through the ocean. This woman was parting the sea.

"Jesus Christ, is she Moses? Shay? Is she fucking Moses?" Shay kept shushing me.

I got out of the water, thinking I wanted no part of this miracle. I climbed out and sat on the deck, hugging my knees like my whole body needed a shield. Tim jumped up high, then took a nosedive onto the sand, his nose bloodied and his pride wounded.

"Tim, oh my god, Tim. Shay. Lindsey. What the fuck is happening?"

The train was getting closer. I couldn't see it, but the sound, the fast chugging was growing louder. I put my palms over my ears and moved closer to Shay.

"They found her body, Renata. Relax." Shay nodded towards Lindsey. The sea parted like in the Old Testament, leaving Lindsay with a path of sand. The water rushed towards her on either side but stopped like Lindsey had her walls up.

But then the train came towards her. I thought conductors blew the whistle as they approached town, or the car of a suicidal person parked on the tracks. But approaching Lindsey, it just got faster, no whistle, no warning. Lindsey turned and looked back at us, just for a second. She smiled and blew a kiss.

And then, the train barreled over her. I screamed. I jumped up, stood with my back against the sliding glass door and yelled, "Lindsey, move!" But she didn't move; she walked right into it and her body turned to smoke. The train made a hard left turn rather than flattening Shay and me. And just like that, Lindsey and the train were gone. It was quiet. The water went back over the tracks, covering the path. Tim swam up to the deck, laughing and trying to clap.

"Jesus Christ. This is how we pass on to Deadtown? By being hit by a train? I swear, Shay, god is not as funny as they think." Shay got back in the water, riding Tim and telling me to calm down.

"Renata, we don't have a body. Who cares if being run over by a train is how we transfer on? How would you like it to go? Would you want the Virgin Mary to float down on a cloud and take you up on a celestial elevator? This is real life, not the Bible, not a children's book. It's real life, real death."

Refusing to accept again that these outlandish little quirks about god don't matter, I asked, "Does everyone go this way, or can we choose another route like we pick at the temple?"

Shay answered, "I've heard that some people are sucked into quicksand, and there's a rumor going around about a guy that was beamed up in a UFO, but that's not been verified."

I can't with this. "Quicksand? Quicksand? What is this, fucking Scooby-Do?"

Shay stood on Tim's back, doing pirouettes and telling him they should take their show on the road. Nothing shook this woman.

Calming down, I wondered where Lindsay was found. I guess the storage unit did finally start to smell like death. I did smile, thinking of her with her dad and her pet poodle. But then I thought of Lola and Lionel. Soon, they'll learn that their mom was shot in the stomach. This will be followed by news that the shooter is their dad.

I'm mad at god.

I know, join the club, right?

Chapter 32

The Eulogy of Lindsey

Lindsey was my best friend. We both grew up in the system. We'd cross paths here and there, for a while staying with the same foster family. I remember us playing with makeup, her putting pink lipstick on me and saying green eyeshadow brought out the yellow in my eyes. Later, we'd be at the same high school, me adopted, her staying with an uncle who somehow passed the social workers' tests, but who we all knew had her because of the check the state sent each month. We'd eat lunch together, and I'd always give her whatever dessert my mom put in my lunch. She'd refuse it, or at least insist that we split it.

Throughout our lives, she always asked how I was. I saw her just a few days after her son,

Lionel, died. But when I'd start to comfort her with words I knew weren't enough, she said, "Enough about me, tell me how you've been." Her son wasn't even in the ground yet. More than anyone I've ever known, Lindsey wanted to know what it was like to be me living my life. She remembered every sob story I ever gave her and would ask me, "So what ever happened with that bitch at work?" Every stupid thing I told her, she remembered. She followed up like a therapist.

Even on her worst days, when she showed up at my house barefoot and with a black eye, she came in, took a shower, then asked if she could make me some tea. She sat cross legged on my couch and said, "I'm dying to ask about that guy you had dinner with last week. Tell me all about it."

And it wasn't deflection. Lindsay was more than happy to tell me the why's and how's of what got her to this place. But no matter what, what energized her, what moved her in this life was genuine curiosity and concern for all of us. Never would she put herself first, even when she knew that it was the only way to stay alive.

Her road wasn't an easy one, after she gave up a daughter for adoption. Being a pregnant, fifteen-year-old foster kid meant she had few choices. I was at the hospital when Lola was born. I watched Lindsay hand her child over to a nun. Even that night, as she recovered from giving birth to a child she'd never see again, she took my hand and said, "I'm sorry Mike broke up with you. Are you doing okay?"

Having Lionel kept her from the streets. We were twenty-five years old then. I had a college degree, and she had a long list of hospitals and rehabs from which she absconded. But having a child she could keep, well this changed everything. She called me the day she was accepted into the nursing program, and I sat with six-year-old Lionel when she got her diploma. I had my own child then, and we embarked on the motherhood journey together. She came to my house when my baby wouldn't latch and magically pushed the baby in just the right angle, giving me the sweet relief one can only get from milk coming in.

Lionel started using around the time I was getting divorced. She'd call and remind me I was beautiful and that my ex-husband didn't deserve me. I'd cry on and on about the love I lost and how my daughter was away every other weekend. Lindsey told me getting a break from my kid was how it should be. What an unfair ask, for us to have our children with us 24/7. We'd plan girls' nights and winery weekends. I'd drivel on, drunk and sad about being single. She'd push my hair out of my eyes and tell me I was the hottest girl on Match.com.

Most of the time, I didn't know her troubles. I'd be the bitch who, after a two-hour phone call about my inability to get laid, would say, "Anyway, how are you?" and she'd say, "I got fired, but enough about me." Or "I reported Lionel missing yesterday, but what else is new? Did you go ahead and buy that dress you were eyeing at the boutique?"

Lindsey spent her life consumed with love. For her son, for me and all of her friends, for the foster parents that gave her a shot. Carrying that love for Lionel was too heavy a burden when he left this world. The streets took Lindsey back, and they weren't the same streets she and I ran twenty years ago. Losing Lindsey didn't just happen last week when she went missing. We lost her months ago, when she went out looking to fill the hole Lionel left behind, when she entered survival mode in the most dangerous way possible.

I remember when I lost her. Six months ago, I took her phone call. I said no, refusing to buy the bus ticket. That was the last time I talked to her and the first time she didn't ask about me.

Let's celebrate today that she is united with Lionel, and with her birth parents, who she

> *never knew. I know the four of them are dancing with the angels tonight. I hope to be there with her eventually, and when I am, I will sit with her and ask question after question about her life. I'll never let her ask me how I am again.*

It never occurred to me that a person would lie about their life in Missingville. I wish Lindsey knew she could tell me the truth. I hoped this transgression didn't stop her from going to The Light Side. Bless her soul.

Chapter 33

After a person watches themselves get re-buried by their murderer, it's arduous to determine what to do next. I felt like I did when a bout of depression would hit me on Earth. That feeling of not knowing what to do with my body, not wanting to be anywhere. Sitting in silence, taking a nap, crying on and off, skipping showers, binging reality TV, none of it helped the ache of unwarranted despair. Take that feeling and multiply it by a thousand. That's what watching Killer move my body did to me.

With my arms wrapped around and through my body, I sat on the deck and rocked back and forth. Tim asked why I wasn't in the water, and I said, "I'm too sad to swim." He told me he thought that was preposterous and sometimes the solution is to do the opposite action.

I asked him what self-help bullshit he was reading, and he said, "Reading is overrated, I never took the time to learn." I realized Tim only went to the school of hard knocks, except it seemed more like easy street, what with his naivete and disgust with cuss words.

"Do tell, Renata. I can't imagine a pain so big, it takes away the desire to swim."

I told Tim the whole story. I described how I was killed, how I loved Kathleen, how Killer hadn't been caught. He bobbed in the water in front of me, saying, "Oh wow, golly, my gosh" a little too often for my liking.

"God is a first-class a-hole, if you ask me, with that stupid fricking helmet," I said, watching my language for a water mammal.

"Renata, even if you take the a-s-s off the word, it's still calling god a bad name. You should watch it," Tim said, looking down his nose at me.

"So, I got lost and found this place. It's called Punishment Prairie and it's like a purgatory for people who did some really bad stuff on Earth," I said, changing the subject.

Tim said he knew never knew there was such a place and thank god he wasn't there.

"You know, good people, good dolphins, can do bad things, Tim."

Taking a holier than thou position, Tim asked, "Don't you humans have rules? Like out here, everyone knows not to eat starfish. It's been established that they're more like art than animals, and though they taste delicious, it's taboo. If my pal Frank ate a starfish, I would never speak to him again."

Even though Tim could speak, he was still more dolphin than human, and I told him things are more complicated when it comes to homo sapiens. He said he heard we're all cut from the same cloth so the rules should be equally dispersed. I told him don't talk to me about cloth cutting as it harkens back to the shortcomings of god.

I then told Tim about Ben. Now this concept Tim understood, having had a few lovers in his lifetime. He got excited hearing the romance part of my story. "Oh my gosh, oh my gosh, Renata. A picnic? A basket with checkered fabric? Oh, my goodness, you're in love. Go see him!"

Tim was naive, which made him mostly right about everything, so I followed his advice.

Chapter 34

When I got to the Prairie, it was dusk, or something like that. Things were in sepia, with an orange hue against a yellow sky. Residents were seated in an amphitheater, rows of bad guys watching a show. I stood in the back and saw a man on the stage, his arms in front of him like Jesus in children's books. He was about three feet tall, wearing a chocolate robe and sandals, and a yellow beard down to his knees. He looked like an extra in a Harry Potter movie. When he spoke, it wasn't in English, but I still understood it mostly. He talked in a singsong, high pitched voice.

"This is a grand opportunity, my fellow dead. You have been granted by god a remarkable opportunity at redemption. I have witnessed noble deeds bestowed on your fellow man here in this Prairie. The data is heavily skewed in your favor. Rejoice in your achievements." He looked and talked like a cult leader, which paired well with suicide; but being that we're all dead, I feared what his grift might be.

The sheep in the crowd, which were all of them, responded, "Rejoice in our achievements!"

He went on to say that, despite their stellar behavior, there were still some who were dying in sin. "Roberta, where are you, sweet lass?" He put his hand to his forehead to block out the spotlights and looked around for his target.

A teenager in a Rolling Stones t-shirt stood up. "Yeah, Enoch, I'm here. What did I do now?"

He walked towards her, arms folded. "I am keenly aware of your transgressions, Robbie. Both god and I saw you steal butter from Henrietta. We saw you stick your leg out and trip Maximilla. I have surveillance footage of you removing amethyst from the altar." Enoch knew the last allegation was the worst. The crowd gasped while I looked around for cameras. I had not considered this.

"Listen, midget, I'm never going to be found. I don't give two shits about getting to Deadtown with a nice little report card. The Prairie is it for me, you can shove your little score card right up your ass." I felt like calling Enoch a midget was worse than Roberta's crimes.

Then, for the first time, I saw the angry side of god unleashed in Missingville. A ten-foot-tall messenger bumped into me as he came barreling into the venue. They wore hot pink leather pants, a bright yellow leather biker jacket, and gold glittery six-inch heels. Their hair was in a black beehive with actual bees buzzing around it and their facial hair was dyed purple on one side of their face, orange on the other. This would have been a gorgeous, inviting human, except for the machete in their hand, gas mask on their face, and a rifle slung over their shoulder.

They ran down the stairs, then bounced on the heads of onlookers to get to Roberta. Enoch yelled, "Your god is not without wrath. Your god is the supreme leader here. They do not tolerate theft, mean spirited pranks, or the desecration of the sacred altar. Persimmon will deal with you now."

Roberta cowered and thrust a bloody toddler in front of her as a shield. This was probably not her best move, considering the situation. Persimmon growled, "You're mine now," and put Roberta over their shoulder. Smoke came out of their heels as they floated upward.

Enoch announced, "There is a place for those that disrespect the Prairie, mock god, and ignore their score cards. Roberta will not be alone there. Persimmon will return to transport a batch of you to No Redemption Road. You know who you are. The rest of you are dismissed."

The dead started running out of the amphitheater like someone had screamed "fire." I was practically run over by a man in a wooden wheelchair. A bloodied nurse was pushing him and said, "Get out of the way, bitch," as I fell backwards. I thought, "Now this woman should be going to The Road."

I turned and ran too, out of the theater and down a hill so steep, I gave up on walking and rolled down. Everyone did the same and ended up at the bottom, rolling right to the edge of a lake. I stood up and followed others into a gondola, floating to the other side and ending up in the Prairie I recognized. Most people went right to the altar, praying, dancing, beating drums. I saw gladiators cry. A professional lion tamer whipped himself. Punching herself in the face, a ballerina with only one hand said, "This is why god allowed me to keep one. I'm so sorry."

I stepped back and saw Ben. He was on his knees with his forehead against the altar. His hands were in a child-like prayer pose and I felt an ache in my stomach as I watched him weep.

This was god and I hated them.

Chapter 35

I squeezed my way between bowing astronauts, kneeling pilots, and sobbing ship captains. The wailing of the crowd turned into cries in unison, "Forgive me, have mercy on me, let me atone."

I approached Ben and put my hand on his back. He turned around and looked at me like a child might when his mom finds him lost and wandering around the amusement park. I took his hand and led him away, back through the dead drivers of things who would never be found. I saw "Challenger" written on the back of a female astronaut's suit. I knew she'd be here forever.

Ben and I kept holding hands after we got to a clearing and slowed our pace, walking in silence toward a pavilion. It was at the end of a walkway, in the center of a lake. Lilly pads and frogs littered the surface, and the croaking sounded like a comfort song.

He sat across from me at a picnic table, wiped his eyes, put his hands on his knees, and said every single thing.

"I killed a pregnant woman. I killed a woman and her baby." He paused and looked up at me.

"Tell me how," I whispered.

And he told me.

"She was thirty-nine weeks pregnant, driving to her weekly doctor's appointment at 3:00 on a Tuesday afternoon. I was laid off that week due to weather. You can't roof a building in a blizzard. I drank and watched every James Bond movie I could find, in order. By the time I got to Pierce Brosnan, I got up to pee and fell on top of my coffee table, which, honestly, was a piece of plywood sitting on milk cartons. I was thirty-eight years old, and I still had a mattress on the floor, a card table in the kitchen, and nothing in the fridge but Sprite to mix with the Titos I kept in the freezer.

On days like this, I would wake up with the shakes. When your body is accustomed to loads of alcohol, and when you start to sober up, the jerks in your hands are like a shorting electrical wire. My hands and legs would tell me I was on empty, that being made of ninety-seven percent water wasn't my preferred makeup. I had to be at seventeen percent vodka just to steady myself. So, I did what any drunk would do. I finished off the last of the vodka until I was calm and still. I fell asleep until the afternoon, and sure as shit, the shakes.

I would wake up soaked. I called it night sweats, but they were just drunk sweats. I remember telling women who slept in my bed that I had a thyroid disorder. I could smell the sour stench of myself. Vodka mixes with sweat and comes out like spoiled milk.

When I woke up, I went to the liquor store for a bottle and orange juice. I sat in a parking lot at a dog park mixing juice and vodka, telling myself the vitamin C was at least good for me. I loved watching dogs and humans interact there. I didn't have a dog, but I felt like this place was what society should be like. Everyone there was full of love for something innocent, talking about their pets with people who also let them lick their faces after they licked their balls. I thought about how I never had a child, a dog, even a goldfish. I thought about how I would never take something under my wing. I would never teach a dog to shake. I'd never teach a son to ride a bike.

I left the park. I don't remember my route. I don't remember the drive from the park to the highway. What I remember next is seeing cars coming towards me on the interstate. I yelled, 'You're all on the wrong side of the road!'

The next thing I knew, I was in field, my car sideways against a tree, the passenger side of my car right up against my right leg. If I'd hit the tree with the driver's side, I'd still be dead, but found and immediately sent to The Dark Side.

My body must have instantly pumped water into my blood, or proteins, or shit, I don't know what happens when a drunk instantly sobers up, but I knew. I knew I killed someone. I didn't see her at first, but before I even got out of my car, I said, 'Ben, you killed someone.'

I crawled out, and there she was. About ten yards from me, a woman was laying on her side, but her head, her head was turned the opposite way. Her body faced away from me, but her bloodied head, her face, they were pointed right at me. I walked towards her, saying, 'no, no, no, no.' I bent down by her. I grabbed her hand and was trying to feel for a pulse. But when I saw her stomach, when I saw she was pregnant, Renata, I ran. I ran away from her. I fucking ran away from her. She could have been alive; the baby, she could have been alive. But I ran."

Ben was facing me but looking down at his feet. Tears dripped onto his boots. I was perfectly still.

"She was so beautiful. With the helmet, I've seen photos of her standing in a field of sunflowers, looking off into the distance, with her hands placed on her belly, one above, one below. I've seen the photo of her husband, kneeling in front of her, kissing her belly. The photo of her glowing face, these rosy cheeks, this curly, auburn hair bouncing around her in a video they played at her funeral. I watched them lower the casket into the ground. I've seen her house, the nursery, the crib, the rows of tiny clothes, the diapers and cream organized on a table, the quiet of the place since her husband was never able to go home. Just yesterday, I saw her mom call her boss, quit her job, and drive to a psychiatric hospital. Last week, her brother sat alone in a college dorm room, saying her name and cutting his own thigh. Her dad, he likes the bottle too. He hasn't walked a straight line in months.

While I was running, I heard the sirens. I kept tripping, falling in the woods, my leg dragging, my chest tightening, the pain in my ribs unbearable. My entire pants leg was red with blood. Arteries were cut. Lungs collapsed. Whatever it was, I wish it would have killed me instantly. They would have found me. But no, it was a slow death, the kind I deserved. I ran, fell, crawled, stood, ran, fell, rolled, begging god to take me right to Hell. It felt like I was breathing in fire; every breath was the burn of how I failed my parents, how my mom lay awake at night wondering if I was dead, how my dad lied to his coworkers about how I was doing in college, how I landed that job, when I was actually couch-surfing and pawning his hunting rifles.

I don't know if your whole life flashed before your eyes. I wouldn't say mine did. Instead, every hurt I ever caused surged through me. I saw myself tell my mom I hated her when I was nine. I watched as I taunted a kid on the playground for wearing the wrong shoes. Drunken nights when I called my best friend a faggot, the time I told everyone at a fraternity party how my roommate still slept with his baby blanket, how I pawned a girlfriend's jewelry so I could buy drugs. The time I staggered down the street and punched a homeless man when he called me a drunk.

But the woman. The pregnant woman. I ran from her. I crawled and stumbled and ended up sliding down a hill, right into the same river she posed beside in those photos, holding her baby the only way she would ever get to hold her. I fell into the river and I..."

Ben was sobbing, the same way Newcomers do, the same way living men do when they realize what a mess they've made of it all. He looked up at me with ordinary eyes like all the rest of eyes, with a common brown shade of iris and an average sized pupil. He stuck his tongue out of the corner of his mouth, licking a tear containing the same amount of salt as yours or mine when we were babies and wanted our mothers. Shaking, his shoulders moved up and down the same way shoulders do when we laugh. He brought his hands up to his face and held his cheeks the way people might do when they've walked into a surprise party. He took a long inhale, like he might have done before diving to the bottom of a pool on a summer afternoon with his brother. He blew out a long exhale, the way he might have done after admitting a minor transgression, like speeding or getting written up at work for being late. He closed his eyes and shook his head, the way he did when his grandpa told a joke that touched on a sexual innuendo.

I came over to his side of the table. I straddled the bench and looked at the prominent bridge of his nose, his detached earlobes, the wrinkles around his eyes, the mole that butted up to a dimple his left cheek. I put one hand on the stain from his femoral artery, the other on the back of his head, and put my forehead against his.

Chapter 36

They say Ben and I became the first couple to ever cross the divide between General Population and Punishment Prairie. I find this hard to believe, but when Enoch came to Ben's cabin and interrupted what was my first attempt at dead sex, he said the Council had to have a special meeting about us.

"Make no mistake, you enchanting, fine lovers, we always side with actions nested in such affection, but this has put us in a bit of a quandary." Enoch spoke from the threshold of Ben's front door while I stayed in bed. I had no interest in Enoch, the Council, god.

Ben gave a dead pan expression, and a motion with his hands and eyebrows that said, "And?"

Enoch looked nervous. His eyes darted around, and he said, "Never fear, lad, you can continue as you were. I didn't mean, I wasn't trying to, I didn't intend for, anyway, I shall go now." Ben and I were silent, and after

Enoch walked out, we went right back to figuring out how to put things in things when all of our things were made out of cotton candy.

It went on like this for a few idyllic days. Ben and I hiked, picked raspberries, and planted peonies in front of his cabin. We went to the horse forgiveness brigade, danced around the altar, watched the eulogies of his friends and mine.

I told him about Killer, Kathleen, the time I tripped acid and thought the Post Mates delivery guy was David Bowie. We talked about the future of artificial intelligence and the way buyers of bitcoin not only don't tip, but they also wrote critical notes on restaurant receipts. We played a game called, "What will Hell be like" and I said Nickelback would be on a constant loop. He agreed, saying fans of the band not only don't tip, but they're also mouth breathers who stand too close in check-out lines. Ben had a loud laugh that was always coupled with the tilting back of his head, like a teenager exhaling cigarette smoke. He cried easily like an adolescent girl, about overcrowding animal shelters and the War in Gaza. He whispered when he told the punchline of a joke and enjoyed hand gestures like a finger gun pointed at his head when dead folks got to talking about things like starting a HOA.

He had patience, which he displayed when teaching a city slicker Newcomer how to use a slingshot. He was intolerant of the child molesters and started a committee dedicated to banishing them to Dust Storm Derby. I found him a bit over the top when he opened doors or jars for me. I blushed when he said I was prettier than his famous person crush, Heidi Klum. I said his choice was lame and I expected him to want to fuck someone more distinctive like Juliette Lewis. Shocking him, I revealed that I didn't masturbate until I was twenty-one years old. Shocking me, he said he had a love for anime, which was the most appalling of the tidbits he shared about himself.

I told Ben about my recurring dream where I'm riding a carpet in harem pants, and a Genie grants me the wish of being on a reality dating show. He told me how, even into adulthood, he said in his head, "Don't step on a crack, you'll break your mother's back" when he walked on a sidewalk. He was one of those people that put ranch dressing on things like pizza, a quality I told him paired well with driving a car with red tape stuck to a broken brake light. We had a dad joke competition, with me conceding his win with, "I just found out I'm colorblind. The news came out of the purple." He told me he was afraid of roller coasters and flying, but he enjoyed the claustrophobic feeling of spelunking. I told him not to use the word "spelunking" because it made him sound like a poser. He said the same thing when I used the word, "capricious." Surprisingly, I was the big spoon in bed, and he found kissing to be more intimate than a blow job. He said he wasn't surprised when I told him I was averse to having anything in my mouth that wasn't food. He accepted this and kept his tongue to himself when his mouth was against mine.

For a few days, I almost forgot that I was a soul not yet one with its body. It was lighthearted fun. It was a romcom where the protagonist sees through the tough exterior of her ex-con boyfriend who's trying to better himself. But it felt a little too "high school quarterback dates captain of the cheerleading team" and made me ill at ease. Dead murderers smiled too widely and pointed at us, like we were celebrities holding hands when caught out with commoners at Costco. Occasionally, a soul from the seventeenth century would curtsy as we walked by. If Ben wore a ring, someone would have kissed it.

Enoch returned a second time and again got too verklempt to get to the point. Roberta even returned to the Prairie with a decree from god saying they were thinking twice about punishing her, "in light of recent events," which meant, "If Renata can forgive Ben the murderer, then by golly god can give Robbie another chance."

Maybe it's because of the whole "my murderer is on the loose" thing, but dead me is a more pragmatic me. On Earth, a new crush would have consumed me, distracted me from pricing leggings at work, forced me to put my phone on vibrate so I didn't miss a text, made for anxious Thursday's wondering if my person of the week would hit me up for a weekend meet up. If you're doing these things because of a girl you like, stop it. In hindsight, as a dead person, I see all of this as foolish. You will too. But you could stop it now and avoid the certain regret you'll take into the next life.

So, dead me told Ben I really liked him, and I had a great time, but I had to get back to the business of watching a man jack off on my dead body. Naturally, he understood. I wasn't the first person to tell him such a thing, which barely surprised me.

I said, "Now don't you go getting found by a mushroom hunting hipster while I'm gone."

He said, "All that's left of me is a femur," and gave me an awkward kiss that landed on my eyebrow.

Chapter 37

"Girl, you're a better man than I am," Shay said when I told her about Ben, what landed him in the Prairie, and my celebrity status that made me feel like I wearing polyester.

"Renata," Tim said, "I do not know what to make of this."

I said things like, "But haven't you driven drunk before?" or "Who am I to measure the amount of bad a bad thing is?"

Shay said things like, "Good point, I gotcha, I hear ya."

But I also said things like, "That poor woman's husband" and "I would want Ben dead if I was her family."

Tim said things like, "I still would never make out with a starfish eater."

And I thought that Tim's smugness was the biggest sin here.

Chapter 38

Killer is walking seventeen miles from the murder spot. He's in a town called Sleeper, holding a sign at the only stoplight in town. It reads, "Hungry. Every bite helps." A spelling error, or no? He's wearing ethe same denim shorts and a Mickey Mouse t-shirt. He's filthy, standing in hiking boots with black socked big toes poking out of each. In his pocket are loose peanuts and a toddler's packet of fruit chews.

No one gives him anything. One man stops and yells, "Go back to your meth lab!"

Killer laughs. "Meth lab, meth lab, meth lab, where do I find one of those? Newspaper, Google, internet, I have no internet."

He sits cross-legged on the pavement and whispers, "Are they looking for me, have they found my girl, have they found my girl, where is my girl?" He digs out the peanuts and drops them into an already dry mouth.

He's a yellowish color, in his eyes and on his cheeks. His trembling hands fumble the fruit chews. He can't open the package with his shaking fingers. He squeezes them, shouting, "Why so much plastic? Why is everything enclosed? Why can't things be free? I'm free."

Killer throws the fruit chews on the ground, picks up his backpack, and walks towards the trailhead. "I'm better off in the mud. The sun is shining on me. I'm the sun's son. Sun, sun, moon."

Chapter 39

Killer is back on the trail, twenty-one miles from his last camp and twelve miles from my body. He's got a walking stick and if I look closely, I see the initials "RF" etched in the knotty top. Renata Foster.

He's walking down a steep hill, his toe coming out of his boot with every step. Now there's a hole in the sock. The bottom of each big toe bleeds and the tops hold blackened flesh where there was once a protective nail. He's lost his toenails, but mine are still sitting in a neat row under my phalanges.

I look inside his empty stomach. It's wrinkled and folded, like fabric on a valence. It's various shades of pink, like bridesmaids' dresses. It's quiet here. I can hear Killer's heart beating, but it sounds miles away, not sitting just above me. On to the intestines. They're white and dry. I'm trying to walk through them and I'm expecting slippery bubbles, but it's more like pale paper wadded up in a fireplace.

His heart, a place I've explored before, no longer has the fast, but regular beat of someone sleep-deprived and terrorized by voices. Where before I went through it marching to his deranged drummer, this time it's a staccato beat like thump, thump, thump-thump, thump-thump...thump...thump. I try to move with it, and I feel like I'm doing an interpretive dance entitled, "Madness."

The liver. It's phlegmy in here, pale yellow with streaks of bright orange; the walls are like wiggling maggots. There are bumps in here harder than the rest, where the maggots ignore, like they've already eaten the fat there. I push on the sides of it and the blood spills out, like the mist from a shot gun to the head.

Killer brain. There are neon signs in here. One blinks in blue, "Gray Matter Low." Another, in green, "Glucose Levels < Optimal." There are filing cabinets marked "Memories" with years on each drawer. Pages are flying out, floating to the bottom, back and forth like it's windy in this head.

There's a gauge with levels marked as "Very Low" and labeled "Serotonin, Dopamine, Glutamate." A gauge marked "Music Lyrics" is on "Very High," as is one marked, "Thoughts of Strangling." Surprisingly, "Guilt and Shame" are overflowing, as is "Love for Emily."

Killer is stumbling, shuffling his feet, and landing on his knees with every few steps. He's soaked in sweat that smells like metal or blood. His scalp is sunburned, and his beard has a spider crawling through it. The skin on his palms is still breaking open; he's been scratching at them to recall his last kill. "Last kill, last kill," he's thinking. Last kill?

His thoughts turn to a trailer at the end of a gravel road. The front is overgrown with weeds and red rose bushes; more thorn than rose. In front is a tan Corolla with tarps, duct tape, and bungy cords on the passenger seat. Inside the dark, dusty, paneling-covered kitchen, Killer is sitting at a table overcome with vodka bottles and Taco Bell wrappers. The curtains used to be white, but beige now as the only other thing on the counters are ashtrays and half-smoked Newports. It smells like puss, like a pimple popped on a shoulder.

Killer is hunched over, his elbows on the sticky table, a cigarette hanging out of his mouth, ashes falling on a newspaper in front of him. He's reading, shouting, "Jacqueline Taylor's mother attended a press conference Tuesday where she pleaded for her daughter's safe return."

"Safe return, safe, did you hear that, safe? Safe, safe, safe. Baby, you're safe with me."

Killer remembers her, sitting on the collapsing floral couch saying, "Yes, I love you. Of course I love you. I just can't do this anymore." She's sitting with her legs folded under her, arms crossed around her, her mind trying to decide in what filing cabinet to put the black eye, the punch in the stomach, and the desire she still has to take him to the bedroom.

He stands up, picks up a kitchen towel, and slowly comes to sit beside her. She moves away from him and thinks, “His eyes are still the prettiest I’ve ever seen.” This is her last thought before the towel goes around her neck.

He kills her like he did me, strangling her from behind, kneeling on the couch and pulling, twisting. He then maneuvers in front of her so he can see her eyes when everything goes dark. Next, he’s standing over her. She’s limp and turning blue. He stares at her; his head tilted to the right as he catches his breath.

Squatting, he touches his nose to hers and says, “You were always my favorite birdsong. Song, song, bird.”

Chapter 40

Maybe you predicted this. Maybe you saw it coming. Maybe I was in denial when I was wandering around Killer's insides. I wanted an arrest, a trial, a death sentence, but instead, Killer died today.

I watched him collapse in a valley of pine trees, right along a flowing creek and next to a beaver's den. This would fall under the "Died From Exposure" category, which is a painful, slow way to die, thank god for that. He just dropped, like someone threw him out a window. It wasn't a fainting gesture like on TV. He didn't fall gracefully sideways. Rather, he fell forward, with arms loosely at his side. Face planting on the ground like he was a bag of flour.

During his last hours alive, he thought about dying. Killer was counting his steps, saying "One two, buckle my shoe, three four, I don't want to anymore. Five, six, nothing rhymes with six, seven eight, it's not too late.

Nine, ten, let me meet my maker again."

He imagined a bullet piercing his heart, shot by a county sheriff who would forever celebrate the day he took down my murderer. He was playing out his death, a dramatic showdown with "the authorities" as he "evaded investigators for weeks on end." Wouldn't it be romantic, he thought, if his was a suicide by cop? The fucking pigs had been after him most of his adult life. He'd been harassed enough, for stealing cough syrup from Wal-Mart, passing a bad check, drunk driving, one of which shouldn't have counted because he was drunk in a parked car. Yes, he stalked a sorority girl, but the fuzz never knew that part. Later, there was the domestic assault, but the girlfriend, she just cried all the time, and she did hit him first, so what was he to do?

Ever since he killed me, he imagined his own death. Yes, all killers, for the most part, are narcissists. I guess squeezing the life out of another person requires the sort of self-image that sits on a pedestal. Killer imagined himself a god, or at least something beyond mortal. Like all good antagonists, he wanted to go out with a bullet, or maybe a car run would roll over his midsection. Either way, he wasn't supposed to just fall forward and die the same way good men do, on hiking paths or basketball courts at the local YMCA. He wanted more for his death. He wanted blood at least. But here, lying on his face next to a creek, he only got shit and piss, which, I've already pointed out, happens no matter how you go.

His soul rose up and watched the scene like we all do. His face was turned onto its right side, and drool was slipping down his face during his last exhale. He saw his back for the first time, scratched, sunburned, scabbed. The back of his head had a perfect, swirled cowlick of blond hair, just like it was when he was a baby. He thought of his father. "My dad will be glad I'm finally gone. It will feel like a relief, and I don't blame him."

In his back pocket was a note. It read, "If you find the girl, I killed her. At mile marker 185.5" In a front pocket was my hair tie and my drivers' license. Alongside his body was the walking stick, "FR" carved on the top.

Mother fucker had a conscience.

Chapter 41

I was sitting on my top bunk, and as I removed the helmet, I saw Shay standing next to me, saying, "Yes, take it off, that's good, give it to me."

I handed her the helmet and sat still, staring at her. I whispered, "He's dead."

Shay helped me down and brought me a vodka and cranberry. She guided me outside as my legs felt like they couldn't hold me. I put my head on her shoulder as we walked onto the deck. We sat in our Adirondack chairs and watched the sun set in purple. I couldn't stop shaking my head, rocking with my arms wrapped around my smokey body.

Shay leaned forward, put her hand on my knee, and said, "I know what you're thinking. He'll be found right away."

Knowing she was wrong, I still said, "Yeah, you're right, of course." If I had bones, I would have felt it in them, the discernment of what's coming. If I had a heart, it would be beating in the rhythm of "He's. On. His. Way."

My roommate knew too, but she lied the way a best friend should. "Ok, Renata, let's say he's here in twenty-four hours. He'll go to Punishment Prairie, and you'll just stay away from there. You'll never see him. I bet he'll be here for a few days, tops, and you'll just lay low. Hell, you could be found in a matter of hours. They find him, they find you, he goes to the Dark Side of Deadtown, you go to the Light. Done and done." She did her hands like a blackjack dealer after he distributes the chips.

So many assumptions here. First, that he'll be found at all. Killer and I could bounce around Missingville forever. Shay believes I'll be found. Most presumptuous is her belief that I'm going to the Light Side.

But Shay left something out. I asked, "What about Ben?" I felt instantly embarrassed. I'm thinking about my little boyfriend when the person that killed me is on his way into town.

Shay said I was bigger and better than worrying about some dumb crush. She said, "Just lay low for a few days and then you'll transfer over, so let's just swim with Tim and do a jigsaw puzzle. Let's get drunk." She used the expression, "hunker down," which didn't even sound right coming out of her mouth.

But I did as she suggested.

Chapter 42

I went back to swimming. I still wanted Tim to jump through my arms, but after much practice where Tim repeated, “Atta girl” too many times, we couldn’t get it. He was feeling better about himself lately, less concerned about dolphin tropes floating around Earth and in Missingville. It was a win-win in the self-esteem arena for both of us.

Shay was sitting on the edge of the deck getting her fish pedicure and didn’t look up at me. She was just staring at her hands on her lap.

“The helmet is in the ocean. Sorry about that. I’ve already called Customer Support and asked for a new one,” she said, still looking down.

“Oh, hey, that’s cool, no worry,” I said, as I sat down next to her.

In the middle of the night, Shay threw the helmet into the ocean. She told me there was nothing to see anymore. If one day she got to Deadtown, it would be a shock, and maybe a surprise exit from here would feel more blissful. She didn't want to look at the Earth anymore. After she watched the detective put her file in the "Cold" category on his desktop, she went right to her burial place and saw she wasn't there anymore. She hovered above and said she had a split second where she knew she could go directly to her new resting place, but instead she decided to leave it and come back to our ocean. He moved her, that she knew, but to where would be the question she decided to never answer.

She said, "I'm going to be in Missingville forever and it's about time I made some friends, found some hobbies, maybe took up playing an instrument or making pottery."

I told her I had visited the Craft Carnival just last week and there were sweet old ladies there anxious to teach folks old timey things like using a loom and making soap.

The forever of it, though, it felt like a dark blanket over my head. I thought of the time I had an MRI and was stuck in a tunnel. I thought of being lowered into the ground in a coffin. Forever is something I thought of a lot when I was alive, and it always caused this little flickering in my sternum, like the feeling right after you cut your finger with a knife. You're cutting up carrots, your hand slips, and before the blood even starts, you look at your hands and how they've deceived you. While you fumble through drawers of sticky cough drops and Five Hour Energy, there's the Band Aid. The pulsating in your cuticle dulled by the heaviness in the chest. Forever feels like constant slipped knives, cuts on parts of the body a bandage won't quite wrap around.

I told Shay, "Maybe that one day at time, Alcoholics Anonymous shit is worth subscribing to."

Shay said, "Let's swim," and does her signature swan dive into the water.

Tim, Shay, and I played like kids at a water park. I practiced treading water with my arms in the shape of an oval, asking Tim to give it another try and jump through. It felt like childhood when, at the pool, we say, "Mom, watch this," when we do something dumb like simply jump into three-feet deep water. I'd wear those inflatables on my arms, with fish and mermaids on them. My mom always looked up from her Vogue magazine and said, "Yes, I see, good job."

I wished my mom could see me with Tim. I wish she could see both my water skills and my new home. Knowing I'm dead, making friends and swimming with dolphins would take away twenty-three percent of her sadness. I'm no mathematician, and no grief counselor, but I've watched enough documentaries on the subject of murder and missing people to assess the potential benefit.

Chapter 43

Customer Support hasn't brought the new helmet, which is a blessing, I suppose.

We spent the next twenty-four hours with Tim who said he could tell I was glum, and he'd be happy to let me ride on his back. I asked him if he knew how fucked up it is to be a human. "Oh yes, I don't envy you for a second. You humans and your pesky heartache."

Shay and I worked on a puzzle of kittens, all in beige and white. It gave me a more welcome form of frustration than the situation at hand. I did get drunk as planned, which led to eleven bouts of uncontrollable crying. Shay told me to let it all out.

Sure as shit, twenty-five hours after I saw him drop, Shay and I were sipping cocktails and moved on to a puzzle of a white tiger standing in the snow, equally maddening. I had just found the last piece of the golden eyes. Shay was smiling and doing a little dance, her arms in front of her pumping up and down as she said, "Go Renata, go Renata, go Renata." I was cackling and snorting, telling her I made that tiger my bitch.

And then, Rita appeared on the porch, knocking on the door and smiling bigger than one should when bringing bad news. I let her in, drunk and oblivious to what prompted her visit. "Well, well, well, Rita, welcome to our humble abode. Want some vodka?"

She darted her eyes around nervously, but her voice sounded normal. "Oh no, child. Let's sit for a spell." I bowed down and waved my arm, the drunken gesture of welcoming a queen.

Rita wasn't alone.

"Hello, dear Renata. Please accept my arrival as a message of good tidings and wishes of wellness." It was that bastard, Enoch. He bowed like it was the year 1700, likely the year he died. I knew he was bringing bad tidings.

I wasn't having it. "I know who you are, weirdo. I've been to the Prairie and watched you fuck with people for harmless pranks."

Behind him stood a woman at least 100 years old, wrinkled like a prune, tall but hunched over. She had red hair down to the floor and wore a purple gown covered in sequenced stars. An annoying cliché,' she was holding a crystal ball. She didn't say anything and didn't smile. She sat on the couch and draped her purple cape around herself as if she were posing for a centerfold.

Rita, still too cheerful, said, "Hello, love. I've brought a couple of my dear friends from the Conflict Council. They're experts in...well they're experts in situations such as these. Don't worry, we've got it all worked out." Rita was overly excited as she put her arm around my shoulder, led me to a chair, and kissed me on the top of my head.

I was sobering up.

Enoch chimed in as he climbed onto a chair closest to me. He sat cross legged and leaned towards me, his brown eyes wide and round, with a unibrow that somehow suited him. "So, here we are with a bit of a situation. But never fear, my lady. This is not a novel set of circumstances. I've seen it countless times in my tenure here. We have your precious soul here, a poor victim of such violence. I am ever so sorry. I believe you have come to know that the perpetrator of your demise has passed, his body not yet found. He's just arrived to town, and Jimmy is showing him the Shout Out as we speak. Do not be afraid," he said.

I was afraid, remembering the thing I was ignoring with vodka and puzzles.

"Of course, Killer will go to Punishment Prairie," Enoch explained. "I've only seen a handful of murderers sent elsewhere. Think Dexter. But Killer is no Dexter, as you are keenly aware. It's quite simple. God does not like the messiness of victims being in the company of their murderers, so we've already put the lock and key on the Prairie to keep you out. I recall 340 years ago a murdered man penetrated the Prairie and attacked his murderer, leading to all kinds of repentance resets. Good Lord, we can't have that again, can we, Sylvia?"

The woman in the purple cloak said something that sounded like, "No, sir-y."

"So," Enoch continued. "I've seen this scenario countless times, and yours will come together just like this lovely puzzle you've got here. I suspect everyone will be found soon, including you, and you'll never think of this moment again. Though it will be a shame to see you go. You've got quite an impressive report card. Mostly A minuses and B's, but plenty sufficient."

I felt like news like this should come slower, in a quiet, deep voice. Enochs's loud, shrill tone sounded best suited for "Welcome to the neighborhood," not "The guy who killed you is now your neighbor."

But he continued, "There's one thing I've been asked to mention, though I hate to speak of matters of the heart in this way. Regardless, any a-hem, feelings you may have for a certain soul on the Prairie must be shuttered and stowed away. Missingville isn't a land for lust seeking, of course, is it, Sylvia?"

"No, sir-y." Why was Sylvia here?

Rita chimed in from the kitchen. "Renata, just forget about Ben, okay, sweetheart? God wants things in a nice tidy package, as I know you know."

I yelled in a voice usually used for my mother, “I am well aware of god’s ridiculous rules, Rita.” Peoples’ unwavering support for god is just as off-putting here as it is on Earth.

Sylvia seemed to think she had a part to play here. “Praise god at all times,” she said, staring at me like I played heavy metal records backwards.

Enoch hopped down from his chair, adjusted his robe, and ran a hand through his beard. He looked at Shay, “Now, lass. Do keep an eye on your mate, yes?”

Shay nodded but looked down like a liar.

Chapter 44

Banned from the Prairie, I spent two days eating glazed donuts and drinking espresso Martini's. A combination I never found on Earth, I highly recommend you try it. I did a lot of negative self-talk, telling myself I was childish, a simpleton. Here I am, dead. Here I am, a soul without a body stuck in limbo. Here I am, with a family flogging themselves with worry and a pseudo girlfriend drowning in grief, and what am I worried about? Ben. I'm no psychotherapist, but I diagnosed myself with Narcissism. Again.

I was a Venn diagram. One circle, attachment to Earthly endeavors, like eyebrow waxing and the urge to cut my hair into bangs. The other, the new me, inhabitant of Missingville, enlightened and self-actualized. They overlap in a space I like to call, "Ben." My god, that sounds trite.

Sick of myself, I jumped down from the bunk and went to the water. There were a pair of goggles on the deck that I'd never seen before, purple and sparkly. A locked-away memory comes over me. My dad and Liam and I, playing Marco Polo. I've got that belly one has at nine-years-old, hard and shaped like half an egg. Legs, skinny, knees scabbed. Like every human at this age, when at a swimming pool, the goggles stay on all day. I'm eating a peanut butter and jelly sandwich on a lawn chair. Everything has a greenish hue, sunglasses for a child seeing the world as perfect.

Hoping for that same nostalgic sentiment, I put them on and dove into the ocean. Immediately I was reminded that this is no earthly swimming pool, these are no Dollar Tree goggles.

Underwater, I opened my eyes and saw Punishment Prairie. It was disorientating, being under the sea, opening my eyes expecting to see your run-of-the mill orange fish. Instead, it was more of this virtual reality bullshit.

I got my head up above the water, and damnit, these things were just smaller versions of the helmet. The joke's on me, delivered by Enoch and Company.

I'll tell you what I'm sick of. I'm sick of this place with its surprises; its little gadgets, and councils of messengers. Its neighborhoods, segregated like a prison, no, worse, like a city experiencing the effects of white flight. I've mentioned god's sense of humor, but I think that's just a way of deflecting what I really think, which is that this isn't a joke. God is a twisted and bipolar prick.

I took the stupid purple goggles off so I could get myself out of the water without smashing my skull on the stairs. "This is such bullshit," I yelled as I stomped inside to my drink and a donut. The goggles on top of my head, I thought "I am a child again."

Sticky icing on the roof of my mouth, a coffee mustache on my lips, I again put on the damn goggles. You got me, god. Well played, you jokester.

Albeit in flashes at first, I saw him. Ben is cutting firewood, helping a woman bail hay, spinning the handle of a butter churn. I've seen Little House on the Prairie, though it was way before my time. Ben looked like Pa, a man who would say, "I don't mind getting my hands dirty. The Lord looks favorably on hard work." I hadn't asked Ben about the Lord, or whatever deity he may have fell for when alive. I imagine he's a basic Protestant, but this place may have ruined that. I'll get into his mind shortly, I think, since it's unlikely I'll ever see him again.

Ben is dancing in front of the altar, but not in the joyful way I saw before. Hopping in a jig that looks unnatural, his lips aren't curved into a grin like the other dancers. Rather, they're pressed together like a woman blotting her lipstick. His feet are only coming a few inches off the ground as he dances half-heartedly. Ben's usual dance included knees marching high, coming up to his chin with each step. He's faking. Eyes squinted, he has tears in the inner corners of both. Blinking, he can't stop them. He's crying. No, Ben was sobbing. He stops dancing, puts his hands on his knees, and shakes his head.

A cobbler on the Prairie, a bald, portly man, approaches Ben and puts a hand on his shoulder. He has holes in his shoes, which is unfortunately ironic. That prick, god, won't let the cobbler fix his own shoes, making him, instead, stay exactly as he was when he was bucked from a horse in 1643 Scotland.

"You, okay, mate?" Embarrassed, Ben waves him away and leaves the group.

I see Ben in his cabin. It's the middle of the afternoon, but he's taken to napping as of late. On the hard floor with a thin layer of hay under him, I find him curled up, his hand under a "pillow" made of a potato sack and goose feathers. Eyes open, he whispers, "Get me out of here."

He falls asleep and I leave.

Chapter 45

I lifted the goggles and went back to myself, with my sweet tooth and self-sabotage, but only for a minute. I'm a sucker, okay, or a hopeless romantic, or an optimistic masochist. I went right back to sleeping Ben.

Fuck it, let's skip the niceties and go straight for the skull.

I'm wandering around the lobby, the conference room, the cubicles that make up Ben's brain. I have experience in brain searches now, so I go right to the filing cabinets. Again, like a Narcissist, I look for my name. "Renata" fills seventeen pages in a cabinet labeled, "New Memories, Good Ones." I notice the cabinet is much smaller than the one fastened with a padlock and labeled, "Too Bad to Even Open."

Childhood trauma is all the rage lately, isn't it? Before I died, I was growing tired of the Instagram ads, "Do you see an apple or a butterfly? Click here to identify your strain of trauma." I felt like we should have evolved passed ink blots. I'm no Freud, which is a good thing because, didn't he end up being wrong about everything? My point is, the word "trauma" used to pack some punch. Like "trauma surgeon" or "trauma to the femur bone." Now, we toss it around when we remember the time we cried about a toppled Jenga game and our mom said, "Don't be such a baby." Then she went back to her phone call and cigarette and said, "I swear, Marge, what were we thinking, having children?" A nice memory, no, but trauma?

Flash forward to now, post-death, post big shot of humility, post realizing that my brain, that of the killers, Ben's, even yours, still has to file these shaping moments somewhere, and by gosh, they do matter.

Ben's ego is trying to pull the pages of me out of the cabinets and tear them, but I'm decoupaged onto the paper. He put thick glue over me before filing; I'm flattered. I should feel rejected by his effort to erase me now, but instead I'm sympathetic. I would try to cut me up too, if I felt I deserved flogging, but got a woman who felt like a soft blanket instead.

Sandwiched between the "Too Bad" cabinet, and the "Good," are several cabinets stretching as tall as I can see. "Just the Mundane" is taped on the front of one. I'm reminded that bigger isn't better and size doesn't matter. Curious still, I open a drawer. The first page I pull is Ben sitting on a plane. He ordered a vodka and Coke and spilled it on the woman next to him. He apologized and she said, "Oh, honey, it's fine. I'm drunk too." Next, a time he went to Taco Bell and ordered twelve tacos. Heading home, there was a man at a stoplight, with a sign that said, "Lost my home, but not my faith." Ben reached out and gave him eleven tacos. Another, Ben's neighbor telling him to keep the music down, at least on weekdays. The woman had no eyebrows and a scarf around her head. He came out and said, "Do you have cancer?" and laid in bed that night going over it in his head over and over, like a fool. I go for one more. A Girl Scout selling cookies outside a grocery store. His favorite, Tag-Alongs, had been renamed Peanut Butter Patties. Feeling like it was a personal afront, he told the little Brownie that he decided to boycott their cookies for the rest of his life.

Walking toward the cubicles, there sits photos of his best friend from grade school, his shop teacher who taught him how to make a bird house for his mom, a cousin who always visited him in jail, and a girl he met at a team building thing at work who said he had kind eyes. They're all using a Morse code telegram machine sending into his frontal lobe, "You can be both damaged and cherished at the same time. Stop. It's okay to fall in love, even here. Stop."

Stop right there. Fall in love?

But Ben doesn't know this Morse code. He can't hear his supporters. He can't read their little notes, sealed shut with a red waxed stamp. The dead, pregnant woman's face, the emblem. The cubicle workers are turning their messages into paper airplanes. The shop teacher tells the cousin, "Girl, you're so clever." Paper planes are folded in a rudimentary line vertically down the center, then wings folded over on each side. The shop teacher spits on his fingers to sharpen the nose of the flying pleasantries.

Like every paper airplane I'd ever made, which is exactly two, they stayed airborne for less than a second and then dropped to the carpet. Ben just wasn't in the mood to be emotionally jacked off.

Besides, the poor work husbands and wives had competition. The airplanes might have taken flight if not for the distracting clanging coming from his hypothalamus. I'm irritated by it too, but I go toward it. An ogre, hunchbacked and covered in warts, sits on a mushroom. Everything is in "I just tripped acid" color. The red mushroom is covered with yellow dots. An emerald green cloak envelopes the man in bright, aqua blue, wing tipped shoes. His lips are peeling and bloody and his hair has black, red, white striped snakes crawling through it. A Medusa Man. He's banging pots and pans with a wooden spoon like a toddler. He's shouting, "You killed a woman. You deserve to rot in hell. Don't get too comfortable, asshole. The Prairie is going to spit you out into the shadows. Enjoy the free fall, you baby killer." Now this language, Ben understands.

I come back to the outside of Ben's body. He tells himself aloud to stop being a pussy and walks out of his cabin. The sun makes his sweaty brow sparkle with molecules of self-loathing that I watched run like hell to exit through his pores. Sadness atoms tend to shift a bit when touched by sunshine, I've learned.

Ben takes a long walk to the goats. Some are at the bottom of a steep, rocky hill, while others are standing on the incline like they've got magnets on their feet. A whole mess of children is running around, pulling on goat beards, and feeding them milk. They're clumsy, dropping bottles, tripping over hay, wiping goat shit onto their rolled-up pants. Ben helps a boy who's got a goat standing on his long hair. The little kid is on his back like a cockroach, his arms and leg flailing about. Gingerly, Ben lifts the goat's foot, and the boy runs off, unfortunately no longer a fan of goats. That pesky trauma rears its ugly head again. Ben laughs at a girl who sings, "MY mommy says goats are ALWAYS babies and that's why they take bottles."

At the bottom of a heap of kids, Ben becomes the star of the "Goat Westling Championship" of the world, as little Amos calls it. Ben is crawling on all fours, a pile of preschoolers on his back. Amos is on the sidelines, holding a pitchfork and shouting, "The grown up will win the trophy if he's able to buck everyone off. Stay strong, Molly. You've got this, Laney. Hold on tight, Bobby." Ben is crawling slowly, pretending he can't get them to fall off. Amos, "Five, four, three, two, one. And everyone is still on! The babes win the prize!" The kids jump off and Ben feigns a look of defeat, saying "Shucks" as he snaps his fingers in front of his chest.

I choke a little bit, seeing so many kids in the Prairie. I make a note to ask Rita if they were actors. They've got to be. What four-year-old winds up in PP? Like trauma, another hot topic is attachment. I hear that it's impossible to spoil a baby. Hold him 24/7 if you want. They can't manipulate you. They're just innocent extensions of you. If you let them cry even for a moment, they'll turn into serial killers. Everyone knows now that babies are perfect and innocent until around three or four, then they turn into tiny con artists. Maybe these little youngsters on Ben's back burned a kitten's tail, stomped on a bird nest full of eggs, spit in their mom's coffee, tripped their baby brother when he was just learning to walk. Okay, I bet they're not actors, the little shits.

"Why has it been so long since Renata came around?" Ben asks a goat. I'm startled by this.

"Oh, sir, the answer is so obvious if you look around." I didn't see the goat move its lips, but I sure heard it as Ben did.

The Prairie feels small to him for the first time. He has never tried to leave; he trusted his pals who said it was impossible. With all the chores, one had little time for wanderlust. Ben liked it this way, the contentment of not looking for anything. He settled into the confines of it. Feeling like he had nowhere to go felt like a kind of retirement. The day is full of survival, yes, but not making money, not achievement. When you can't go anywhere else, a person never wonders what they're missing. Ben is free from guilt about not traveling more, rejecting fishing trips, weekend camping. Incapable of saying yes, in Missingville he was equally unburdened by the guilt of saying no. He likes his status of never being invited.

But lately, he wants to venture out. I wonder if this is because of me.

He's frustrated with this hamster wheel. Next, I see him run to the edges of the Prairie, hitting the bubble's interior surface, bouncing off it like it's an upright trampoline. I have secondhand embarrassment seeing him run again and again into the wall. I can't watch. I rip off the stupid, purple, sparkly goggles.

I'm really getting sick of helmets and goggles and schlepping around the innards of men.

Chapter 46

I'm the walking dead, in ways beyond the obvious. More and more I feel like I did years ago, a memory that's in the filing called, "Crystal Clear Moments of Childhood." I'm on a road trip with my family. We went on a simple summer vacation to sticky Texas to visit my mom's family. Texas, in my opinion, is second only to Florida in the worst places on the planet. I have evidence of both, but for now, we're talking about one thing that makes me hate Texas; that is, this memory.

I was that typical kid, thinking a hotel swimming pool was the best thing ever, not a catalyst for yeast infections and bloody pee. We ate at a Cracker Barrel, because that's what you do when you're traveling through the Southern United States of America. The apple cobbler came up in chunks so big I wondered if somehow, I had never learned how to chew. Vomiting on the side of the highway, the car shaking as every semi passed, I kept thinking, "What if I can't swim at the pool when we get to the hotel?"

That night, my mom and I shared one of the two queen beds. My brother and dad were at the pool; I just knew it. But my mom lied and said they went to buy some ginger ale and Saltines. My eyes burned, my shins hurt, as I watched Barney the dinosaur jumping from one bed to the other. He was saying something about a moat below and I shivered in my mom's arms, terrified of the crocodiles on the floor. I saw fish jumping out of the water, hitting the ceiling, and coming down bloody on the beds. I was afraid Barney would fall into the green, mossy water, or be a victim to quicksand we all know now doesn't even exist. Kid fears I'm sure you've outgrown too. But that night, anything was possible. There were rabid bats caught in my hair, a baby bunny whispering, "Why do you only pay attention to me on Easter?" Mary Poppins pulling a candelabra out of her carpet bag.

This. This here. This Missingville is a fever dream.

I'm looking back fondly on Barney and the bats. Being out of your mind isn't a bad place to be, especially when your mom holds you during the spell. Falling into a moat sounds adventurous and talking rabbits are always a good time. Fever dreams stop, usually ending with a restless sleep. But being dead and not found is potentially endless, or it ends with a transfer on to another forever. I want to get out of the redundant confines of my own mind.

So, I goggle up and visit Killer.

Chapter 47

I want to talk to Shay first, but she's at candle-making class. I thought of checking in with Rita, or Enoch, but I don't feel like being patronized. So, I chatted with Tim.

He's extra jumpy today, torpedoing through my arms with a fervor I've not seen before. I tell him isn't he a spunky boy today and he says he's reached a point in his life where it's just not worth it to worry about humans and their genocide of Earth's marine life. I ask him if he's ever felt psychotic and he says he's never heard of it, but he has certainly felt trepidation and is that the same? In response to my question about falling in love, he tells me he's heard loyalty is better. He says I'm not myself today. I respond, "I don't think you knew who I was in the first place." Persistent, he urges me to let my guard down. Ashamed, I pet his back and thank him for being such a faithful friend.

I can't say Tim empowered me to goggle myself into The Prairie, but I did feel a sense of camaraderie. Knowing that Tim would always be there for me, that was enough to take the plunge.

Except I don't plunge. The task I'm about to embark on is one done best sitting upright at a table. It feels like business, not some kind of beach read one might do on a reclining chair on the beach, or in this case, the deck of an afterlife Tahitian hut. No, this calls for feet planted on the floor and hands wrapped around something responsible like a coffee mug. I'd put a shawl around my shoulders, if I had one, and make like a grandma. I did braid my hair and wrapped it in a matronly bun. Armed with timid, apprehensive curiosity, I became a voyeur, again.

I see Killer. He's falling, fast at first like we all do, then softly landing on Missingville's soil. We're all the same, sinners and saints, putting our pants on one leg at a time, free falling into the next life.

Thin, he's shirtless with his fifth and sixth ribs protruding, or are they the first and second? I'm no anatomy instructor, but it's the bottom two. It looks like I could stick a cupped hand underneath them and fling him into the air, like a boomerang that keeps coming back. Sunburned in a way that should have killed him, he's got patches of scarring on his shoulders where the sun was like a razor and skimmed off the top layer. His back is still scratched and bitten. His legs are white under his shorts, but brown from the knee down. This tan makes him look like a child. His hands are still full of open cuts, the threads from my strangulation rope imbedded into his wounds.

The length of his eyelashes shifts him from handsome to pretty, in a way very few masculine men can pull off. He's been told by more than woman that he was beautiful. I imagine that at his core, the place I'll end up creeping through, he's the kind of man that detests this compliment, the kind armed with layers of fragile masculinity.

The exquisite bastard's body has no visible blood, no track marks, no strangulation bruises. He's got a bump on his forehead from falling flat on his face, but it's mostly covered by those precious whisps of golden hair.

What I'm trying to say is that this is my effort to see him purely, without the bias one might carry if they were murdered by him. I want you to know that it's true what they say on Investigation Discovery, the monster lies inside the boy next door. Clichés bore me, and I don't want to bore you either. It's just that this man, I would have called him 'my type' if I met him at a gym or microbrewery. He might have been a beer-maker. I might have sat at his bar, talked to him about the weather, and smiled with my mouth and my eyes when he said, "Good choice. I never met an IPA I didn't like." I see me in this encounter thinking, "I want to put my mouth on his shoulder."

I wished we'd met this way. I mean, of course. But not just because I'd be alive, but because I would have fallen in love with him. I know this the same way I know the basics. Yellow and green make blue. Hanging wallpaper with one's spouse leads to divorce. If you voted for Trump, you've never invited a trans person to dinner. Since dying, I've had increased confidence in my convictions. While I used to tell myself not to believe everything I think, here, everything I think is accurate. Imagine wondering if you were annoying at the lunch thing with your work team but knowing unequivocally that you were not. I met someone here from the sixteenth century and knew that he, too, hated the texture of cheese in his mouth. I would have loved Killer despite his schizophrenia, substance use disorder, anti-social personality disorder, obsessive compulsive disorder, and post-concussive syndrome.

He lands in Missingville and looks like a lost man in a forest, being hunted by ghosts. He's bending his knees, holding up his hands in a karate kind of pose, and pivoting so he can look behind him, all around him. Most citizens of this place, when they land, do ridiculous things, like fight the Welcome Committee. If god wanted to accentuate their sense of humor, they'd have a ring doorbell camera recording everyone's arrival. Play it on the television in a constant loop, like bloopers. I'll have to bring this idea to Rita.

Killer continues in the way you expect. "Who's there? Who's here? Where am I?" He continues to spin and pivot. I wonder if the dead can get dizzy from such rotations.

I'm waiting for Rita to appear, and just when I think that would be a betrayal, enter stage right, a middle-aged man wearing a pest control uniform. He's holding a container in one hand, a wand in the other, but the top of the bug spray is blown off. He's got skin and an ear hanging off the left side of his face.

God, you are clever, though a bit predictable. The guy conducting escorts to the Prairie, of course he's a bug man. Who else do you use as the angel of death? A garbage man, a pool boy skimming the water with that net for the bugs, leaves, twigs? Someone who takes things out, that's who greets Killer.

"It's okay, just relax. Take a minute," bug man tells Killer. Killer charges towards him, puts his hands around his throat and takes him to the ground.

"Who are you? Where am I?" Killer thinks he's murdering bug man, but Joe from pest control just goes limp and smiles, trying to gurgle out, "It's okay, get it out of your system."

Strangling someone, it takes time and a heck of a lot of strength. The bottom person will kick and flail around, so the strangler must be committed, especially when going rogue and doing it with bare hands. But Joe is still, frustrating Killer more.

"We're both already dead, son." Joe repeats it a few more times until the vein popping out of Killer's forehead goes flat. Killer's hands start to loosen as well. His mouth relaxes, his teeth no longer grinding against each other.

Killer lets go, his breathing becomes regular, and he says, "Say it again, what you just said, say it again." Joe tells him they're both dead, and Killer finally does the thing we all do. While still straddling Joe's body, Killer hugs himself, the hands going right through. The cotton candy moment. He slides off Joe.

Joe gives the same spiel: look at the temple, choose the place that speaks to you, when you're ready we'll go inside. How long do you think it took Killer to calm down, think clearly, and pick a location? Longer than usual, I'd say. Resistance looked different on him. There's the typical disbelief about being dead and all, which understandably takes some time. But what's the average half-life of death denial? I'll have to ask Rita sometime, but I feel confident that the 2.5 hours of Killer resisting and bullying Joe was uncalled for. The insufferable murderer, with his aforementioned mental health disorders, plus one I hadn't mentioned before, narcissistic personality disorder, he just wouldn't accept that he was unalive.

While dying came as a surprise to me too, I didn't waste all this time on questioning my own pesky mortality. Jesus Christ, Killer, get over yourself. It's like it never dawned on him that he'd expire. In love with his own reflection, Killer Narcissus has been stuck his whole pathetic life wondering why he's no longer the center of attention. He was a beautiful baby, and the first son born on his mother's side of the family in years. He had a sister and eight cousins, all girls. They practically crowned him when he was born, and grandparents, great grandparents, aunts, uncles, even longtime family friends thought him some kind of miracle. He was born in 1981, but you'd think it was 1681 the way they celebrated the passing on of the family name. The joke's on you, people. Killer never married and never had a son, at least none he's aware of.

So, along he went, wondering year after year why he slipped from adoration. Grown men all over the world are practically trying to slither their way back into the birth canal, and Killer is no exception. Living in the world, just a man, albeit an attractive one, wasn't met with the praise he received in his first five years of life. Kindergarten shocked him when he was told everyone had to lie on their mat for nap time, and no he couldn't go outside instead. The rest of childhood felt like the slamming of doors inches from his nose.

His neurotic self-love confused him. Why wasn't he picked first, or god help him, at least second or third, for kickball? What was so great about Tommy Lawson that he was chosen as teacher's helper twice in one month? Who did Cindy St. Clair think she was, refusing his attempt at a first kiss in sixth grade? Why wasn't the whole block at his birthday party? So, Narcissus took his sweet time accepting that he was dead. It's like when narrow-minded imbeciles say, "I don't agree with it, but I have no problem with the gays." Like it's a notion calling for consensus. You can't agree that water is two parts hydrogen, one part oxygen, but go for it, if you must wrestle with science.

Finally, Killer finally decides on a location. During his incessant denial I had to stretch, move around my room doing lunges and a few planks to pass the time. Finally, like the rest of us, Killer succumbed to the receipt of the Shout Out.

If you had to guess what place this waste of human tissue chose, what would you pick? Where would Narcissus go if said mythological figure had sprinklings of psychosis in his frontal lobe? If he spent his time looking at his own reflection and then turned into a flower, where would he go when his petals fell out and he died of thirst? A football game where he's the star quarterback? Landing on the moon for the first time, since we all know that 1960 moon landing was faked? A rotunda where he receives a Pulitzer Prize for his work on how to charm a woman who won't give consent? Maybe prom night where he's king and the hottest chick in school goes down on him in the back of a limo?

Well, you'd be wrong. Killer is not two dimensional, you see.

The man picks a field of lilac with a thousand puppies tumbling around as they're learning to walk. Killer is sitting on a blanket with a bottle of wine and strawberries. Unsteady Beagles are licking his face, climbing onto his crisscrossed legs, whispering into his ears that they're glad he's here and life was overrated anyway. There's a woman beside him and she runs her fingers through the hair at the base of his neck. She's enamored with the puppies too and tells him she's bought a house big enough for all of them. He leans over and kisses her on the forehead just before he's knocked down onto his back, giddy puppies jumping on his chest. He's laughing and the woman is too. She's wearing a sun dress with yellow ties on the shoulders. She's got a mess of black hair, blowing behind her like they're sitting on a motorcycle. The sky is blue, but plenty of bloated clouds pass through the sky in front of the sun in the way you want it to when you're trying to look East in the morning. The puppies make the grass look brown, black, and white.

Killer stands up, a puppy over his shoulder like an infant. He holds onto the woman's hand but lets go as he walks away.

Joe from Pest Control, says, "Follow me. It will all make sense, I promise." They tip toe through puppies until they're at a clearing, under a gigantic willow tree. Killer and Joe sit on a checkered blanket as Killer pats the baby Beagle's back, like it's time to burp. Joe hands him a rolled-up piece of yellowed paper, a red ribbon tied around its center.

Killer is relaxed now, for the first time since his seventh birthday when his parents rented a bounce house. That was the last year he was treated like royalty, and the beginning of the first year he realized he was no prince.

He unrolls the scroll, clumsily, as he's still supporting the head of the newborn puppy.

> *Welcome to Missingville. Let me assure you that you are exactly where you belong because I said so. Whatever your religion (a word I don't like to use, but I must for the newcomers), know that I did not kill you. I do not cause death, but I do think it's endearing that so many of you believe so much of that thing you call "The Old Testament."*
>
> *I made a few mistakes in my making of humankind. I also think it's a shame that for so long you simply called humankind "man." Geez, people, I had higher expectations of you. Anyhoo, I forgot to make a rule that bad things do not happen. That's a lie, I did not forget. I chose not to. I decided to let there be suffering. I had some kind of holier-than-thou moment where I wanted to separate you all from me, from my angels, from the nonhuman. I thought suffering was the best option. Boy, was I mistaken.*

When people say the biggest riddle is "Can God make a boulder so big he can't move it?" the answer is, "Yes, except the proper pronoun is 'they'."

But since I made this error, here we are. Humans suffer, their bodies suffer, and their bodies get lost. This is certainly not something I thought of when I was cutting the molds. Lost bodies? Who woulda thunk? Yes, souls go to a place after life, called Deadtown, and there, decisions are made on where to send you all for eternity. Think Heaven and Hell, but without clouds or fire. You silly humans and your metaphors!

It pains me, though, that you caused so much suffering in your pathetic, self-serving life. I'm not sure who scrambled your brain, but I have my suspicions. Regardless, you had that brilliant thing called free will. I gave it to you, this gift. Squandered it, you did! No, you desecrated it. You defiled it, boy. You were sent down by me to the United States of America, for my sake. In the year 1981 when you had running water, electricity, and later, the world wide web. You were born a male, with good looks, a proper gestation period, without a cord wrapped around your neck, and without jaundice. I even gave you loving parents. You lived in an exceptional school district. You had your own bedroom!

Not so much as an open hand ever slapped you. You weren't forced into child labor. You had ten fingers and ten toes and genetically exceptional organs. (You of course destroyed them with your drinking, that poor liver.) You were blond haired and blue eyed and were a solid 7.5 or 8.2 on the beauty scale. You were the crème de la crème.

Do you not realize what you started with? Why middle-class white men, who have avoided the draft and the black plague, go on killing people I'll never understand. So, your parents stopped worshipping you. Lots of humans stopped praising me and you don't see me going on killing people.

I digress, but only because chaps like you make me feel bipolar. Which I know you understand, since you have the same affliction. Get over yourself.

I realized when one of the first humans died that I needed a stop gap. He was chased and attacked by a monster, or as I have learned, what humans call 'dinosaurs.' His tribe could not find his body. When he passed over, he came before me, and I realized that he needed a body in Deadtown. I like things tidy, final, calculated... think tides, moon phases, DNA, the way pi is an infinite but necessary number. Gosh, I love pi! I was so thrilled when I heard that humans

> *celebrate it on what you call March fourteenth. Very clever! Greeting the mauled man while his body was in a creek, while his family looked for him, I could not let him in yet. I do not deal in unfinished business.*
>
> *I created Missingville, where you will stay until your body is found. When I feel better about the order of things, that is, your body and your soul united, I will send you over to Deadtown. We will have a chat then. You're no dummy. You even had a high IQ, also squandered. It's not going to come as a shock to you when I say that right now the cards are stacked against you and the likelihood of you going the Dark Side is a solid ninety-three percent. But I suppose you could redeem yourself here. I highly doubt it if I'm honest, and well, I don't know how else to be.*
>
> *You're headed next to Punishment Prairies. Do not question this. Do not try to argue with me. I'm not having it, not today when an entire school bus of Norwegian teenagers went off a cliff and haven't been found for twenty-six hours. I have bigger fish to fry, child.*

I love god sometimes. Don't you?

Chapter 48

Shay returned from sourdough bread-making class, and it was high time I took a break from these vicarious little romps around the minds of men who either killed me or started to fall for me after killing another woman. It makes for a long day.

I told her about Killer's little puppy party and who would have guessed that, and no, I stopped watching just when he got to the Prairie and his escort was a pest control guy which ultimately was apropos of nothing.

Shay said she met a fine man at the class who did the dead equivalent of asking for her number. He asked her where she was staying and if she had a roommate. The question about having a roommate did lean towards a hook up, but turns out, that's exactly what she's in the mood for. Looking at me as if to say, "Get my drift?" I said, "Oh, oh, yes, of course, I was so needing to get out of these four walls, my gosh." I kissed her on the cheek and quickly walked out, passing a man who looked like People Magazine's Handsomest Man Alive from the seventies. Lucky her.

I decided to attend a eulogy. Not of someone I know, just a rando. I needed to get my mind off myself. I took a seat in a church basement, with a low drop ceiling and the smell of fried chicken. I sat in a folding metal chair and took in the sight of fake rhododendrons poised on either side of an open casket. Who's inside, I don't know, as I chose not to approach. Hoping for a lighthearted send off to someone decent, I waited.

Median age of the crowd, seventy-three.

Size of the crowd, nineteen.

My grandma used to talk about her schedule being jam packed with funerals. Pointing to her paper, spiral bound calendar, she'd say, "Renata, I swear, the only places I go to are doctors' appointments and funerals." Patting her hair in curlers, she'd add, "Oh well, it gives me a chance to make myself presentable." She'd be wearing a zebra print caftan and lipstick that failed to take years off her face. I appreciated her attitude and made a note to take her out to a movie, or to Sonic for a slushy. And, no, I never actually took her. If you've thought lately about spending more time with your Nana, stop reading right now and go pick her up. My ramblings will be here when you get back.

A woman walked down the aisle between the hard chairs. She wore a polyester number, something I thought died out in the early '80's, but this beige get-up, coupled with the bright orange scarf, it suited her. She wore thick panty hose and navy pumps, her feet bulging out of the tops. Knowing she hadn't been out of slippers in months, I appreciated her efforts.

Pushing huge, square glasses up her nose, she coughed. Pulling a wadded-up tissue from her cuff and a piece of flimsy paper from her pocket, she began.

> *Rose, my dearest Rose.*
>
> *I want to celebrate her today, and I know all of you here can easily conjure up memories of this lovely woman. You see her bringing you a pie, folding your palm leaves into crosses, putting flags on Veterans' graves. Or maybe your go-to memory is her calling numbers at BINGO, celebrating each winner with, "Praise the Lord." I like to think of her playing Canasta, drinking her sweet tea and asking her friends how on Earth young people can afford to live, what with the price of trash pick-up and coffee creamer.*
>
> *Rose was also a doting mother. Reginald and Catherine have gone before her, and I'm sure she's with them now, holding them and reminding them that she did her best. Harold is sitting with them, the family reunited now in Christ.*
>
> *I was the last person to see Rose alive, and the one that initiated the Silver Alert. She stopped*

by with banana bread, and we drank coffee in my kitchen. She mentioned buying a Precious Moments statue on Facebook Marketplace and gave me the address of where she was headed. I hugged her goodbye, and poof, she vanished. The Precious Moments seller claims Rose never showed up, but Rose's car was found right around the corner from the woman's apartment.

I am grateful for those of you that helped search for her. I know your failing sight and hearing made the walks along the interstate perilous. When I found her Medicare Advantage card in a ditch, I knew Rose had passed over.

The nine days it took for her to be found were the worst days of my life, and that says a lot since I've had to euthanize eleven precious dogs during my lifetime. I felt her presence during that time. A candle would blow out despite there being no wind. My radio turned on by itself, blaring that Barry Manilow song she loved, "Mandy." The most profound visit from her was that where she told me to look for her behind the prosthetic leg store on Route 22.

Call it intuition, call it a sign from God. Whatever it was, it called me to the field, the pile of leaves, the body of my dear friend. Rose told me where she was, just like she did in life when she'd call and say, "Whatcha doing? I'm waiting in another god damn podiatrist's office." Those of you who have speculated about me, shame on you. Steadfast in my love for my friend, I am here....

She stopped talking and looked at the back of the room, her mouth hanging open. All twenty of us craned our necks to watch two men in suits, and four uniformed police walk up the aisle. "Ms. June Brown, you're under arrest for the murder of Rose Slayton. You have the right to remain..."

A man at least 110 years old stood up with his cane, shouting, "I knew it! I told you!" Except his vocal cords were also 110 years old, so it was a yell whisper. I wondered if it was just that no one could hear him when he tried to say June was a murderer.

June Brown tried to run, or rather, she tried to saunter off. Knee replacements and a trick hip made for an awkward attempt to flee the police. They spun her around, bringing her hands behind her back as she said, "But I loved Rose." I laughed when a cop said, "Yeah, lady, we get that a lot from people. You always hurt the ones you love."

Putting up the kind of fight only a woman of eighty-six can exhibit, June was escorted outside. Not knowing what to do next, a woman walked to the front and started singing Amazing Grace. It lacked originality and reminded me of Barack Obama, but I still stood and sang with the group.

I'm not sure about grace, really, and I'm certainly not buying that it's amazing. What I do know is that we've all got to go through way too many dangers, toils, and snares to feel like anything is even close to mercy.

Chapter 49

"What I'm looking for is a spy of sorts," I say to the girl on a smoke break from the "Murdered by a Stranger" support group.

Charlotte and I had become fast friends after, at my first meeting, we exchanged glances and a smile when a hitchhiker who died in 1973 was defending herself to a room full of snowflake millennials. "Trust me when I say it was safe back then. Washington wasn't the serial killer capital of the world yet, okay? You careless girls have Tinder hook ups in all kinds of dark alleys, but I'm the one who should have known better?"

Margie, the group's chair, was bruised in purple and yellows from her face to her toes, which was obvious in her granny panties and Maidenform bra. She said, "Now Linda, let's not discriminate based on age. Millennials deserve compassion too, even if they are the pussies we understand them to be."

Charlotte was intrigued. "A spy, huh? Sure, that sounds fun," she said as she puffed on an American Spirit. Her Green hair, Metallica t-shirt, and eyebrow piercing put her in the category I like to call, "People I Would Make Fun of on Earth." But my guidelines are different here.

Charlotte was deadpan, like I was reciting the tax code, as I told her about my death, Killer, Ben. I don't know, maybe I'm just hungry for some simple, "No way, Girl, shut up!" sort of Earthly interaction when I talk to women. You know what I mean. Aren't we all telling stories for ourselves, for the satisfaction of a reaction? I'm imaging you saying "Shut up" at least every few pages as you read this, which is very much not fiction. Join me, will you, ladies, in our collective effort to at least feign interest when another woman tells a story. It goes a long way.

Niceties like this, Charlotte hadn't been taught. She nodded a few times when I told her I was strangled, said, "Mm-hmm," when I said I had a crush on a guy named Ben. Expecting her to ask, I said, "Don't even ask me why Ben is there, because I'm not telling you." She looked at me blankly, with no intention of asking me one thing about Ben or the rest of it.

"You can hear me, right?" I snapped, wondering if she was high or deaf.

"Yep" is all I got in return.

Chapter 50

Today's helmet wearing exercise is brought to you by the letters, "F" and "U."

Kathleen is in a nondescript room at a Podunk police department in Tennessee, the one closest to the spot Kathleen was standing when she realized I was in trouble. The Marshall County Sheriff's Department boasts four solved murder cases in its tenure, which is not what you think once you learn that twenty-nine murder investigations have been based out of this office. I'm no mathematician, but I'm pretty sure twelve percent is not exactly a winning streak.

Lucky for me, I guess, is that the State Police, the Highway Patrol, and the FBI are here too. Why we need so many sections of law enforcement, I don't understand. I've always thought this was a little bit over the top, but its explanation lies in the number of men who want to wear uniforms and carry guns. Wait, that's way too easy. It's more about the men who want to tase other men, make women feel ashamed, and compensate for small appendages. Whatever the reason, all the big boys with crime solving pedigrees were joining forces for me.

Purple half circles sit under the lower part of Kathleen's bloodshot eyes. Her hands are holding up her tired head, elbows on her knees. "Ok, I'll say it again. I last saw Renata at mile marker 184, something like that. We stopped for a snack and then kept going."

Interrupting already, a cop says, "Something like that? Something like that isn't going to fly, Ms. O'Bryan. We need you to be clear on exactly where you were when you last saw her."

Closing her eyes tightly, she's picturing us eating apples and beef jerky. I'm complaining. She's comforting me. We're laughing. The moment is clear, but it takes the kind of calculations her brain just can't do right now to decipher where we were. She tells them again that she was at 184 when she realized I wasn't within ear shot behind her. This is where she turned around and walked back, calling my name, and panicking.

"And, Ms. O'Bryan, am I correct that you and Ms. Foster were lovers?" This guy looks more important than the other one, but it might just be because he's standing up and his hair is gray. "Or is it more accurate that you wanted a relationship with Ms. Foster, and she wasn't interested in you romantically?"

I see where things stand. I hadn't told anyone about Kathleen. Call it homophobia, call it just typical "the lover always does it," but as you'd expect, Kathleen was suspect number one. While I'm not surprised by this, I'm disgusted. Over seventy-five percent of murders are committed by someone known by the victim. When it comes to women, over seventy-five percent are committed by an "intimate partner." If Kathleen were straight, I'm sure they would have moved on to, oh, I don't know, the theory that there are lots of unwell people living along the Appalachian Trail. If I was hiking with a boyfriend, the guy would already be locked up, so maybe they did cut a little break for Kathleen.

The cops got statements from my family and friends like, "She went hiking with her friend, Kathleen. Oh no, Renata is straight, it's not like that."

Kathleen tells them it's not that simple, it's not all black and white. Investigators want to know if we'd had sex, as if this one act of a body being against or inside another body was the linchpin for solving my murder. Some people would have just said, "Yes, we were intimate." Kathleen wasn't a person to let the elephant in the room galivant around unchecked.

"Listen," she said. "Renata and I have been friends for several months. We spent a lot of time together, playing tennis at first, then going for coffee or dinner, then spending the night together. We were very close, but our relationship wasn't defined like that. I wasn't her girlfriend, she wasn't mine, per se. I love her. I think she loves me, and the parameters of what that meant for us were yet to be determined. It has nothing to do with why I'm in this room right now or what you have to do to find her. I didn't want more from her than what she was willing to give. I'm not some dyke trying to coerce straight women into fucking me. Renata isn't a naive child being lured into some homosexual lifestyle." She put finger quotes around "homosexual lifestyle."

She told them I wasn't an experienced hiker; she felt terrible for pushing me to take this trip, and worse for getting so far ahead of me. She said she was going back on the trail right now and will show them where she was when this, this, and this happened, but please stop asking her who she fucks and how she fucks.

"Ms. O'Rourke, we have a search crew out there now, and the places you already described have been marked. We have more questions for you."

And in that moment, Kathleen thought, "This is when they'll turn the story into the unrequited love of a hiking lesbian." She asked if she was under arrest. They said no. She got up and walked out.

Unfortunately, she passed my parents who were giving a statement to the press. I watched my mom watch her. Kathleen was doing a walk-run right into the street, headed toward the closest trail head. But to my mom, Kathleen looked like a woman refusing to cooperate. She looked like someone about to lawyer up.

Worse, two cops came next, trying to catch up with her. Both my parents heard them say, "We've got to stay on her, she may be leading us to the body."

None of this is a surprise to me. Are you surprised?

Chapter 51

Charlotte returned from the Prairie. I chose well; she's a smart cookie. We met at the Lover's Quarrel Lighthouse. We sat on a picnic table at the lighthouse base, looking out onto the ocean. At the bottom of the cliff, there were teenagers drinking beer and spinning pigs on beach fire spickets. They all had legs and arms protruding in wrong directions, with their necks cocked to the side. Jumping off cliffs makes for a dreadful after death body.

Equipped with a notebook, a bodycam, and an old dictation machine, my spy recorded her visit to Punishment Prairie better than I expected. I brought her a carton of cigarettes and a CD of a live Black Sabbath concert. Maintaining an apathetic expression, Charlotte took both and nodded what I took as a thank you.

"There's some whacky shit going on over there. If I were you, I'd just be wishing I were dead, or more dead.

Found, you know." She picked a piece of tobacco off her tongue, which I noticed had a purple ball pierced into its center.

We started with the notebook.

Killer has a cabin about half a mile from Ben.
Killer's roommate is a woman who drowned her children.
Killer participated in the altar dance today, weird...he's a good dancer.
A man who was stabbed by his pimp has a crush on Killer.
Ben isn't talking much. He did bring me a cup of coffee, but he stayed quiet.
The horse brigade decided collectively not to offer Killer forgiveness.
I see no evidence that anyone knows who Killer killed.

On to the body cam:

Charlotte is sitting around a campfire. "I got lost, I'm sorry, I shouldn't be here," she says to a woman dressed in 1800's London upper-class regalia, with cushions under her dress making her unable to walk through doorways without turning sideways. She's wearing a white wig two feet high; the white powder on her skin is smeared with blood, under her nose and trickling out of the corner of her mouth.

"We hear that all the time. I'll take your word for it, though I'm not persuaded to find you truthful." The woman gives Charlotte a pair of gloves that don't fit her, and walks away, leaving Charlotte alone.

My spy is easily bored. Within a minute she's wandering around the Prairie. I can see cabins with their bright doors, goats and chickens, the blacksmith, the women squatting in vegetable gardens. A few people pass her and nod. One, a man with a hatchet in his skull, another, a teenager with one arm and no legs, floating around in a tank top and sweatband, a boombox on his shoulder. Wearing roller skates, a teenage girl hands Charlotte a Slurpy from Seven-Eleven as she passes her, shouting, "You deserve a treat today, sinner!"

Charlotte is approaching another fire pit, another circle of dead folks surrounding it. They're passing around a jug and wiping their mouths with the backs of their hands. A long-bearded, bald man wearing a kilt and a chest plate hollers, "Hey, modern woman, come join the heathens." He leans over to a woman next to him and says, "The real party always starts when an outsider shows up."

"Uh, sorry, I'm lost," Charlotte says, convincing no one.

"I'm growing weary of the gawkers, aren't you, mate?" Says a weathered man with a dead sheep over his shoulders. The mate, a child not more than five says, "Yes, Pa, I'm tired of decent people."

Charlotte, who cares about nothing really, has a keen ability to ignore, and for this, I thank her. She takes swigs of moonshine, puts logs on the fire, and raises her eyebrows when appropriate, like when the shepherd said, "I swear, my murder wasn't as horrifying as being accused of mating with my flock."

Killer approaches the fire circle. He's stumbling and talking to himself like when he was alive, "Baby, I'm coming for you." And then, the haunting chuckle.

There is an uneasy silence when he sits down and Killer says, "Geez, who died?" Everyone laughs, a joke I'm quite surprised I hadn't heard yet. I feel a churn in my stomach and realize I'm delighted by Killer's sense of humor.

Ice feels broken. Someone gets up and hands the jug to Killer, saying, "Welcome, Newcomer." The circle responds in unison, "Welcome Newcomer!"

Charlotte goes to hunt for twigs, and I say to her, "My god, woman, why did you walk away?" She tells me to shut up and watch.

Clever spy that she is, when she returns with sticks, she positions herself directly across from Killer. "Oh, my bad," I say.

There's chatter about what the fire needs, whose turn it is to brush the horses, what time is the baptism reenactment at the river, and a rundown of who left the Prairie recently. Someone puts their arm around a sobbing little girl and says, "Chin up, lass. Your ma being found means you're next. Don't fret."

There's a lull in conversation, like everyone collectively realized where they were. It's exhausting, even for the dead, to feign acceptance. The best hooch in the world, or this world, can't numb this level of shame. It looks like everyone just realized the limbo they're in is endless and black.

And then, Killer breaks the silence. "So, I guess I gotta be nice to all you vagabonds? Is that the way this little game works? That jokester god is marking his spreadsheet as we speak? I've died and woke up under a microscope?" He tilts his head back and looks up, "Are you watching me, big man?" Then laughter.

The outlaw circle is quiet. Even those bound for the Dark Side can tell when something extra sinister is in their mists. I can see people folding into themself, hugging their cotton candy bodies, crossing their legs, looking at their hands. Someone whispers to a young, pretty girl with a gunshot wound to her eye, "I think you should go on to bed, sweetheart."

A grandpa kind of guy says, "Run along" to the boy sitting on his lap. A woman in a wedding dress, algae falling out of her hair says, "I bid you all adieu," and bows before walking off. The group keeps thinning out, and it's obvious; murders, rapists, animal abusers, child molesters, even they're put off by Killer.

Charlotte though, my dear infiltrating mole, she's no snowflake. She stays. Killer is surveying her. Charlotte tells me that in this moment she's looking right at him.

She says, "I felt like a kid in a staring contest, and I won." I tell her she's my spirit animal. She ignores me.

"What are you looking at, poser?" Killer asks. "I feel like I knew you in high school, but then again, I didn't really hang with your type, I just liked having girls like you go down on me."

"Girls like me?" Charlotte asks. Killer snorts, choking on his laughter. He looks around like he's searching for a bro in the group to join him in his favorite past time of degrading women. But the people in this circle, they drank the tracking-good-deeds-spreadsheet Kool-Aid. They were watching their P's and Q's.

Charlotte went for it, the little firecracker that she is. I might have had a crush on her in this moment, but wouldn't you feel the same? "So, what are you here for, blondie? Kill a stray cat, did you? Put a BB through your brother's eye? Wait, no, I know your kind, you killed a defenseless woman, didn't you? After you raped her? That's your thing, isn't it? I can tell by your hands that you like to kill girls."

Killer takes a swig from the jug and laughs. "I bet you're thinking I'll deny it, aren't you, honey? Yeah, I killed a girl or two. Loved every second of it. My only regret is that I didn't wear gloves," he says as he holds up his blistered hands.

Charlotte pressed pause and looked at me like a friend. "Are you sure you want to watch this?" she asked. I told her I wasn't sure.

"There's a lot coming. Your boyfriend never came around, at least not until the next night."

"Do you like to swim?" I asked Charlotte. She shrugged, which for Charlotte is an enthusiastic "Yes."

I invited her to come to my place the next day. "Let's watch your next visit with some cocktails and a swim with my dolphin friend."

"That sounds lame, but okay, I'll see you tomorrow," she said.

Chapter 52

Charlotte arrived with what looked like a pep in her step. Which, for Charlotte, means she wasn't slouching, and her hair was brushed away from her eyes. She even greeted me with mild jubilation, "What's up, girlie?"

"There's a swimsuit on the bottom bunk. Meet me outside."

Charlotte appeared instead in her bra and underwear, saying, "I don't wear anything with 'suit' in the name." She lit a cigarette and sat down, bored already.

I told her about Tim, how he's a great friend to swim with, but he also has a fragile ego so it's best to compliment him a bunch before playing with him.

"You're asking me to stroke a dolphin's ego?" She asked, which coming out of her mouth, did sound ridiculous.

"Let's watch another video first," I said, thinking Tim might not be able to handle a girl like her.

I imagine this is as close as I'll ever get to being a mother, this mama bear commitment I've acquired, protecting Tim's fragility.

Today's video is brought to you by the letters "W.T.F."

Charlotte said this recording is of the next morning. This genius of a little mole slept in the Prairie, in a hammock near the horses. I asked her if she was afraid to sleep there and I don't have to tell you that she said, "Fuck no."

She's approaching another campfire, this one with a grate and a tin pot of coffee percolating on top. The fire is in a perfect triangular, tee-pee shape, with a line of smoke rising to a blueberry popsicle colored sky. There's a lot of flannel worn by the group, but also a teenager in fur, and a middle-aged woman in a blood-soaked toga.

Ben's head is hanging between his knees again, a posture most often seen in members of AA, or people waiting for their name to be called in traffic court.

My spy is sitting next to Ben this time, with Killer on his other side. Killer is not in a shame posture, but instead has his legs stretched out in front of him, ankles crossed, arms folded against his chest. He's wearing the smirk of a person with no regrets. I don't find him attractive, and I'm relieved.

No one is talking, which is making me anxious. I'm gnawing at the inside of my mouth, waiting for one of these bad boys to start speaking, humming, praying, anything. Dead murderers, rapists, animal harmers are extra scary when they're quiet. Have you ever watched those true crime shows that air an uninterrupted confession? The silent ones, the ones that look the detectives in the eyes with no sound, those are the ones dismembering grandmas in the bathtub. I also notice that no one is looking at another person. Fire does that to people though, doesn't it? It makes a person stare into the fire, like something might come out of it to give us the true motivation of god, or how in the Dark Side do we get out of Missingville and to the Light side of Deadtown?

Charlotte stokes the fire and accepts a black coffee from Ben. He looks unrested, his hair standing up straight at the top of his head. His beard has a few days of growth and when the fire cracks I can see silver sparkles on his chin.

A woman with a rope around her neck sits down and comments on the weather. Killer and Ben nod. It looks like a normal camping trip, save the rope and the woman's crooked neck. Ben starts frying eggs and passing out plates. Everyone is quiet, except for "thank you's" and pleasantries about how they slept the night before, how much wood needs to be cut for the day, how the eggs aren't too runny, just like they like them. Killer says he couldn't sleep so he chopped wood most of the night.

"It's uneventful now, but just wait," Charlotte said, seemingly invested in the job I've given her.

Killer looks nervously at the ground, then at the broken necked woman, and asks her how long it took to die. She says, "Not long. I almost wanted it to take longer, that's how sick I am." She introduces herself as "Mary. Yes, the one married to the film director." Even when you're dead, you'll look around a group of people with the same expression you have now, asking, "Do you know who the hell she's talking about?" And you'll do that slight movement of your chin, the way you crinkle it up and curl in your bottom lip to tell the dead group, "I have no idea."

The film director's wife is also just like the alive, in that she totally misses the group's collective gestures which said, "Can you tell us a movie he made at least?" She just goes on.

"I'm not sure if the suicide landed me here, or if it's all the other transgressions. If I only knew which thing I had to atone for, it would be easier for me to repent, ya know? I desperately want to know if my body will be found. My husband cut me down from the rafters at our Tahoe house and threw me in the lake. I know, you've never heard of such a thing. Me either. The man didn't want people to blame him for my suicide. Holy cow, the press would have a field day. He might be uninvited to Russell Crowe's birthday party. The bastard thought it would be easier on his reputation to let the world think I was missing, kidnapped, murdered. Hell, I don't know what he was thinking. I mean, I just, shit,

I just wanted to be carefully untied and buried next to my mom. Yes, I know you all know who she is too."

Again, chins wrinkling up, heads turning this way and that, asking each other, "Who is this broad's mom?"

She just can't stop herself. "I don't want to pry, but I've been asking about other people's sins, to make more sense of my own. Ya know, trying to figure out why I'm here, what's the threshold for other people to land here. Is it the suicide or the other shit, ya know? Can you boys tell me how you think you landed here?" She pulled her skirt up a bit and blinked her fake lashes quickly.

"It's a little early in the morning for confessions, isn't it, Mary?" Ben says as he flips a pancake.

Killer is looking at her with a slight grin. He sighs loudly, his cheeks bellowing out as he exhales.

Killer sounds normal. He's not chuckling. He's not wide eyed and picking at his skin.

"Isn't it just a religious scare tactic, the whole 'go to hell if you kill yourself' thing? I mean, the Catholics sure believe it, and probably the Lutherans, but the god who wrote that Shout Out, is he sending the suicides to the Dark Side?"

A collective "they" chimes in from the group.

The film director's wife says god was vague in her shout out, so she can't be sure.

Killer thinks he's an expert, "My guess is you're in Punishment Prairie for other things you did, lady."

Killer seems lucid. I'm waiting for his laugh, for his wild-eyed stare, for the pulsating to start in his forehead. I'm zooming in on the video, staring at Killer, pausing it, rewinding, playing it again.

"I know, girl, I thought the same thing. This guy has his wits about him, at least sometimes," Charlotte says, crossing her legs and kicking her foot.

Mary tells Killer she was raised Lutheran, as a matter of fact, and yes, suicide sends you to hell. "I wasn't a practicing anything, but before I stepped off the ladder, I prayed to god to send me to Heaven despite it."

Ben stays quiet. Killer is nodding his head like a therapist. He's interested and goes on. "I used to go to AA. I had to 'take a moral inventory,' which meant writing in a notebook what a piece of shit I was. Did it keep me from drinking? No. It just made me feel more guilt, which made me drink some more. I had a guy who called himself my sponsor. He made me read it to him, everything I listed, from stealing from my parents to pushing my girlfriend. We sat in a coffee shop, and I sobbed across the table from this old man who congratulated me on finishing the fourth step, or whatever it was. I never saw him again and I never went to another church basement for that bullshit. But I kept the notebook. Since I died, I keep seeing that notebook, and my list of mistakes. I did something really terrible just before I died, and I deserve to be here for that alone, but when I picture that notebook, I think I was a prick all along. I hurt people, Mary. All my life, I hurt people. Did you?" Killer's voice is deeper than I remember it, soft and measured. He's leaning forward, looking at Mary like she mattered.

Mary clears her throat. "I was an unavailable mother. I had around the clock nannies and sent my kids to boarding school. Lying, making up stories, that was also a favorite past time. I left one husband after an affair with a young pool boy if you can believe that." Mary shakes her head.

Ben is quietly watching the two of them. He scratches his head, fidgets on his tree stump, glances at Mary, Killer, the ground, the fire. He looks on guard, like a man who knows certain conversations in Missingville are sticky like syrup, oozing over people who have a damn good reason to lose their shit.

"All of that seems pretty minor, if you ask me," Killer says. "I tormented the people who loved me. I don't mean a lie here and there. I don't mean I cheated on my girlfriend. Fucking the pool boy and letting your kids be watched by professionals, that seems par for the course, a lady like you. Married to a movie producer, you had to lean into the cliché of yourself, didn't you? I mean, when in Rome, right?" The movie producer's wife smiles, and it cracks her cheeks like this was her first time.

Killer says it was a shame to see a woman like her choosing to hang from the rafters. "You haven't mentioned why you ended up with a rope around your neck. I've been there, with a rope, a few bottles of pills, a gun, and my god, I thought about letting myself off the hook, just like you. I thought a bunch about it during my life, so I don't blame you a bit, not even for a second. I sure don't. But a lady like you, pretty, rich, famous, what sent you over the line?"

Mary says, "A little bit of everything?"

Nodding, Killer says, "Well, I suppose that's about all I need to know. A little bit of everything sure seems like enough. I hate it for you though. I mean, you had a choice, and Hell, maybe I did too."

Killer explains, like an ordinary person, "I made my sister worry every day that I would die or kill someone else. The women in my family watched the news every morning and every night to be sure I wasn't on it. My mom took me to hospitals where I was strapped down and drugged up, and she left every psych ward a little more broken. I didn't just cheat the system. I didn't just lie. I methodically took every bit of compassion anyone ever gave me, and I made it feel like poison in their guts. I can't count the number of times a woman I loved sobbed and shook as she asked me why I couldn't just stay on track. One woman, I asked her to marry me. She said yes and then a week before the wedding skipped town, telling my family it was the only way she could be free of the mental gymnastics she had to do to love me. I actually tortured her, ya know?

My jealousy, paranoia, bursts of rage, and then begging. My god, I begged for her to come back just so I could kick her down. I took the hearts right out of people, threw them on the ground, and stomped all over them, often dancing and singing like the lunatic I really am."

Mary looks at Ben. Ben looks at Killer.

"Come on, man, don't do this to yourself," Ben says, wanting to be washed of this sticky situation.

Killer's eyes look watery. Tears fall down his cheeks, and he wipes them with his shirt. "Mary, I'm sure you're only here because of that noose around your neck. You're not like me."

Ben tries again. "Let me get you some more coffee, man. It can't be that bad, man."

Killer isn't looking for accolades. He isn't interested in comfort he knows he doesn't deserve. "It is that bad. I've been strapped down onto beds, injected with things to keep me from clawing my own eyes out. I wallowed in self-pity. I didn't think about the people I hurt, or the women I killed." He blinks hard a few times, his head twitches.

"Anyway. I'm fine, like cherry wine, like wine, like cherries." Killer starts tapping his feet. He purses his lips, willing himself to stop crying. Tilting his head back, he blows out a heavy breath again. Raising and lowering his shoulders, he opens his eyes wide, staring at Mary. No, staring through Mary.

And then, the laughter. And then, "Baby, I'm coming for you."

And then, "Mary, I don't suppose you ever killed anyone. At least no one but yourself." Bellowing laughter. "Killed anyone? Killed anyone? Anyone? Anyone? Killed? Killed?"

Ben and Mary look at each other. Mary backs up.

"I killed a girl, killed a girl, killed, killed. Two girls, two girls. It was on the Appalachian Trail, maybe you've heard of it? The AT? Pretty, rich girls come to hike it like they know something. I'm minding my own business, it's my business, mine, not yours. She fell, bloodied those bony knees. Her little girlfriend abandoned her. Girlfriend. That girl had a girlfriend, crazy, isn't it?" He's up now, walking in long strides around the fire.

Ben stands up, his fist already clenched. "You did what? Who? Who did you kill? When?"

Killer is skipping around the fire, like a girl on a playground. "There once was a girl from Nashville, who I killed before I landed in Missingville. I strangle her by a fire. The situation is quite dire." Laughing, louder and louder, he doesn't stop when Ben tackles him.

"Who did you kill? Who?" Ben's hands are around Killer's neck.

Mary screams, "No, you can't do that, god is watching you. You'll go to the Dark Side." She tries to pull Ben off him.

Killer's legs are wildly moving. He's struggling to breathe even though there's no breath in him to begin with.

And then, I ask Charlotte to adjust the volume. The crickets stopped chirping; the fire stopped crackling. "It's not the volume, Renata." Charlotte reaches out and holds my hand.

The Earth around the huddle that is Killer and Ben widens. The ground opens up and the train comes. Ben stands up, and then Killer is kneeling, looking all around him, his mouth open in a scream, but there's no sound. And he's gone.

The bastard's body was found before mine.

Chapter 53

I probably don't have to tell you that I ran to the Prairie. I probably don't have to tell you that I ran to Ben.

This is a predictable part of the story, isn't it? It's trite, to be honest with you. A romance in the afterlife. There's nothing special about it except that he's a man that killed a woman and I'm a woman killed by a man. I stayed in Punishment Prairie for a day. Ben and I danced around the altar, drank whiskey by the fire, visited the horses, and tried death sex, again.

I told him how I often think of the talent I displayed while playing four-square in the sixth grade and how I have no memory of ever eating a funnel cake. I told him how I count on my fingers for numbers containing eights or sevens and that I thought of killing myself during the time in school meant for learning the multiplication tables. He said it was weird that teachers said, "It's time to learn *your* multiplication tables" as if we had some kind of ownership of math. I told him I'd never thought of that and that equally weird is that we were forced to say the Pledge of Allegiance like we were in North Korea. He said it wasn't anywhere close to the same thing, and I said I appreciated his naivete.

But I came home to Shay. I said goodbye without any fanfare, even though we both knew I was headed to Deadtown. I don't know if it's a soulmate thing, or a dead love thing, but there was a knowing between us that would have been trivialized with discussion.

I didn't come here to fall in love. I didn't come here to play house, or master cotton candy body intercourse. I never meant for this to be a love story. Romance novels are for the desperate and daft.

You might think I'm going to tell you what I did come here for, but god is a real son of a bitch and didn't tell me. Like a scientist who puts rats in cages to see how they feel about heroin when they have lots of friends, god is simply curious and looks past the victimization of his subjects. They don't care about you is what I'm trying to say, and I'm only a smidge sorry.

I managed to use the last of my ghostly energy to put this book on the front steps of the religion writer for the New York Times. I imagine that you're reading it now because she believed me. I imagine the little "miracles" I pulled convinced the world that this is a true account from the dead. Yes, my actions might have been dramatic, and I'm sorry you thought the world was ending.

I probably could have skipped that part where I freed all the world's zoo animals, but I stand by the sudden and synchronized death by heart attack suffered by all of the planet's billionaires. Putting money into the hands of every breathing human on earth was an undertaking I'm most proud of, though I suspect you humans will still manage to muck it up.

I do have a request in return for letting it all hang out. I'd like to ask you to google "missing person near me," and whatever story comes up, read up on it, watch some documentaries, listen to a podcast, and then go search for them. Look in the woods first and don't stop looking at the boyfriend. Get a party together. Normalize buying beers for pals to help search for the dead.

With the millions you just got, go ahead and buy trackers for your loved ones. To those of you in the United States, forget about your pesky right to privacy for a minute. Use the technology available and go right ahead and chip your babies. Your kitten doesn't mind it, and your kid won't either, not when he's being strangled on a trail while a boy he loves is walking miles ahead. Your grandma won't complain when she wanders off to search for Colonel Sanders and you find her before she walks in front of a train. Let's beat god at their own game, and while we're at it, let's keep families from wondering about bodies decomposing in piles of leaves.

Aren't you sick of stories of the missing? Don't you want more from your new society where the billionaires got what was coming to them and you never have to wait again until pay day to buy a pair of shoes? Maybe you're scared now, and you want to be sure you never wind up in that shallow grave; go chip yourself.

I'm sitting here on the deck, watching Shay and Tim and their commitment to synchronized swimming. Shay's legs are haphazardly doing splits while Tim is trying to jump through them. I hear Tim say, "Is Renata leaving soon?" Shay says probably and Tim says I inspired him to break from conventional paradigms. I watch them like I'm a mom at the park, smiling at shenanigans I don't want them to grow out of. I'm telling myself that breaking the eleventh commandment will be worth it. I'm having a pep talk where I assure myself that I've lived a worthwhile death.

I have to put my pen down, my friend, I hear a train coming.

www.ingramcontent.com/pod-product-compliance
Ingram Content Group UK Ltd.
Pitfield, Milton Keynes, MK11 3LW, UK
UKHW041631190726
13854UKWH00006B/2437

9 798994 939109